*Christopher*

*Raymont*

# THE MARINERS LIBRARY

1. SAILING ALONE AROUND THE WORLD
   by Captain Joshua Slocum

2. A CHILD UNDER SAIL by Elizabeth Linklater

3. THE VENTURESOME VOYAGES OF CAPTAIN VOSS

4. DEEP WATER AND SHOAL by W. A. Robinson

5. THE CRUISE OF THE TEDDY by Erling Tambs

6. GALLIONS REACH by H. M. Tomlinson

7. DOWN CHANNEL by R. T. McMullen

8. ACROSS THREE OCEANS by Conor O Brien

9. ROUGH PASSAGE by Commander R. D. Graham

10. The CRUISE OF THE AMARYLLIS
    by G. H. P. Muhlhauser

11. SAILING ALL SEAS IN THE IDLE HOUR
    by Dwight Long

12. AROUND THE WORLD SINGLE-HANDED
    by Harry Pidgeon

13. FROM THREE YACHTS by Conor O Brien

14. THE £200 MILLIONAIRE by Weston Martyr

15. THE FALCON ON THE BALTIC by E. F. Knight

16. THAMES TO TAHITI by Sidney Howard

17. A GIPSY OF THE HORN by Rex Clements

18. ON SAILING THE SEA by Hilaire Belloc

19. 1,700 MILES IN OPEN BOATS by Capt. Cecil Foster

20. THE MARY CELESTE and Other Strange Tales of the Sea
    by J. G. Lockhart

21. THE CRUISE OF THE ALERTE by E. F. Knight

*Others in preparation*

RUPERT HART-DAVIS LIMITED
36 Soho Square, London, W.1

THE MARINERS LIBRARY

# Gallions Reach

## A ROMANCE

*by*

# H. M. TOMLINSON

LONDON
RUPERT HART-DAVIS
1955

First published 1927
This edition published 1949
Second impression 1952
Third impression 1955

TO

CHARLES E. HANDS
FOR SHARING WITH ME HIS
OUTLOOK ON GALLIONS

REPRINTED BY LITHOGRAPHY IN GREAT BRITAIN
BY JARROLD AND SONS LIMITED, NORWICH

# CHAPTER I

THE steamer moved up river at half-speed, and the sounds of life fell with the sun. The shores grew blurred. The quiet was the dusk. The ship itself was hushed, and her men about their duties appeared at a task spectrally, out of nowhere. She might have been trying to reach her destination unobserved. The tired air spilling over the steamer's bows hardly reached the bridge. The bridge caught the last of the light, and a trace of anger that flushed the mirk banked in the west, to which the ship was moving, was reflected in the face of an officer there, and gave him the distinction of a being regnant and stern. He was superior, and seemed to be brooding down over some passengers sitting in a group on the indistinct foredeck. They were murmuring in conversation, with a child asleep on a shawl beside one of the chairs.

Yellow glims appeared low down in the shadows that were Kent and Essex. That day of summer had gone. Only the wan river and the sky remembered it. A figure rose from the group on the foredeck, and his voice, surprisingly uplifted, was as if he had been compelled to an important announcement. "There's the smoke of it. London."

The child sat up quickly. He stared up and ahead, as his elders were doing. He wanted to see what London meant. He saw only the solid black angle of the bows, and the faint smear of crimson beyond. He heard waters muttering, and edged closer to the shadow of his mother. Her hand sought his bare head, and rumpled his hair.

"Nearly home, Jim."

The sound of the waters, the quiet that was neither day nor night, and that grave word which announced the unknown, brought the child to his feet. He felt as he did when he heard the old clock talking to itself at night in its case, or saw a star watching him through the bedroom curtains when everybody was asleep, and he was wondering what the clock was saying. He did not know what he expected to see; but if it were there it would be better to look at it. So he stood up. But nothing was there that he knew. It was the world. He did not know what it meant. The ship was going towards a darkness which reached almost to the top of the pale sky. It seemed to have blood in it. "There you are, Jim Colet," said his father. "See it? London, my boy." But he could see only a darkness.

He looked at his father. But his elders had forgotten him. They continued their confidential talk.

"You know, I haven't seen this river since the year of the *Princess Alice*."

Who was that princess? It did not look like a place for princesses. Sometimes his father did not mean what he said. He never smiled when he was joking with you. It looked as if the ship were going to where night hides in the daytime. He did not know what they were all talking about.

"Never heard from him afterwards."

Their quiet words came out of the shadows without being joined together.

"I remember. He was afraid of it, but he went."

It was nearly as hard to hear the talkers as to see them. Who was afraid? Where did he go?

"Yes, but he was afraid of his own shadow."

Why were they speaking so quietly?

"Well, his shadow was enough to make any man nervous."

There was a little laugh. Jim thought they were talking as if they did not want some one to hear them.

"Called it fortune. His luck, or fate, I forget. The same old dream. I suppose we can't live without dreaming. He didn't want to go, and yet he never came back. This river has seen a lot of men of that sort. It is a river of dreams."

A woman's voice came with more distinction. "Some of them came true, though. There's London to prove it."

The ship seemed to have reached the hiding-place of night. It was almost quite dark. The ship was going deeper into it. Low yellow stars moved past on either side, as though they were fixed in the darkness which had come to meet them. The night was sweeping past. The ship was trembling. It was getting cold. Jim could hardly keep from shivering.

"Proof they come true? What proof do we want?" said a voice. "The dream is true, if you have it. There is nothing else." The speaker stood up. "I know, I tell you. It is true if you have it. Better than London, or any other proof. If I had my time over again. . . ."

The speaker was tall but misty, yet Jim could see he was an old man. His voice was like the sound of water. He was staring over their heads, at the darkness, at London.

"Staying away or coming back makes no difference. There are other worlds."

Nobody answered him. The tall stranger continued to stare ahead, and was silent. Then another voice asked, "Where are we now?"

The old man remained standing. He did not seem to hear the question. The only answer to it was the murmuring of the tide. The standing figure seemed to have forgotten them. The boy looked up at the tall old man, who continued to gaze over the heads of the others. Was he looking to another world? The tide continued its muttering. The lights went by in silence. Then the old man sighed. He spoke again, in a voice that seemed far away in something deep.

7

"Gallions Reach," he said, as if he thought he had better let them know it, after all. As he spoke, out of the night, across the water, as though to show that he was right, there came a fluttering of the air, and that broke into a sombre answer, the call of an unseen ship.

# CHAPTER II

THERE is a region of grey limestone and glass, horizontally stratified into floors, intersected by narrow ravines called avenues, and honeycombed by shipping and commercial offices, which lies between Fenchurch and Leadenhall Streets. Billiter Avenue is one of its intersecting clefts. This secluded corner of the city must be traversed on foot, because its narrow paths are marked out only for its cliff climbers; but nobody ever goes into it except they who are concerned with the secrets of its caves. The wealth of the cave of Sinbad, compared with that of most of the offices in this canton of the city, would have seemed but a careless disposal of the superfluous, yet within the guarded recesses of the cliffs of Billiter Avenue no treasure is ever visible. It may be viewed at all only by confidential initiates, and even they cannot see it except as symbols in ledgers, bills of lading, bank drafts, warrants, indents, manifests, and in other forms designed to puzzle moths and official liquidators in their work of corruption. It has no beauty. It is not like the streets of jasper. It does not smell of myrrh. Its gates are not praise. There is no joy in it even for the privileged. A life devoted to the cherishing of this treasure gives to a devotee a countenance as grave as would golf or the obsequies of a dear friend. One rose in the sunlight, or a snail on the thorn, might seem to be above its dry and papery fame. Still, its virtue is there, powerful, though abstract and incredible. The attraction of the hidden treasure of this region, if as baffling to strangers as the beauty of the innumerable brass name-plates at its doors, is dominant, nevertheless.

9

There are acres of its lower walls covered with names. They are, nearly all of them, inscribed in brass. A chance wayfarer might think he had found abundant evidence of a local craving for immortality. He might think the inscriptions to be the marks of anxious men who desired a lasting impress of their insignificance, for to him the names would be no more important, famous, or delectable than those cut into trees or on tombstones, or scrawled in convenient recesses.

James Colet was one of the multitude which entered this region every morning at nine o'clock and deserted it about six in the evening. Between those hours the arid and hollow limestone, where nothing grows but cyphers, is thronged with a legion as intent and single-minded as that of a vast formicarium. Before those hours, and at night, it is as silent as the ruins of Memphis, and as empty, except for a few vestals with brooms and pails who haunt the temporary solitude on their ministration to whatever joss presides over numerals.

An explorer, questing those acres of brass plates for a clue to a man he desired to find, could never happen on Colet at all, unless he had divined him behind a plate which announced Perriams, Limited, First Floor. That name did not seem more significant than the numerous other inscriptions on the wall within the stone and iron portal of the building in Billiter Avenue. Yet it is famous, in its own place. There it is as familiar a word as Colombo, Rangoon, Penang, Borneo, or China. Perriam is synonymous with produce. It is rubber, copra, nutmegs, tea, gums, pepper, sugar, rattans, tortoise-shell and much else which can be induced by native labour out of tropical prodigality disciplined by western accountancy. It is other things, too, of course, but in a chronicle of commerce they would be as irrelevant as the sayings of Jesus of Nazareth. One should not expect come-liness to be one of the inherencies of a brass plate. Nobody desires that the balance-sheet of most moment to him should get its chief virtue from what is apostolic. So nobody could love the house of Perriam for its graces and inward beauty, nor would they question a cheque which, indubitably, bore its sign-manual.

There was a Perriam who had been master and part-owner of an opium clipper. There is no need to say any more about him. He had been the master of an opium smuggler, and he was the origin of the firm. When a visitor is left in the waiting-room of the modern house of Perriam, and is idle and impatient sufficiently long to feel a diminution of his consequence, to feel the matter of his call dwindle to something which is scarcely worth discussion in circumstances so imposing, he then has time to note a portrait of the founder of that house, above a Nankin jar on the mantelpiece; a stylish head, in a rakish marine cap garnished around with an escape of abundant hair, with sombre but truculent eyes, side-whiskers, and a shaven mouth and chin which might once or more have confronted mutiny, and, without a word, caused it to shuffle backwards a little in irresolution. Those eyes would dwell from their height and from the past upon a visitor, with fixity and stern indictment, and thus he might feel the less opinionative when at last a member of the house of Perriam snatched a brief release from matters more urgent to incline a polite ear to his humble petition. Beyond the waiting-room, and within the sanctuary itself, was a corridor of frosted glass and mahogany. The closed doors on either hand bore the names of the principals. One announced Mr. Colet. There were others, and the last of them, just where the office broadened into a spacious array of desks and clerks, had the name of Mr. Perriam upon it.

It was an interior of imperturbable calm. It was a house whose establishment and power was unquestioned. A voice was never raised there. It would have been impious to fracture its lucid stillness with a rude note. In its hush the pens could be heard adding to the treasure of numerals. The clerks were bent over their desks with devout heads. When one of them was wanted his bell rang on the ceiling overhead, a brief peremptory summons to the principal's room. The bell in Mr. Colet's room whirred, and his door of frosted glass opened instantly. Colet crossed the corridor swiftly and deferentially. He wondered what was the trouble now. That sudden noise in the plaster heaven of the office was the harsh and imperious warning of absolutism. Now what the hell was the matter with Him?

Mr. Perriam was standing at his table. He did not look up as his assistant entered. He continued to regard, in disfavour, some papers on his table, upon which one hand was outspread. He was a tall, middle-aged man, bowed forward as if by the great weight of his affairs on his broad shoulders, and he bore a disconcerting likeness to the portrait in the waiting-room, except that he was bald, and his florid and massive face was clean-shaven. Colet waited, an insurgent antipathy to the arrogance of that grim face mingling with his apprehension as to what it was going to announce. This confusion of feelings constricted his throat. He feared he might not be able to answer the brute, if he had an answer to make. Perriam paid his men well. Colet's chair was an enviable seat.

"I've told you before, Colet, I've told you before, that I cannot allow our men at the warehouse to argue with us about the hours they will work. That's our affair. Why have you passed this question on to me? Why haven't you settled it?"

Mr. Perriam did not look up. He waited, with his expression of disfavour downcast to the offending papers.

Colet fingered the point of his neat little brown beard. Mr. Perriam's logic was certainly right. But was that all? Jimmy had been induced to grow that beard through the firm suggestion of the rigid mouth and aggressive chin of the portrait of the master of the opium clipper, a portrait he had admired as a boy in that office, though of late years his admiration had been maintained only by the strength of habit and the traditions of the office. His own red lips were really dissimilar, and not in the tradition. His friendly hazel eyes were now troubled. He did not answer at once. He only moved his feet. He could not think of words which would help him.

"Well?" demanded Mr. Perriam. The principal fumbled a glance at his assistant's face, and then dodged his eyes away to the wall beyond, for Mr. Perriam never looked at a fellow-creature for more than a second. Mr. Perriam remained still, though Colet noticed that his watch-guard was trembling, as though through the suppressed energy of a powerful engine. It kept the mind active and resourceful, working for this man, but Colet used to insist to himself that this was good for the mind. Kept it ready and taut.

"I'm waiting, Colet."

"Isn't it outside my province, Mr. Perriam? Their hours are fixed by their union. You know that. Isn't it for you to say whether or not you'll sack the lot?"

"Don't put it on to me. What are you here for? You seem unable to face your job, young man. I was afraid I'd noticed it. I don't like it. You haven't tackled those fellows. Are you afraid of them?"

"I'm on good terms with them. . . ."

"Your good terms! I'm not interested in them; my work must be done my way. This house can't waste time disputing with a gang of warehousemen. When I put you over that department it was to serve Perriams, not our labourers."

"Their union. . . ."

"Now you need recognise no unity except that with us. That is what pays you and me." Mr. Perriam struck the papers before him with his palm. "I care less for this document than for the way you have handled it. That is serious, in my opinion. You know, Colet, you are being tried? Very well. Here is failure, in a better post. You would be foolish to fail there too soon, don't you think?" Mr. Perriam thrust the papers across to Colet. They cracked like a shot. "Let your good terms be with me. I shall be back on Monday night. See me then. That will do."

Colet retreated to his own room. As he crossed the corridor the clerks in the office eyed him furtively. They wanted a clue to any change that was imminent. Changes there were frequent and unexpected. It was a change for Colet to be in that room of his own. But Jimmy was merely twisting the point of his beard as he crossed the corridor. He was thirty-five; he had worked there for twenty years, and his reward had come but recently with this handsome advance. He sat at his desk, looking absently at Kuan-yin. She stood upon some papers, a benign and demure little image, the Chinese madonna, in porcelain the colour of ivory. Jimmy had bought her at a junk shop on the day he was promoted. He thought he would like her to preside over his work. She appeared to be looking down on his paper when he was writing. Her comeliness was admonitory. Her colour and form, there so exotic and lenitive, would qualify his impulse to act the full part of Perriam. She was different. She would keep him reminded of what was beyond.

But though he was looking at her now he did not know it. What could he do with those men? Useless to argue with them. Then sack the lot? But be damned to that. They were good fellows. They were reasonable. They knew their work. The work would not suffer. Stupid to get rid of what was good over a matter of cranky principle. But either he was to go, or they. There was no sense in it. These sacred business rules were as idiotic as taboos. Nothing to do with reason. Money was worse than ever Moloch could have been. Into the fiery belly to-day with any decent feeling! Pop in even common sense, if it won't kowtow to money! People always went crazy before whatever they worshipped. Perriam was just the same as a priest of Baal.

Still, there Baal was. No escape. Serve the god, or be offered up. Only gradually did Kuan-yin, a luminous symbol of benignity amid alien things, show through the heated whirl of his thoughts. If he left that place, what else was there to do? His father had told him he was made, when he went there. Made into what? The idol kept her eyes lowered to his writing-pad. Everybody in that neighbourhood the other day said how lucky he was. He had stood the boys champagne at "The Ship" when he got that chair. Yet he had never felt it was really his chair, even with half a bottle of wine inside him. How was that? Perriam was right. Some kind of secret reservation, only dimly felt by himself, warned him that he was not in his element. Never had been in his element; always had felt that he was only partly on the spot, even as a boy in the city. Not all there, perhaps. But there was something rum about commerce, as if it asked for only half of a man, and that the worst and cleverest half. Yet it was enjoyable. That disorder before him of enigmatical samples of tropical produce was as good as a scatter of choice books. It had smells you could snuff and snuff again.

He fingered one of the specifying labels. All the samples were labelled, though the marks on the tags were as mysterious as the stuff they indicated. They announced merely the names of ships, and seasons, and the cabalistic port-marks of consignors. The objects mostly were but mummied relics, odorous suggestions entirely foreign, so that they gave Jimmy's room at Perriam's, to a caller, an indefinable air, as though it were concerned with the subtle traffic of Oriental mysteries. But Colet himself did not know the origin of most of the samples which littered his desk, nor what form they had when alive in whichever far islands and coasts were their homes. He did not always know for what purposes they were used here. Some were in bottles, with names, like collars, about their necks. Others were in trays, in packets of blue paper, in bundles of sticks. They were but names and markets to Colet. They were good names, though: mace, turmeric, myrobalans, cinnamon, benzoin, lac, gambir, annatto. So were the names of the ships which brought over the stuff, names of eastern cities and countries, names out of the Iliad, names out of English literature. But he never saw even the ships. They, too, were but names. Nothing of all this was alive. There was not a whisper of the voyages of the ships, except a rare call from the river when he was working late, the city was quiet, and the wind was south-west and wet. That was a strange warning, the voice of a ship. He would never get used to it. When he heard it, he stopped and listened. It was like Kuan-yin. It did not belong to his world, and was disturbing as well as heartening. It would be impossible to continue amid the unrealities of the city, with its yet certain penalties for the misreading of its arbitrary symbols, without those warnings of a life and beauty beyond. The call of a ship at night, the strange smell of a sample, at times seemed to diminish Perriams to an unimportance which he half deplored; but there he was, one of its figures. It is bad to guess the relativity of one's urgent and onerous duties. That begins a creeping paralysis.

Jimmy absently assembled his letters for the post. He glanced at the clock. Saturday, and nearly one. An office boy came in. "Mr. Perriam's just gone, sir."

# CHAPTER III

COLET was the last to leave the office. He paused on that
first-floor landing. Had he forgotten anything? He stood
contemplating the handle of his unrefined ash stick as
though divining the portent of reflections in the heart of a
crystal. Ought to be ebony, that stick, with a silver knob,
in that place. His stick was not in harmony with mahogany
and plate glass. Neither was he. Trousers were rather rustic,
too. They made him look as if he had not clearly decided
whether he belonged there or not. He had accepted his fate,
but his trousers were all against it. Was it possible to change
such trousers? Anyhow, it was Saturday afternoon. No need
to change them in freedom's hour.

"Morning, sir! " A junior clerk went off with the letters for
the post. As soon as the lad was round the bend of the stairs
he began to whistle cheerfully. The lucky young devil. He
had not been there twenty years. Well, the work was all
right. It was good fun, plotting round difficulties and making
them flourish into profit.

But that was only a game for children. He was good at the
game, but his zest merely filled up empty time. This really
was nothing to do with him. All very well, though, talking
like that. What was his work? Where was it? Perhaps a
man never found his place in the world. No blessed angel
ever was on hand to conduct a fellow to his pew on earth.
There was no way of learning whether you were in the right
place. Well, if Perriams was the wrong pitch for him, and
not his game, he'd shown most of them how to play it.

Yet what a game it was. Perriam was an artful old dog.

You couldn't help admiring him, in weak moments. He could not help succeeding, that watchful and predatory monster. Saw his advantage and took it before the next chap knew there was anything to be got. He deserved to succeed. Success? "Always keep your light so shining, a little in front of the next." There it was. But what a light! Only good enough for card-sharpers and ravenous stomachs. Kipling's light was a resin flare. Rollicking smoke and splashes of flame. Very picturesque, but no illumination at all. Suited that place fine. A pity, though, that commerce could not flourish except on the morality of the *Mary Gloster*. Commerce would suit a fellow, he could do something with it, if it wasn't gutted of everything soft and warm. The romance of commerce! Romance, but with bowels of iron piping. One day they'd make workmen of aluminium and clockwork. Wind 'em up and set 'em going every Monday. Light to handle. Reliable. Go the week without watching.

He closed the door of Perriams. It was almost a sacramental act. Wouldn't be there again for nearly two days. That romance of commerce. The snap of the lock was like the amen to a benediction. Jimmy breathed as if free air was his at last. The very stairs looked different from Monday's apprehension of laboured stone ascent. Now they seemed to be leading out to life. Something must be wrong with the other days of the week when Saturday seemed so different. What was it? Very likely none but the Perriams of the world really feel this cold-blooded lust for things of which most men know the names, but no meanings. There must be another sort of life beyond, if a fellow were only bold enough to smash the cage which had got him. No matter. His cage might be smashed for him anyway. Perriam wouldn't think twice about it, if he were in the mood. Then what? O, to hell with Perriam.

In a porch of the court below was Saturday's accustomed elderly harpist sitting on a camp-stool, Silenus himself playing a love song, the old rascal, listening close to his crooning strings while his bowed face seemed bursting with wine. What was it Wells said of that sort of carbuncular red moon of a face? Botryoidal! A jolly good word. Jimmy gave the harpist a shilling. A lovely orbicular face. Booze and the harp had done it. Perhaps as good as rectitude and invoices. That harp was foreign to the avenue. A pity it could not move those stones, as once a harp moved some rocks. No harp would ever shift those stones. Nothing would ever shift them. Nothing but a flaming comet from God.

Round the corner in Lime Street Jimmy stopped to peer into a warehouse door. The Hudson's Bay Company. That was a very queer smell. It was like the whiff of something old, something lost and mouldering in the Arctic. He thought of Ballantyne. It was a reminder of the past. Once, through Ballantyne's heartiness, he wanted to go out to Rupert's Land and trade with Indians from a fort of logs. His boyish application might have saved him from Billiter Avenue. But no answer. Nothing doing. Fate and duty to a father whose influence intrigued a lucky berth for him had marked him for Perriams before ever he knew the name of that house. His fortune had been planted while he wasn't looking. He tucked his stick under his arm and strolled towards Leadenhall Street. Across the street he saw facing him a row of pictures decorating the P. & O. office; regal steamers amid seas and skies as good as the invitation to glory. He knew them all, those ships, by name. There was no reality about them. They were only gaudy inducements unable to induce.

Past East India Avenue, with a side glance, and a regret that he had gone to the city too late to see the old home of John Company. Names, then, meant something, after all. The implication of a word could haunt a man like a ghost.

He was a fool! Well, Lamb felt the same about South Sea House. Yet Lamb stuck to Leadenhall Street till he was pensioned. "The barren mahogany!" Barren then? How did such a man hold out for so long? The sentimentalists had given Lamb the wrong name, the Gentle Elia. That name just suited the sentimentalists. It made Lamb one of themselves, with brains of mush and syrup! Lamb could have endured anything, if he'd thought he ought to. He'd have have had a sly joke if the heavens fell. He had a heart stout enough to furnish a dozen bold explorers, but it pumped out its years on an office stool. He'd endured enough to make any man take to gin. Entitled to a drop of gin, old dear, to take the taste away.

Jimmy felt his sleeve plucked. A man hurrying past with a rose bush had caught his arm with a thorn. Spring had caught him by the arm. He saw it was an April morning and the light was of good growing weather. There was a chance that the mind had a budding season, too, as if some spring, though not in the almanac, could penetrate to the root of the matter in its due season. Jimmy turned to look at the man. Younger than himself. No doubts bothered that eager figure. There was happiness in its spry legs. Some girl at home to make him hurry like that, with a rose bush. On Sunday morning he would put on a pipe, and plant his bush, with the earth smelling good. He was all right. He had found the centre of his world.

Ah, Helen Denny! Jimmy looked at his watch. Early yet. Not till four, outside the British Museum. He felt glad of that. She confused him. He must see her, and yet, somehow, she reminded him of Perriam. Better not think that out. Some feelings made less trouble if unexamined. God only knew to what some threads would lead reason, if it were too curious, and persisted to the ugly end of the line.

Along Gracechurch Street. Plenty of time. There was a good bookshop in that street. Jimmy stood for some minutes searching its windows for insinuations and conjectural words. To see the words on the backs of books was like smelling the samples with the eyes shut, and guessing.

Words were good. In the beginning was the word. Perriam never read. Perriam picked up *Past and Present* one day from his desk, looked at it as if it were odd, flicked its pages, forgot it was in his hand as he talked, and put it down because he knew nothing else to do with it. Asked nothing about it. Some day another word would come along, as it did at the beginning, and the Perriams, the whole lot of them, would look like ten a penny. The little words counted—if you waited long enough. How long? The right word would shift Leadenhall Street, shift London. It wanted some doing, though. Look at it! How long to wait?

People kept pushing him off his standing-place. He was a post in the hurrying tide. Couldn't hold fast in that Saturday pour of humanity. Better to flow with the stream. On the footpath of London Bridge the converging streams congested into a viscous mass—the city was slowly emptying itself over Surrey. He leaned on the parapet above British and Foreign Wharf and looked down to the plan of a steamer's deck. There was a smell of oranges. There was a ship. He was, like many other fellows in London, always writing the names of ships, but he knew nothing about them, and never would, though ships kept the city alive. Astonishing, that men should be so incurious, should be satisfied with names, and never try to get hold of life, to learn the feel of it. Civilisation made eunuchs of men. Their minds grew as infertile as emasculated tomcats, and they lost all interest except in food and safe warm corners.

The torrent behind him undulated past, shuffling and husky, over the stones. Voices floated by as though bubbles had burst. He looked sideways at the continually advancing faces, but they were set and vacant. If you fixed on one it melted in the next wave. A girl's smile appeared for a moment in the tide and sank in it. But that smile was there, somewhere, as though the sun had touched the stream. The sad and desperate current had been sweetened. What was it that once was addressed to a figure in this mass of nameless life? "Even the hairs of your head are all numbered." Jimmy looked again.

No. You couldn't number even the heads. Each head only existed for a second or two. This was the homogeneous spate of flesh, flowing for thousands of years, for which Christ died. But it didn't know it. Didn't even know now that ships and the sea were under its myriad feet, the interminable and horrific caterpillar. Didn't seem to know anything. The hairs numbered of that tide of heads? Poor little man on a cross! Humanity poured through time like a senseless fluid. It now turned the mills of industry, but it never learned why the wheels went round.

That ship below was more intelligible. She was going somewhere preordained. She was solid and confident in repose, waiting to act a part designed. You might die for a ship. You would know what you were doing. But die for a sea of humanity? That would have no effect on its tides. A wisp of steam leisurely ascended from the ship's funnel. She had intelligence about her. She was made to a conscious purpose. The river down which she headed was wide, bright, and unencumbered. The river went past the waiting ship to the open world with the sun on it. Freedom seemed to be down there. But men, they never broke free from what held them. What enchantment was it held him to the barren mahogany?

Perhaps Lamb was right, though. Perhaps instinct and habit knew better than the man himself what he ought to do, and held him, against his will and reason, to his place in the unseen ceremony of creation. There might be some unknown but inexorable law of being which would have obedience at all costs. Though it broke your heart, it would make you do some of its work. Well, then, all right; but Perriam was a damned funny agent to be in the mystic employ of the Creator.

He edged and dawdled back to Cannon Street against the human stream. The roads were full of huge red buses, their foreheads announcing eccentric destinations, places he had never heard of. A girl's voice fluttered at his elbow. "He's a dear." He turned to see what she was like. Nobody there. A ghost, perhaps. It had melted in the crowd. Where he had heard that voice there was a bus which was going to Theydon Bois. And where was that? London was too big to know itself. It was congested with anxious people and nervous engines, and at the same time a man might just as well be on Crusoe's island. There would be more in a parrot than in all these people. The angel Gabriel himself couldn't make a chart of London. He would never know from whom the words came which floated up to the blue calms out of those swirling miles of uproar and confusion. But Crusoe could be in less doubt about his parrot.

It was terrifying, if you thought about it. London was like the dream in which you stood by yourself at night and saw all the stars break loose and stream down the sky. Jimmy paused by the London Stone at the thought of that boyish dream. And that was strange, too. His dream persisted, which only he himself knew, just as did that oldest stone in London, which had come from nobody knew what age and place. What irrelevant things to survive in so long and immense a show! But that dream, the stars out of law and falling down the sky, was like the spectacle of London on a Saturday afternoon. Terrifying! None of the books had ever proved whether it all mattered, or whether it did not. Whether everything was happening so because it had to, or whether it was all worse than shove-ha'penny. Cosmic shove-ha'penny?

He crossed over by Cannon Street Railway Station. From there he could see, dominant over the confusion and the noise, with a lambent cloud behind it, the triumphant dilation of St. Paul's, holding above the capital its mysterious symbol to the sun. By Jove, though, man did that. He even divined the culminating mystery. Not much shove-ha'penny about that. Jimmy watched a sad woman, in clothes women do not wear unless they must, go by a dreary fellow standing by the kerb, pause, fumble in her handbag, and return to give the chap something, though she hardly looked at him. Was that a chance hint? But a man never knew when he was tipped a crafty wink out of the welter of the alien tumult. Jimmy warmed with a sudden confidence, anyhow, that the shabby woman was as important as Wren's masterpiece, as anything in London. She was a vestal to the god of April. He had seen her compassion for a wreck, and she didn't know it. There must be something inherent in this chaos which informed it. Perhaps in the beginning it got the word and had remembered it, without knowing what it meant. These people were all right. They would work out what had to be done, in spite of all the Perriams, and without knowing what they were doing.

That thought, outside the fruiterer's, gave him the freedom to admire a favourite shop. Better than any Bond Street jeweller's, that place. The greengrocer trafficked with the raw material of the poet. Sonnets and lyrics by the pound. You could come to any generous and hopeful decision before that shop window. It accorded with the dome of St. Paul's, and a white cloud, and the poor woman whose pity was moved by misfortune. If the earth were not a good place, when it could do that, then what would you call it? If the good fortune of that window was just the chance luck of time and rain, like that woman's pity, then it was good luck. It could not have been better if divinely planned. Those massed grapes were the translucent globules, purple and gold, of the juice of our own star. Enough to make the sun laugh, to see what he had done. Jimmy lit a pipe as he surveyed the show. Those colours would put it across Helen's artist pals at Hampstead. What an artist, to get those dyes out of mixing mud and sunlight! Helen herself couldn't get that hint of green light in those topaz lanterns, the melons. The rank of geometrical pines was a rich joke. The oranges were the congealed drops of the glow of luxurious noons. No doubt about the earth being a baby, when you saw the skin of a peach. Plenty of time for it to grow. Only fools get impatient with a baby.

Jimmy found himself, without knowing how he got there, by Blackfriars Bridge. "Premier's Grave Speech." The newsboys were running along, holding placards like slovenly aprons. You felt anxious to learn what made the boys run in excitement, got a stimulating hint from a word or two, and then a draught blew the placard open to merely that full announcement. Speeches were always grave. That was the joke of a speech by a statesman; it was wind to keep the ignorant shivering. Wasted on a fine Saturday, anyhow. A little group stood near him, eagerly talking, with a policeman in the midst. The constable hurried away from it, with a lady's silk reticule in his hand. He looked comical, the helmeted and serious man, with so incongruous a little dainty in his fist. The women in the group watched him go away with it, but they did not smile. They were all talking together.

"Couldn't stop her. I was as near as I am to you, that I was."

"Yes. Just dropped that bag, and over she went. Nice girl she looked."

"In a green coat. Never said a word."

Perplexing, with that thought of a nice girl in a green coat who had gone out of April so abruptly, to worry through the eager throng of home-goers hurrying along from Ludgate Circus. They knew nothing about it. Only one of the bubbles had gone from that stream of life. Episodic, a girl who drops over a bridge when others feel jolly on a half-holiday. At the corner by the Circus he felt he would like a drink. Must have it. He left the daylight and went into a crypt, vaulted and cool, under the railway. Lamps were alight in there. It opened into other low caves with roofs arched and dim. Casks stood in rows by the walls with tiny white pails under their spigots. A famous literary man, whom Jimmy recognised because he was even more pleasing than the familiar and outrageous caricature of him, sat by himself, a black cloak falling from his shoulders, at a round table which was like a toy out of a doll's house beside that expansive rotundity. He was nursing a comparatively minute bulb of wine on his knee with an expression of child-like faith and dreamy beatitude. Men stood about talking to each other with the rapid confidential amiability released by alcohol. Some high stools with exiguous seats were ranged along a counter. Jimmy mounted a stool next to a hulk whose taut hinder-parts bulged spherically over their pedestal. The hulk was turned the other way, consulting anxiously with another man. Jimmy got some Burgundy and a plate of sandwiches. He thought of the unknown girl in a green coat while looking at a picture on the wall illustrating high wassail, in which a nymph was emerging from a wine-glass to advertise a famous brand of champagne to two men in evening dress.

"Not me," he heard the hulk say earnestly at last to his friend. "Not me, Charley. I can't. I can't go back. I couldn't apologise to Harmsworth."

"No," murmured his little companion meditatively. "No. He never waits for an apology, does he? But couldn't you go back without trying to apologise? He mightn't notice you were there."

Jimmy was drinking when he heard that, and he made a bubbling sound in his glass, which he lowered too quickly. The barmaid glanced at him at once in cold dislike. He was a stranger there. They might think he had been eaves-dropping. He left the place. Of course, those caves were for the retirement of journalists. Another world surrounded those caves. Another? No. Probably only an extension of the world he knew, complete with its Perriams and idiotic fears which meant nothing except to those whose alarms were roused by the only taboos and fetishes they knew.

Here he was. The retired front of the British Museum, frowning darkly in its retirement with its wealth of the mind, unsolicitous of attention, does not induce the stranger within its gates of iron. Beyond the austere guardians in their uniform at its outer ward an intervening desert of gravel is chiefly interesting for its doves. The doves are alive. They make love unashamed under the shadow of wisdom. You may watch them, through the iron railings, without going in. No need to cross that desert of gravel. All the urgency of life, insistent on the unknown word which first set it going, is in the iridescent neck of the gentleman who struts briskly after the coy lady: "By God, madam, but you must." What is inside the dark portals of the building is only the sublimation of the iridescent throat of a dove in spring.

That high, massive, and grim colonnade, the last strange consequence of love, is not to be entered by humble and ignorant mortals. They are intimidated. They have the play of the doves to watch, which is easier than summoning up the courage to mount the spacious terrace of temple steps to the interior gloom. But Jimmy turned in without a thought. Man, he knew, had done something with the passionate bloom on a dove's throat. He thought the Museum was the best thing in London except the Abbey at Evensong. He became positive when he was in the Museum. His sporadic hints concentrated into a confidence which he could not explain. Why explain, when you know? Man was aware of something better than the things to which he was daily compelled. There, about you in the Museum, the confirmation was, whichever way you looked.

Jimmy did not consult his watch. He did not know the

time, as he mounted, his mind at ease, the steps to the temple which enshrined the proofs of the ardent experiments of his fellows. He was not thinking of time. He went inside, surrendered his stick, and then, irresolutely, because he was trying to think of something he could not bring to the front of his memory, went up the stairs past the stones teeming with the figures from the Indian tope of Amaravati. What had he come to that place to see? He considered this vaguely, while noticing that a wasp-waisted creature, with exaggerated breasts and hips, seemed to be moving sinuously out of the stonework. The stones moved with seductive little forms. One might suppose it was inevitable that those breasts and hips should have developed from the teachings of Buddha. Whatever man did, he found it hard to keep that from his thoughts. He gave his temples to the adoration of the baby. Quite right too. The temples began with that, and they would end with it. Things must be kept going, while we are here. But those Hindu waists were too slight. They were sensual. Adoration of the mere form of good was likely to make the generative gods shy.

He became lost among carved ivory oddments from Japan, translucent Chinese bowls of jade, lacquered boxes, and jolly dolls of the traditional Japanese puppet shows. In those things the fond human mind was at play. Its very fun was better than all the ledgers of British commerce. He wandered on, past Samian ware, and some hints of Rome in a land where the Cæsars at last came down to nothing but the unresolved litter of their imperial state. It served them right. What did they expect to do with lawyers and soldiers? At the far end of a corridor was an obeisant figure, black but comely, spreading out to him its robe, edged with gold, in gracious salutation. He felt that he and that figure were alone in the place, and that it had known he was sure to come. Nobody else was there. It was plain that the figure watched him as he approached. He went straight to that exquisite idol spreading its cloak, offering a lotus bud in its right hand, in invitation to a shrine of peace lost somewhere now in the jungle of Burma. But there was no attaining to the spirit which created that figure, and the assurance of the far grove where it was at home. Too late?

Yet some other image was sternly eyeing him. He had known that all the time. He did not turn his head at once to meet its lofty regard. That required a little resolution. He had been there before, and he knew. With a sigh at last, under compulsion, he turned to the other idol, the supreme example of human handiwork in the Museum. It was the challenge of the Orient to the west, that great representative of the mind, one of Buddha's men. London city could not answer that critical glance. If it were not condemnation, at least it reduced Leadenhall Street to a skittle-alley. That image of a Lohan, haughty and challenging, though in complete repose, was a little awesome. He could not turn away from it. He had not the nerve. He backed slowly from it. It followed him with its unspoken and unanswerable challenge. He knew he had no adequate apology to make. But if it could only answer questions!

When out of that room, he looked at his watch. Five o'clock! There was no doubt at all that Helen Denny would not have waited an hour for him.

## CHAPTER IV

No diner at the Gridiron should flatter another diner by noticing his capriciousness. That would betray his surprise, which he ought not to feel. If he were not singular, he would not be there. For that restaurant is not only in Soho, but it is hard to discover unless one who knows it is clever enough to think you are equal to it, and so conducts you to its primrose door between a dubious tobacconist's shop and a large window of many small panes that are screened by dark-white curtains. No outside symbol betrays the Gridiron. Its frequenters are so pleased with the secret of its choice attractions that they take their friends to it. It is sufficient that it should be known to those who deserve it. If you should enter that restaurant with the bare guess that it is a place for refreshment, and because you have noticed that one place where food is sold is much like the others in any neighbourhood, you will be stopped in a narrow passage by a sinister waiter, who will slyly question you. Should you answer him in any way you will be admitted; should you not answer him at all you will be allowed in.

Even though your nature is so mild that it would permit without impatience a casual policeman to scatter the contents of your bureau as rudely as would a burglar, that is nothing. It is sure to be the sport of gay caprice at the Gridiron. For it is but just to allow the deserving some protest against conformity after they have suffered it virtuously all day; and caprice for an evening in a secluded chamber which we trust is Bohemian is all the revolt most of us can manage against the spell cast over us by custom and habit. The Gridiron is the only place in London where you may get Italian dishes you do not want.

So the proud voice of the great musician Suvretta, as he conversed there with a lady noticeable because of the distance between her burst of orange-coloured hair and the upper margin of her green frock, drew no attention. Everybody behaved as though the musician had the place and the lady to himself. Yet Suvretta knew that the best of his harsh drollery would appear presently, neatly glossed by a journalist who then was missing nothing of it, in one of those illustrated papers which give us the soothing illusion that we are not far from where the important people move in the brightness of their wit with better manners amid their improvements on life.

Helen Denny, at the other end of the saloon, while watching the door, could not help a glance idling occasionally towards the musician. She knew the vulgarity that face betrayed, but it was a masculine face. That arrogant mouth would never soften in surrender to a gentle appeal, except in condescension. And condescension is savoury, especially to those who themselves compel others with a show of pride and indifference. His sullen eyes were arbitrary and poaching. He knew she had been looking at him. The lines of his broad face were as definite as those of a mastiff's. He was a savage, but savages had their way. Jimmy had not come. It was getting late. Would the duffer remember where they would be that night? Jimmy was a strange fellow. It was not easy to see whether he was as simple as a child, or was as experienced as sin, and so was not particularly interested. No, not experienced; that was unfair. She liked his quiet informality. That looked very like wisdom. You could be sure of Jimmy. But his restraint was tantalising. Restraint was a puzzling attribute of informality.

She turned, in a petulant dismissal of Jimmy, to her companions. She was wasting her evening. It did not matter

31

where he was. He reserved too much. He would never be touched by life. Probably he was still dutiful at the office, making quite sure the things that worried him went their proper roads. You could never tell what was in his mind. He only looked as if he knew. His usual answer to any bright word of a friend was a happy chuckle. He might say something about it to her, hours later. But if his comment was surprising then, it was too late, and was wasted. Jim was either careless of the opinions of others, or else he was unaware that people were curious and critical. It was not easy to see which it was in a man whose eyes were often fixed elsewhere and distantly when his friends were drawn together by something which had aroused them, and who, if he spoke at all then, did so as one who was good-humoured but had something else to think about. If he had anything better, what was it? She wished she knew.

Doris Oliver was looking at Helen with her black eyebrows arched over her childish face in an expression of querulous languor. Her elbows were on the table, and her pale hands drooped towards each other like two lilies which had been communing on their stalks, but had fallen asleep. Doris was a wily elf, Helen thought. Helen wondered whether a girl ought to wear her hair like that. It was as smooth as an Indian carving in ebony, and so coaxed down to her thin cheeks that it left only a white triangle of forehead, and was coiled into neat bosses over her ears. Could there be a prim wanton? Doris looked like it, fastidious but hungry. A pallid little Quakeress with florid lips.

"I saw Jimmy this afternoon."

"Yes? What had he to say? Haven't seen him for a week."

"Oh, he didn't see me. Jimmy never sees any one." Doris picked at her necklace of limpid crystals and swayed it with a tired hand. "I'd been to hear the 'Twelfth Mass' at Saffron Hill. He was in Ludgate Circus, looking as if he'd just come away from an interview with his Maker, and was dissatisfied.

Then a bus intervened. He vanished. Translated in a fiery motor, perhaps. All gone."

A plump young man sitting next to Doris, whose happy grin, which never left him, suggested that he was cherishing a ridiculous world because it was so amusing, leaned forward eagerly, as though he were going to add a jocund comment, but he saw that Helen's attention had wandered. He checked himself, with his mouth a little open. His good teeth, and his fair hair which stood upright as if in constant astonishment, made it right for him to smile with his mouth a little open in cheerful interest. He thought, as he appreciated Helen, that Jim Colet must be a cool customer. Helen distinguished their table. She was the picture of the place. That is, if you liked 'em heroic. Too classical for him. She might be warm, but not cosy. A little haughty, except with those she acknowledged. He did not think she had accepted him. It was hard to learn that from a woman whose profile was like—it would have been like Brynhild's, only she was too quick for a Teutonic goddess. She was wasted on a chap whose game was bales and casks and all that. Such a fellow could do nothing with a bosom which was meant for privileged joy. Beside her, Doris was a peevish child. All the same it would not be pleasant to annoy Helen. Those little lines were not at the corners of her mouth for nothing. Things had fallen a bit flat this evening. He must talk.

"I say, Doris," he said, "I've been reading that book of new poems you lent me. Many thanks. But what's it about?"

Doris was swaying her beads. "I wondered whether you'd ask that when I lent it, but I might have known you would. You ought to get some change from biology."

His grin broadened. "All I can say is, my dear, give me the old songs, though I can't sing them, if they're the new. What does poetry want with foot-notes about psychoanalysis and negro mythology?"

"Suppose," some one asked him, "that you don't know anything about them?"

"Well, I couldn't get them out of footnotes and the poetry all in one stride, could I? But Doris, they were very clever and insulting poems, I think. Sing a song of mockery. Is that the latest? But it was a surprising little book, though it smelt like the dissection of bad innards."

There was a quiet chuckle above him.

"Hullo, Jim. We've been waiting for you. Come on. Only as far as the soup, and no hope of progress much before midnight."

"This place is only known to the elect," said Doris.

"And so the waiters have no time," continued the light-hearted young man. "Sit down and let Suvretta refresh you. Look at the Princess Olga. And there's a table full of Russian dancers over there. *Hors d'œuvres* all over the room."

Jimmy blinked obediently towards the princess, but saw no distinguishing back in that direction. The Russian dancers, entertained by a newspaper proprietor, were very engaging. The long room, with its vistas deepening into a sort of maroon haze, was warm and chromatic, and sparkling with eager noises at the level of the table lights. Everybody seemed to be enjoying it. He looked at Helen with some concern, but she was talking calmly to Doris. The biologist was relating a story happily to a girl Colet did not know. Plenty of cheerful common sense about that scientist. A healthy boy. A waiter came, performed some legerdemain at the table swiftly but noiselessly, bent over him in confidential and unexpected solicitation, and left him. He could hear only fragments of the conversation.

"Got no time for him. When I open that man's books, only a little lymph comes out," said the biologist.

Helen was gazing absently into her wine, rotating her glass reflectively on the table, as if admiring the gleams of its ruby light. It sent a flush upwards to drift about her throat.

34

"What would you expect, Walcott; blood, these days?"

"Don't be silly. But I'd like to know why you literary critics are so keen over those morbid symptoms. Why not cut up dogfish with me?"

The critic looked sadly but tolerantly at the biologist, and smiled. Walcott was so young that he was lively. The kindly critic did not appear to think it was necessary to answer. He guarded the secret of literature with a pleasant but superior smile.

"Well, give me something I can enjoy. I've always thought literature was above my laboratory, but from the modern books Doris presses on me for my good I've been thinking it must be the same thing as the dissecting slab, only more smelly."

"If you are able to find books you can enjoy, why not enjoy them? There's something for all of us," the critic murmured.

"I know. But consider the young learner. Isn't the best meant for enjoyment, these days?"

"Obviously it depends on what you can enjoy." The critic's gentle but deprecating smile showed that he was not to be idly provoked. "Why not keep, for a time, to Lamb and Dickens and—and the approved entertainments?"

Jimmy turned quickly to the speaker. The man seemed to mean it. Perhaps he would regard death with a gentle sneer. He did not appear to be expecting applause for an original remark.

The amusement of the biologist, however, was now a little embarrassed, as though he had become conspicuous with a childish enthusiasm. His forehead was pink. Doris watched him with a trace of affected weariness in her eyes.

"I should like to know what you think is important in literature—if, of course, I may be told."

"Important?" The critic was slow and deliberate. "I never said that literature has anything of importance to say. If you were to ask me, I should say that I don't think it has.

Its importance, if we were honest enough to admit it, is but in its manner, which is a matter of taste. One need not insist on one's own taste."

The critic was patient, and spoke as if this belief, like all else, afforded him no pleasure. If the truth was insisted on, well, there it was.

"Sorry. I'll give thanks for my dogfish then. I found a new parasite in the liver of one yesterday. Might be the same as the truth in literature."

"You stick to your protozoa, my lad," said Doris.

"Yes, I must. It seems as if anything more than unicellular is probably fake."

"No, not fake," wisdom assured him. "There again you are imputing idealism where it cannot be found. Why name it?"

Colet moved as if to ask the critic a question, but relaxed again. He refrained. The conversation continued, facile and inconsequential as an air-balloon to the touches of children. Were these people serious? Very likely such evenings were only the desperation of empty existences. But he looked again at the critic to confirm a sense of loss. He felt as if something of value had been withdrawn, by an authority who was able to declare, if pressed, that literature has nothing of more importance to say than a dado. Choose your dado to taste. Yet he had always read that critic's contributions to the more serious reviews with respect, if bewilderment.

Walcott, who had evoked this disillusion, saw Colet's interest. The critic was now, in ironic humour, elaborating his views to Helen and Doris, tapping the edge of the table with a forefinger. The young ladies were as attentive as though he were a priest.

"Look at his tie-pin," whispered the biologist.

Colet looked. It was an opal, but it was an opaque blue. There was no light in it.

"Even his opal looks like the eye of a dead fish. Now he's giving the girls the outlook of Bloomsbury."

"Don't know it. What's that like?"

"The prospect of a dead fish. Nothing really matters. That's all. But you ought to show good taste, though, and that is fairly easy if you consider other people's preferences are very funny."

A girl danced languidly down the room between the tables as if she were expected to do it and were getting it over. She avoided the eyes of the diners, but only a few of the men looked at her as she approached, and the elder women glanced after her critically when she had passed their table. Colet watched her go by, and felt still more humiliated. Helen saw his detachment, and his dislike as the dancer swam past. The critic had not amused her. Things, she understood, were certainly good if you thought they were, and if you thought they were poor they could be entertaining, sometimes. She was glad Jimmy was different. He was not an intellectual. You could hold on to him—more like a coarse man. She had mocked his beard, but after all it was the only one in the room. Just under the reddish cheekbones it was golden, but it was grizzled already by the sides of the mouth, and under the lower lip. She had not noticed this before. When he turned his head to young Walcott— they seemed very friendly this evening—a muscle stretched like a strong cable from his ear to his throat. He looked solid, and as if he would last. There he was. The evening could be a success after all.

But when Colet chanced to see her face Helen had turned it, in the idleness of contentment, to the Russians. She was an admirer of that critic, he thought. Used to recommend his stuff to him. She was part of this place. He was an outsider. Better be off. Most of these people were a little queer, like the pictures painted on the walls. Over their table was a puzzle of heterogeneous yellow and crimson geometry, in which he could make out a one-eyed woman who would have been nude but for the chance intervention

37

of a greenish rhomb. There were no vitals to the room. It was heartless. Night was outside, and you could wander there alone, and would not have to listen to anything clever. He rose, and squeezed the shoulder of the biologist. "I'll be off. I'll leave you to it."

Outside, the look of the stars above the parapets of the houses opposite, and even the smell, on a still night, of London's pavements that had been heated all day by the sun, were better. Nothing ingenious about that, even if it had no meaning. No false contact. He stood by the kerb, free again, deciding which way he should turn.

"I'm coming too, Jimmy, I could see you were bored. So was I. Come along." Helen laid her hand on his arm.

"You were?" He hesitated.

"Of course. Did you think you were going to escape like this?" She laughed quietly, in confidence. She could rely on Jimmy.

He, though, was suspicious that the friendly night was being taken from him as soon as he had found it. He was reluctant to share the street with any one. It surprised him that she had left her friends. Why was that? He could trust himself, when alone. There was safety in the night, but he knew he could not be sure of himself if she were close to him. Then he was largely in abeyance. It was as if most other human creatures were inimical. They were so remarkably not the same that they were uncanny. He felt strongly drawn to that clever, supple woman beside him, and resented her for that reason. There was no privacy with a woman. The soul got mauled about.

Besides, she had not left that dinner-table because its talk was glib and sparkling. She liked that. She'd brought that atmosphere with her. She admired those people in there. They were all clever, and he felt a slow fool. But if they were clever, perhaps that only meant they could justify their hollow insides. They could make their dry and dusty cavities seem more like nature than having guts. Lord, they could make a heart feel ashamed, compared with an interior that had a thick settlement of knowledge on its hard ledges. If that was Bloomsbury, give him Billiter Avenue. You knew there where you were.

"It's better out here, Jimmy."

He found it hard to believe she meant that. She meant it at the moment; that was all. But what an autocrat she was in that cloak. He wanted to believe her. If he could do that he would surrender. Here was luck, for a woman like this to show she wanted him. Helen was as clever as they were made. Then why did she want him? Even the pictures she painted were malicious, as if her insight were diabolical. Sometimes her designs and figures were as though she was contemptuous of the world, and wanted to expose it. He would sooner look at the traffic now, and have no reason to talk. He would not accept her; she did not belong to him. It didn't do to look at that full throat of hers, and then at her eyes. Common sense went then. Was it time it did?

As they walked, and she stepped in unison with him no matter how in irritation he broke his stride, for she was nearly as tall as himself, he felt her intended touch now and then, and was stirred. She pointed to something comic in the upturned faces of a crowd that was watching an electric sky-sign, a baby's feeding-bottle that constantly emptied and refilled to the joy repeated as intermittent jerky lights in the face of a gigantic cherub, and Jimmy stopped and laughed aloud. The crowd might have been watching the heavens unroll as a scroll.

They got into a taxi-cab. Helen could see his profile, salient and thoughtful, in an occasional light, and his nearness was evident to her. He suggested faintly—what was it?— tonka beans. That was Perriam's warehouse. Or his tobacco. She remembered it. She broke into gaiety over what they had heard at dinner. He heard, in surprise, his own dubiety

39

expressed in positive wit. Was that what she was thinking while listening to the critic with such apparent respect? Poor man of letters! Perhaps women were like chameleons, and could swiftly assume the colour which circumstance required. But he liked it. It was pleasant to feel a woman so close who could be as comically shrewd as that over people who had mocked his verities.

Helen knew he was coming over to her. "How's the ogre? How's old Perriam?" she asked. "You haven't said a thing yet. Talk to me."

He outlined the latest manifestation in the city. He put his hand on hers. "So, you see, if I'm to go on, they're to get out."

She took possession of his fist. "Don't let those people trouble you. That's what you always do."

He did not answer.

"You are ridiculous. You want to treat a crude earth as if it were porcelain. You waste feeling on what will never know it. No doubt about it, men are the sentimentalists. Haven't you learned yet that the art of commerce is the art of doing without more feeling than you need for luck? "

His fist was clenched on her knee. She opened his hand, and laid it limply flat.

"If it were daylight, I'd read your fortune. You're too easy with those men. No daylight wanted to read that. If they hurt you, get others who won't."

The cab bumped. His hat fell to the floor. He withdrew his hand to pick it up, and then folded his arms.

"Those men knew well enough, of course, that either they would win, or else you would. They asked for it. Why let them win?"

He could not answer that. Such an argument came from a different order of assumptions. That was the way Perriam looked at it.

They went up to her rooms. There she was, cool, clever,

and luxurious, with her books and pictures about her, the best that London could offer a man. And here he was, like a grey long-eared one, out of sympathy. She welcomed him with a restrained little gesture, and for a second met his eyes in candour and intimacy. They might have been alone in the city. He was sure her eyes could look the Lohan serenely in the face, though that disciple of Buddha were in the flesh. That would give the Lohan something to do.

He did not sit down. He stood with an elbow on the mantelpiece, and examined a Tanagra figurine. It was not unlike Helen in miniature.

"There you are, Jim. Where's your pipe?" She lifted an arm, which would have delighted him in Grecian marble, and pressed his shoulder. He noticed the turquoise on her white hand. He sank into the chair. She sat on the arm of it, and he did not hear what she was saying, for her voice was as far as something just remembered. The bold curves of the thigh beside him, instead of satisfying him, as would that of a statue, so disturbed him that its proximity gave him anxiety. It was dangerous; and she had said "get rid of them." He could not forget that. He was not going to blaspheme life. There was no fellowship here. He stood up and met her glance. She was patiently watching him in enchanting perplexity.

"Why, aren't you going to stay?" She looked down, and paused. "You've only just come," she said very quietly. He did not answer, and she said more. He vaguely wondered whether he rightly understood her. The courage of this woman! He dared not look at her. His own sensations were baffling, but somehow he remained rigidly outside himself, so that his body could not act, as though he were afraid, not of her, but of coming too close to himself. There was something more important. She took a step back, and her arm, which had been raised towards him, fell to her side, as though she had forgotten it was raised. He had no sense.

# CHAPTER V

At Brixton on Monday evening, Mr. Perriam was trying to leave his house. It was his address, or his house; he never called it his home. He had but just come from Manchester, and the fact that the train had been late gave him the impression that he was an overtasked man to whom even time was an enemy. But he could do it all. He was a strong man. He could continue till he had steeled the indecision into which his affairs had softened in his absence. But it was imperative that he should go to Billiter Avenue at once. He was incensed by the impediments placed by the stupid in the straight course of a just man single-minded in his devotion to good order and commonsense. His menservants, with an air of solicitude, and in swift obedience to his peremptory exactions, were silently cursing him, and doing things awry. Mr. Perriam had been in a hurry when he arrived, he was in desperation to leave, and was moving about the hall with an abrupt and heavy celerity which could have been mistaken for craziness, or at best black temper, except that he was so evidently controlling with dignity his righteous impatience over the follies of inferior creatures.

His wife was not there. She had withdrawn unnoticed to a secluded upper room at the first wave of disturbance sent before Mr. Perriam's car as it entered the outer gates of his residence, as it passed in fact between the two giant pineapples in stone which guarded their Brixton privet hedge. Mrs. Perriam was represented in the hall by the silently protesting surrogation of some Chinese silk tapestry, and a few comforting rugs and prints. They did not accord with the magnificent Indian furniture of Mr. Perriam's importation, but they did give something on which the eye could rest. But Mr. Perriam's eye did not rest upon them. He was unaware that his wife was in any way represented. The reproach he felt because she was not there to assuage for an anxious man the torment of the foolishness about him gave his countenance a shadow of proud resignation. His thoughts concentrated on his grave decision, that he must ignore his dinner, and go instantly to his office to examine his letters. He knew his fear was both natural and scrupulous, that ignorance and folly, while he was away, had deflected the orderly directions of his authority.

Jimmy was wondering when his chief would come. The offices of Perriams were deserted. It was past six o'clock. The only light was in his room. Jimmy had to wait. The church clock in St. Mary Axe chimed a quarter-past, half past; and its echo in the empty office where the shadows were deepening was like the memory of things gone in a place where the stir of men would be seen no more. Colet's surviving light might have been a meaningless obstinacy in the face of advancing night. The desks in the big room were cleared of their books, and the bare mahogany surfaces gleamed in cold patches in the dusk. One of the cats of the building strolled across the linoleum. Jimmy stood up and nervously stretched himself. He saw that cat. Ah! another creature was alive there. He called to it. But the cat only twitched her tail and went on. She was nothing to him; she was only a familiar, native to the desert.

But why should he wait? There was really nothing to wait for. He did not want to see Perriam. And perhaps the boss was not coming after all. It was impossible to do any work. If Perriam came there was no report he could make which could be called good. He could give nothing to the place; and it had nothing for him except a cat which considered he was a stranger to the time and the occasion. By going now he could save London from one little eddying turmoil, make one quarrel the less in its vast meaningless jangle. That was worth thinking over. It was impossible to know by how much the air was kept sweet through saving it from but one quarrel.

Jimmy, in abstraction, was placing Kuan-yin so that he could consider her from various angles. Then the telephone bell menaced. (Yes, yes. . . . Certainly. . . He was waiting.)

The office no longer seemed so abandoned now he had heard Perriam's voice. But he was not thinking of his chief. He was considering the Chinese image. Kuan-yin was meek and passive, however she was viewed. She accepted just what happened to her. At whatever angle she was seen her grace was distinguished only by its gentleness and composure. She was not like the cat, which flicked an insulting tail. Kuan-yin was possibly a mistake. This passive acceptance might be all right in the East, or in Jerusalem, but it was a poor substitute for assertion among western steam-engines. He had been passive all his life. He had never felt himself other than an outsider, watching the show. Somehow, the show never seemed to have much to do with him. He had taken the place in it to which chance had led him. He was sitting in that chair because his father pushed him that way. One place was as good as another. If he had followed his instinct ten minutes ago he would not have been there when Perriam was at the telephone. Which was right, the cat or Kuan-yin? There he was now, waiting for something unpleasant to happen, through a sense of duty no more admirable than the reason the cat had for crossing the floor.

And there was Helen. To her he had, without knowing why he did it, casually declined life. He had got out of its way. Actually, in its most adorable form, he had refused it. That would be hard to explain, when the sense of his distance from what was warm and living, from what was shaping the world, was like a drouth. The outer office was the picture of what he had done; cold and empty. But it is not always easy to tell whether one is accepting or declining, whether one is going with the tendency of life, or against it.

Perriam was late. He would be glad to get this over. Then he would be free from two perplexities. He would escape into another existence which, whatever it might prove to be, would be free from the worst consequences of the past. He would be born again. That Chinese image of acceptance had her back turned to him. Should he turn his back on her? Perhaps not. These little things might mean a lot. She might represent something better than he knew. Perhaps the damned steam-engine was on the wrong line, after all.

Eh? There at last was Perriam. He was coming up the stairs in heavy deliberation, like destiny. No escape now; might kill the beggar, though. Jimmy smiled at the thought. But to fling a bomb into Moloch's fiery belly and do in the brute god would be decrepit backsliding. Not much spiritual acceptance, in that act, of the ultimate unimportance of material bellies, fiery or otherwise. Let the fiery belly burn itself out.

Mr. Perriam was filled, in fact, with resolute calm. He was not burning. He was content, for now he knew that control of his affairs was in his hands again. He and they were safe. He walked slowly to his door. Jimmy heard it close. The reflections of another light confused the darkness of the outer office.

Jimmy considered it. Should he go in? No. Better to wait until he was called. He heard his principal moving about. Then there was silence, a long silence. Then his bell rang. Jimmy was glad to hear it.

Mr. Perriam was sitting at his table, magisterial, but at his ease. His hands were spread on the arms of his chair. He did not look at his assistant. He was as if inspecting the central air, his eyes half-closed, in the sad knowledge that there could be no right answers to his searching inquisition;

45

as if slovenly men could never satisfy demands that were so austere and irrefragable. He was anticipating, in weariness, a coming dissatisfaction.

He asked some questions about the drift of the office; and, as no fault could be found with the answers, he made no comment. He merely took his eyes from their inspection of the invisible to look at his signet ring. He rubbed his nose. He leaned forward, with his arms on the table, and he himself began to surmise that he had wasted his time. He might have left all this till the morning. Jimmy began to feel more at his ease. The boss seemed almost human, after all. He had been exaggerating this problem.

"See, now. I'd forgotten. There's another little thing. When do the men go at our warehouse—the fellows who don't want to stay? This week or next?"

Jimmy did not reflect. "Haven't heard," he said brightly. Let chance answer for him.

Perriam was drumming on the table with his fingers, but he stopped. It seemed a long time before he spoke again.

"When will you know?"

"Well, they haven't told me, and I haven't asked."

The principal pushed his chair back noisily, paused, and then rose in pointed slowness. He began to pace the room, his head bowed in thought. As he walked, he snapped his fingers once or twice, and his resentment began to glow anew at the frivolity of this frustration of reason. He considered, with his back to Jimmy, a picture of a ship on the wall. Jimmy knew it, the old *Chrysolite*. Important once; now that rare lithograph. Without turning, Mr. Perriam asked, "What is your reason for saying that?"

"No reason for it. I merely report the fact."

"What are you going to do about it?"

"Nothing."

Here was a man Mr. Perriam admired. He had not expected this. It was very good. Colet was a stouter fellow than he had imagined. Any one who coolly ignored the aggressiveness with which Mr. Perriam disguised his own simple hesitances was sure of his secret approbation. A sly smile moved round his set mouth, but Jimmy did not see it. Still, this young man would have to be disciplined, to get him back to his place. When Mr. Perriam swung about his face was flushed and grim, and even fanatical in its assumed determination. The principal of that important house began, with sonorous sententiousness, for his task was not easy, to advise his assistant what young Colet was, when he came there, and what he had become in that fostering office. Mr. Perriam had all the command of rhetoric of a romantic man of affairs luxuriating in the waywardness of fools. He was solemn, and eloquently reasonable. He was enjoying this. He moved hither and thither with the energy of his warm periods, as if this was a meeting, and he could not help an appeal to the better feelings of a thoughtless generation, which might, nevertheless, do well, if it would but listen to him.

Colet hardly heard him, after the initial outburst. There was but a continuous and strenuous noise. He was meek and enduring. The room grew hot. This must end some day. But Perriam, he could see, was a figure of lasting power, able to continue, and the logic of his monomania was unanswerable. Jimmy merely waited patiently for silence to fall. It did not occur to him that he might laugh and walk out of the room and away. Nothing occurred to him.

But his meek submission to ill-luck, which to Mr. Perriam seemed but a show of proud and enduring reserve, caused his chief to believe that this appeal for gratitude and common sense was in vain, a further offence that made Mr. Perriam flounder in his periods. He was convinced by his own eloquence. His sense of an injustice became genuine, and too quick for his words. They were not ready for his heartfelt sincerity. He began to accuse Colet with an emphasis which he felt was all too weak. He saw that this was because he was not near enough for his assistant to get a full impression. He approached Colet, with his voice raised. Jimmy looked at him then, in dreary apprehension of a puerile but menacing apparition.

"A man like you," Mr. Perriam was saying, "has no right to be here. There are better men. I'll tell you what it is to take a place you can't fill. It's swindling. You are a fraud. That damned quietness and good-nature cheats the people who pay you."

Jimmy was not listening. His principal, close to him, raised an arm in trenchant reprobation. Colet glanced at the threat with indifference, and then an uncalled surge of abhorrence turned him black. He saw Perriam's near mask as the front of all arrogant swinishness. He struck it.

Mr. Perriam behaved as though he had no bones. He dropped, face downwards, and his unexpected falling weight, which his assistant tried to catch, sent Colet floundering. He sat on the floor, legs spread out, deferentially waiting, as it seemed, for Mr. Perriam to rise first. But Mr. Perriam did not move. Colet eyed his chief in astonishment. The room was silent. Mr. Perriam remained on the carpet, with one arm awkwardly folded under him. His bald head, resting on the Axminster roses, was absurdly out of place. His boots with their spats were spread unnaturally. The assistant scrambled to his chief's aid, and turned him round. Some effort was necessary; and Jimmy was as surprised as if, succouring the figure of a man, he found it had the head of a tailor's dummy. Mr. Perriam's face was a bad parody in wax. His mouth was open, and his teeth looked dry. His tongue was large and fatuous. Mr. Perriam stared at the ceiling.

Jimmy shook him, and called to him, in the sudden anger of dismay. Mr. Perriam continued to stare at the ceiling. Jimmy loosened his chief's collar in fumbling haste, swore at the knot of the neck-cloth, tore roughly at the

48

starch which held the collar-stud; but Mr. Perriam did not object. His big rough chin was warm but docile. His limp submission was horrible. Jimmy saw that he was dead; and waited on his knees, hoping that some one would come in. The church clock chimed nine. Only the cat looked in at the door, in round-eyed surprise, but did not enter.

Jimmy went to his own room, grabbed his hat to hurry for assistance, yet returned irresolutely to his principal's room, because, naturally, one would expect to see Mr. Perriam in his chair. But he was still on the floor. Colet left the office, in the confused intention to escape from that object, to get help, to think it over, to call the police.

# CHAPTER VI

COLET was surprised to find that the night outside was in cool and spacious repose. Its indifference stopped his rush. The Avenue was empty. He could hear the traffic as usual in Leadenhall Street. It was still there. And then he could hear also the lonely sound of his footsteps quickly following him. That sound startled yet steadied him. As he approached Billiter Street a policeman strolled into view, paused, and yawned. Jimmy was looking for a policeman, but not for one who yawned. That sign of boredom confused him, for he was nearing the constable. His distress would have checked him with an impulse to confide, but his legs did not know that, and so he was carried on.

He found himself in Fenchurch Street. He was walking east, but without any reason. He had merely turned to the left. He was just walking, and somewhat too hurriedly, so he slowed down. Then he came to Aldgate Pump, which is the starting-point in London for all solitary and extravagant adventures. He stopped, though not because he recognised a starting-point. He knew that pump. He was astonished to see it there. It had not changed. It was the first impartial and certain landmark to show distinctly since he took his eyes off the Axminster carpet.

What should he do? He thought of this as he continued to walk eastwards. He did not know what he expected to find in that direction, but the vista ahead, he had seen, was more friendly with a larger crowd. The crowd, somehow, looked helpful. He wanted to get into it. One more does not seem to matter so much when the crowd is large. Nobody looked at him. This steadied him still more. He did not want to be looked at.

Something ought to be done. Should he telephone to Mrs. Perriam? "Is that Mrs. Perriam? I have just killed your husband. I couldn't help it." Seemed rather silly. She might be upset.

Was there anything he could do? He considered that, and continued his easterly drift. Perhaps there was nothing he could do. Now and again the image of that yawning policeman came before him, to be instantly expunged. That fellow would not understand; he didn't know Perriams, and never saw the boss with his arm up, bullying, and that look on his big flushed face. The look wasn't on his face now. Where had it gone? No good trying to produce it in evidence. The little things which really count can never be shown in evidence. They do the trick, and then they vanish.

Nobody could help Perriam now. He ought not to have died like that. Too idiotic. A man who could die so easily should have kept quiet. Bad as a swindle. He would never have believed it. Any one would think the heart was just waiting for an excuse to stop. Heavens, you couldn't stop a decent heart like that.

Had he really hit his chief? He did not remember doing it. He could not recall the feel of the contact. The violent old fool just dropped. Poor old fellow. A pity he waited till that telephone bell rang. Perriam would be alive now if he hadn't. It was odd that he couldn't remember the blow. But that wouldn't do. No good, that. Either he hit the man, or else God knocked him out. Perhaps a bit of both. All the same to the police. Easy for God to prove an alibi.

He found himself by the stalls of Aldgate. There was a distraction of hissing naphtha flares, and illuminated trams which interlaced on many tracks like short lengths of lighted streets on the move; and a confused slow tide of faces, masks that were vacant, foreign, indifferent, which expected nothing. They seemed to be upborne on shadows. They went slowly past, bobbing on the surface of nothing, and had no names, and were going nowhere. Each face had but a brief existence by the favour of a chance light, and then was gone.

That made the matter worse. It was meaningless. The faces just glanced once, and then went out. Eyes in a never-ending stream, that came into existence with one look of indifference as they passed into a light, and then were done. He went into a tavern to get out of it. There were many eyes floating past, a ceaseless drift of stares.

His thoughts would not stop, and yet they did not help him. Perhaps the morning would help him. It would be all cut and dried by then. No escape. He could stand up to it then. But to what? What would there be? Only the usual cold and compelling logic of the old confusion, and those eyes all round looking on indifferently.

He was not sure what he wanted in a public-house. A brisk potman appeared to know what, and served him. The potman had a squint. That was a good squint. It made the chap seem polite. He sat on a bench near a tough who was thumping a table with a heavy hand to emphasise a matter which had to be whispered, though huskily, to a companion who listened with his eyes shut, while sucking a pipe. "I arst yer. What would you 'ave done?" The lean man did not open his eyes. He nodded his head solemnly.

The talker glanced furtively at Jimmy beside him, who was gazing in evident abstraction at a glass globe in its haze of tobacco smoke. The man had no collar, and he eased his thick moist neck from a constricting shirt-band with a finger, and grimaced in impatient discomfort. "I'd 'ad enough of the bitch. Too much of it. But that stopped her jaw. An' there you are, Bill. I shan't turn up in the mornin'."

The other fellow removed his pipe. "Police know?" he asked.

Jimmy moved instantly at that word to look at them. The tough felt his movement, and swung sharply upon him with his great hands clenched on the greasy knees of his trousers. He contemplated Jimmy with lowering insolence in silence, head thrust forward, for some seconds.

"'Ere, you—you with the whiskers. You listening to us? Know anything? By cripes, you shift your ear, or it'll get thick."

Jimmy felt a change of thought. It went over him with a glow of pleasure. He smiled kindly at the tough. Good, good, that fellow was a weight.

"Don't be alarmed," he said. "I don't know what you are talking about."

"Alarmed!" The big fellow inclined his head to his friend. "'Ear 'im, Bill? Arsts me if I'm alarmed." His face came round with decision. "Don't you wait 'ere any longer than you must, whiskers. This pub is unhealthy. Understand what I mean? You got anything else to do, go and do it."

The distraction grew still more pleasing, though Jimmy thought it might be better to go. Yet not too soon. He maintained his friendly smile, and took a drink.

"Plenty of other things to do, when I feel like it. Don't let me keep you from your interesting conversation with your friend."

The man steadily took stock of Jimmy, hesitated, and turned away, to mumble to his companion. Jimmy presently rose, wished him good night, and left the tavern. He paused, when in the shades beyond, to watch the door. The two men came out, surveyed the traffic carefully, and walked towards him. This would never do. He kept close to the wall, and continued. He took a dark and handy by-way, and lost himself in it. Those two fellows did not appear to enter it. No use having more trouble. He had an unlucky fist.

Where was he? But it did not matter where he was. Any

circumstance would do now, for he had lost the old set. Lost it? Not so easily lost as that. Anyhow, he might as well walk off his feelings till morning, when he would have to own up.

Queer place, this. There was a wall beside him which was Cyclopean. A straight section of primordial night, like the beginning of the way down to Erebus. The just and pre-destined path for him. He would follow it to whatever was at the bottom of it. He did not know that it was, anciently, but the beginning of Ratcliffe Highway. The night was brooding and overcast. He could only guess that he was still going east. There were no stars. Why go east? Well, when the stars have fallen out of the sky, of course they are not there for use.

When he came to a street lamp he could see the wall was only dingy brickwork, but it looked like the palpable residue of old chaos, something which had never seen daylight. It ranged upwards beyond the glim in the street. No end to it, above. The glass of the lamp was broken, and its flame, shaken by a draught, caused irresolution in the revealed area of the wall, which contracted and expanded, as though immemorial night were resilient, but too vast to be moved by a little light except as a local jest.

He continued along by the wall, which was so vague that sometimes his hand knocked it. Then he remembered he had a body. Damn! He was still there. He was not a dis-embodied spirit yet walking in a chaste nightshirt down to Hades. But there was no need of a grave-cloth for him, to get the appropriate feeling. Was Apollyon anywhere about? It would be a pleasure to meet him. Give a fellow something to do. The trouble with Belial is that you can get no nearer to him than when in abstraction you bark your knuckles. Pretty lonely, that kind of conflict, in the valley of the shadow. The worst thing in Hell is that nobody else is there, no devil, no fire that has the merit of being everlasting, no pal, no light, no way out, and the way in behind you gone like yesterday morning.

Were they houses, opposite? They might be houses. They were more like that than anything else. Some were the complement of the wall beside him, and the roofs of others came down almost to his level. The irregular penumbra opposite was sprinkled with lighted squares. The squares showed, surprisingly, that there might be others beside himself in this abiding-place of night; he could see into their lighted caves. Who and what were they? At times the shadow of a colossal and distorted head would appear on a window-blind, a protean shape which confused a newcomer with its grotesque mockery of order and shapeliness, reduced itself to a sudden knob, and faded off. The others here had that scope. They could take any shape they liked, and diminish to nothing suddenly while you watched. Occasionally there were wanderers like himself on the other side of the way, figures with no character, in no hurry. They only moved. Perhaps they were shapes which had come off the blinds for a change.

At times he heard voices, but they belonged to nobody. Nobody was there to speak. Once there was a single eldritch cry. Jimmy stopped. It came from a narrow opening in the dark on the other side, to which depth was given by a distant bracket lamp on a wall. He could see nothing but the lamp up there. Its light flattened and turned blue in a gust, and then flared again, as though it had got over that trouble. Maybe the lamp had shrieked in its loneliness. A figure, which reminded Jimmy of a man, leaned against a post at the bottom of the turning. It did not stir. It did not move to look at the lamp which had screamed. Perhaps it was used to the cries of loneliness in the dark.

Jimmy felt it was time to make out what the shapes were that haunted this region. He crossed over to see. But the figure did not look at him. Its head was on its breast, studying the road, perhaps trying to see daylight on a path that was far below the reach of daylight. There came along three other forms which appeared to be two women and a man, and they shambled together past him, singing with drawling and doleful remorse. The yowling whine of the women was almost human in its discordance with the subjugating dark to which it was addressed.

Jimmy, nearing another lamp, was thoughtfully regarding a truncated monument which stood under it. What did that commemorate? The top of it moved, and turned a human face to him. It was a policeman. "Good night," said the policeman, as Jimmy got within that brief circle of knowledge.

"Good evening," said Jimmy, and stopped.

"Having a midnight prowl, sir?" asked the policeman.

"Yes," said Jimmy. "This is a strange parish."

"Oh, I dunno. Not to us. We're used to it. Not so bad as it's painted."

"I thought it looked like a place where everything was hidden away."

"Not it. Don't you believe it. No good for hiding in. Too many looking on. No good to come here, after a little upset like, thinking that you can get lost. Though some people do say so. I read a book the other day . . . funny things get into books. All about this place. But not like it is when you know it, same as I do."

Jimmy turned over the keys in his pocket. There wasn't much to talk about, if you didn't want to say anything.

"I heard an unpleasant scream just now, at the turning above."

"Yers; they're always nasty to hear. But there's nothing in it. Take no notice, that's the thing to do. No screams, guv'nor, take it from me, when some one's really getting it in the neck. They take good care of that. As a rule. Only amateurs let 'em scream." The constable was amused. "If they began with a loud noise our job would be as easy as kiss your hand. Go straight to it, couldn't we? But they don't oblige us. We have to find 'em afterwards."

The officer seemed glad of some one to talk to. He eased his helmet.

"Take it from me, sir." He jerked his left thumb over his shoulder. "Why, only last week a young feller up there, he tried it on. Came from another part of London. People always think they're safe when they dunno where they are, like. Reckoned, I suppose, that anything could happen here and nobody would notice it. God bless me, the fact that he was here gave him away. What was he doing here? Of course, everybody asked that. Wouldn't come here for pleasure, as you might say." The constable chuckled again. "And there you are."

"Where does this road lead to?"

"Same sort of thing all the way along. Comes out by Stepney Station. Go on far enough, and you'll have to walk back, this time o' night. Far to go?"

"I think I'll be getting along, then."

"Well, speaking for myself, I'd sooner be indoors. But, of course, if it's the first time you've done it, it's an experience. I hope you'll enjoy it, sir."

Jimmy hesitated, but then went his way. He strolled away from the light, but without knowing whether he was continuing in the same direction. He was not thinking of that. He took a side alley without knowing it, and continued to take whichever opening in the obscurity was the next one. No good trying to believe morning would ever come to that precinct. But he wanted the morning, he wanted it as soon as it could come.

This place looked like the forgotten lumber-yard of creation. Objects that could not be published had been abandoned there. They held together because they had never been disturbed. The echoes of his footsteps might shake them down, so he made less noise. This was the very bottom of the night, and he had sunk to it by his own weight. One by-way left him in a narrow passage, under a gas-jet, where he had to choose between right and left. He could see what used to be there. It used to be warehouses. He looked above, as if in appeal, for a suggestion of sky. There might have been one, but the ancient walls were close, and leaned towards each other, as if the weight of night with its density would bury that foundered corner. Jimmy felt that he was sunk profoundly from all communion with his fellows. The gas-jet made hardly any hollow in the gloom. It but selected for illumination a worn iron post, a scatter of chaff on cobblestones, horse droppings, and a few barrel-hoops. Then, almost melted into the dusk beyond the chaff on the cobbles, he saw a dog watching him. He saw its yellow eyes. It was a dog? Here, old fellow! When he moved that way it became only an ugly little noise, and was not there. An unseen hoop sprang from under his tread and bit him on the hand. But he did not cry out. Almost immediately he saw it was only a hoop.

As though it had only opened in the darkness since he came, he noticed before him a cleft in the wall. It could have been an outlet there. It was a lighter patch. While he wondered whether it was an outlet a green planet moved across it, midway, from side to side. The planet appeared suddenly, was bright for a few seconds, and then was eclipsed. As though that green light had caused it, he felt a cool draught blow steadily from across the way. What was there? Then a red star appeared midway, in the midst of a travelling cluster of white stars. Lord, a ship!

He listened rigidly. He could hear the plunging of a propeller. He made a guess. A red light? Then she was going east. She was bound outwards. He crossed over and walked down that slit in the dark till he felt only outer space was before him. There were remote points of light in a void. He stopped, and fumbled with his hand. Yes, this was the edge of his world.

He sat down on it. In a little while he could hear water talking quietly somewhere below him. It might have been near or far. It was invisible. Perhaps that was the tide running by the Southern Cross. That was a long sheer cold drop.

"Ahoy!" It was a clear but minute call from straight before him. "Aho-o-y!"

"I'm here," said Jimmy to himself. "I'm coming."

That caller would take some finding. How far to go? He sat looking at that idea till his plight, the monody of the waters, the far points of light, and a thin drizzle which began, all blurred into a stillness within which his waking mind became like one of the stars sunk deeply in the void. He was hardly there.

Had he been asleep? It had been raining. He was wet. When he stood on the edge, he heard, as if from across the river, a clock strike three. Three tiny ones. Not much longer to wait now. Better get moving. Nobody about yet.

The same old walls continued in a city that was dead. Funny name that, over a shop. Couldn't be right. Perhaps he was getting light-headed. Wu Fu Li. Better not see people about when they had such names. This ashy solitude was interminable, and morning never came to it.

He rambled up to the centre of a bridge which seemed to rise above the shadows, and saw beyond him the inky grotesques of chimneys and house ridges against a low pallor. He leaned over the parapet. So there it began, that day for him. Below the bridge was a stream, soundless and raven, which became outlined in the bottom of night even as he watched. Its banks were of mud. They were livid like the water, but they did not move. The water uncoiled slowly and so it could be seen. A careened barge was below, a lump melting into the sludge. It would take old Charon some time to shift that. But this was his river, all right. The old boy was probably waiting asleep under that gasometer.

A group of men passed him, going the same way. But

they were brisk. Their noisy footsteps meant purpose and direction. Something was ahead of them, and they were going to it. That was more like life. Where they could go, so could he. He followed them, more like life. People were about, glum but purposeful. This was an early world, where railway lines were mixed with the streets, factories with the homes, and an unborn ship stood immense in her skeleton womb above the tenements. The day was broad, when, surmounting grey fields and sheds with low roofs of iron, the scarlet funnel of a liner stood up like a noble beacon. Beyond her was a blue funnel with yellow bands. The vista of low buildings was overtopped by a long diminishing array of cranes and jibs, masts, and the vivid colours of smokestacks, one beyond the other. A broad new world this, but with some smells he knew. Where did this road end? Some lascars in blue muslin and red turbans were crouched under a railway station. A clock was suspended over the deserted platform. It proclaimed a quite impossible hour. Time, perhaps, had lost its way. Or there was no time here. He might have got beyond the range of the schedules. He looked up at the clock, and saw a sparrow's nest in its works. Time was stopped here to let the birds nest. At the other end of the platform was a name-board above the palings, its letters big and positive enough to announce that locality to a great distance, *Gallions*.

## CHAPTER VII

AFTER a little respite of sleep in the hotel at the dock-head, Jimmy went down through a dull corridor to the coffee-room. He was surprised, when he opened its door, by the attack of an interior light which was theatrical in its early brilliance. Four or five men at a table near the window looked as if they were beginning the day. Breakfast then? He got an impression of a room which was set, in a surprisingly good imitation of morning, for an act in a play. The dour figures of the men at coffee and newspapers were very like life. One of them looked up at him over his spectacles in critical fixity, as if he had interrupted a private rehearsal. In his embarrassment Jimmy shut the door at once, without going in. Thought it was time for tea. Perhaps his watch had stopped.

"Who was that?" asked the spectacled man of his neighbour.

"Don't know. Didn't see him."

"Thought it might be the man who got the *Altair*. He was supposed to join her yesterday."

Another man lowered his cup. "The *Altair* is my ship," he said.

"So that's that. Pleased to meet you, sir. She's anchored astern of mine, the *Harlow*." His paper went aside. "Nothing in that," he grumbled, "I always go to it as if it could no more be missed than the chronometer, but somehow I can never get the time by it. Anything in your radical rag, doctor? And don't keep those rolls."

The elderly doctor smiled sideways. "Why, yes, Captain Bennett, plenty in it. You are unjust. You must have missed

61

a whole page of bargains in Oxford Street. And I see our owner's horse is fancied for the Derby. You didn't see that? It struck me as strange that racing stables should be run on ships that never will pay."

"Get away. If that horse is like the *Harlow*, he'll want some stoking to raise the knots out of him. But I know what you mean. I don't like your talk. You're too fond of showing notions by the arse-end."

Jimmy went out of the hotel. The look of that room had lessened his specific gravity. Quite a hopeful hint in the air, that day, of Rip van Winkle. Perhaps he had not, like Rip, secured a very long advantage on the dear old home; he could not have left it so securely far behind. For his beard was about the same. It was not venerable. How much of the calendar had he dodged? Through a slip in the celestial cogs he might have been wangled into another year. What year was this? It was a buoyant thought, it ascended as a morning grace, and at least he could continue to enjoy it till he reached a newsboy and the truth. There was enough about him to justify brief enjoyment of the idea. Evidently Gallions was outside the world which used to have him. Its railway station clock was timed to a sparrow's nest. If time is one of man's devices, like fish-knives and drains, then alter the clock when its current hour is unsympathetic. Choose your own time, if the local duration feels untimely. To the devil with Greenwich, if it is out of your date. Settle on your own meridian, and stick to it. He paused to take in a noisy group of lascars.

The station was busy with a life that was foreign to him. This was a boundary where diversities melted, Hindus, white men, Chinese, negroes, as if Gallions served as a common denominator of men; turbans, woolly knobs, silk hats, and caps. No wonder the clock was abandoned to nesting-time. A rough and dusty enclosure at the back of a shed was cumbered with vans that were loaded with packages port-marked for coasts that were only names in London.

Even the vans here had more faith than the far thought had a reality. What you had to do was to follow it up. Only custom and timidity prevent us from stepping over the last row of the cabbage plot.

A newsboy offered him a paper. Had he better take it? It was certain that paper did not belong to the day he hoped he had reached. Cowardly to step back. That boy was handing him a line of return to Billiter Avenue. But perhaps there was no choice. The boy was destiny right enough, though destiny ought to wipe its nose. He took the paper, opened it.

Nothing was in it. Not a name he knew, not a name which concerned him. No big type for such as he. Useless for the unenterprising to kill anybody. He looked at the date. He had lost a day. This was to-morrow morning. He would have to keep to his own time. The night before last was with the Kings of Memphis. He dropped the paper, returned to the hotel, and went into the coffee-room with a spurious confidence which was almost complete that he knew where he was, and when. Jimmy took a seat beside the master of the *Altair*.

At that moment, on the other side of the captain, the diffident doctor was contemplating the master furtively, for the doctor wished to speak to him, and this bearded stranger who was just sitting down had changed the atmosphere a trifle, and he had not yet spoken to the captain. The *Altair* was to make an interesting voyage. The doctor sighed. It was years since he himself coasted in the China Sea. Out there were the coasts of youth. Probably he would never sit again in the verandah of that place he knew in Singapore, and watch the various and unaccountable East go by, at sunset. Never smell tropical overgrowth again. He would like another chance to visit the ruins of Angkor. The *Altair*'s captain was staring absently across the table to the window light, which was broad from the river. That light gave him away. The elderly and experienced doctor wondered, for a moment, while he judged his neighbour, what the merchant service was coming to, when a man like that could have command of a ship. A negative figure; thin hair, an insignificant mouth and nose; even his moustache was trifling. A lot of interest Bangkok, or the ruins of a forgotten civilisation, would be to him. No character. The doctor had long ago decided that England was decadent, for an unassailable reason; he had found it impossible to get an appointment ashore better than the quackery of humouring the willing victims of bad habits and unoccupied minds, and as a ship's surgeon he was sent on uninteresting routes.

"You know Bangkok, Cambodia, those places, sir?" he asked.

The skipper started nervously. "Eh? No, well, I haven't been that way since I was a junior."

"An interesting coast."

"Yes? You know it? Any coast has to be that, though, when one is there."

Captain Bennett laughed rudely. "Interesting! That's it. That's the way my surgeon talks. You ought to sail with him." He shook a rebuking fork at the doctor in pride. "I tell you he's even interested in the cockroaches. Keeps 'em in bottles. He'd measure the head of any bumboatman who came alongside. The interest of a coast is to keep off it. It's a fine coast when you're clear of it."

"It's only a point of view, captain."

"Point of view! Five fathoms, and a draught of twenty-six feet. There's a point of view. You always talk as if a ship were a peep-show or Noah's Ark. You ought to know by now it's more like a pawn-shop owned by a Welshman. No Cardiff man here? Every damned rivet is tallied. Doctor, you are too late. You should have signed articles with Noah."

"Well, captain, don't you think Noah would be more interested in your ship than you would be in his old ark?"

64

Captain Bennett was entangled for a moment. He frowned at the doctor while getting this notion free. Jimmy took a look at him. A rosy but truculent old dog. This was one of his favourite pastimes, to quarrel in play. The sly doctor enjoyed pulling his leg. Bennett grunted.

"That ark, dirtier than a cattle-ship, what with monkeys and elephants. Didn't her old man have to beat about because the only port was under water? Weather as thick as hell. All the same, no trouble with soundings. Yes, doctor, I guess old Noah would have been glad of a gin and bitters on the *Harlow*. But you knew all right what I meant. Our world isn't new, but Noah's was the first voyage, wasn't it? You'd have seen everything for the first time with him."

The doctor was offensively quiet and kind. "Do you think we ever see anything at all? There's nothing but names in the world, captain. Most of the names are old. They hide the things. We look at the names and see nothing."

"Now what's he getting at? That's the way he goes on, quietly pushing the soup off the table to start a nice little conversation with me. Him and our engineer. If you could hear the pair of them at it, you'd think the earth was only a fog, as near as I can make out. Not enough solid rock in it to scrape the heads off wet matches."

"Oh, come . . ."

"I say yes. All very well for a doctor to talk like that, when his job's just guess-work, but it beats me to hear an engineer doing it."

"Playing with words, doctor?" suggested the *Altair*'s master; "taking soundings with words, and finding no bottom?"

Hullo, thought the doctor, more in this chap than I supposed. He felt more at home.

"It can be a very dangerous game," he said. "Find the right set of words, and you can make almost anything with them, a steam-engine, God, a war, or a pleasant little suggestion to upset everybody. I was thinking of a brother of mine, who is surgeon in one of the New York liners. I know her captain. No more nonsense in him than in you, Captain Bennett. My brother told me yesterday that last voyage they had a lovely upset. It's down in the log, it's reported to the Board of Trade, and one large and decorated form of the story—which depended no more on the facts, I need not say, than my ship's voyage depends on me—appeared in a New York paper, and created some prejudice against the cruel captain of the liner. The master, just before dinner one day half-way on the outward voyage, my brother told me, got a message that somebody was overboard. The sea was calm, so they had a chance to save him. The ship was put about. There appears to have been no doubt about it. Three ladies on the saloon promenade-deck had seen the figure drop from the boat-deck into the sea. The skipper questioned the witnesses, but each most emphatically had the same yarn, a man's figure whirling into the sea from above. Naturally, that captain knows all ladies, or some of them, are charming, but he has been so long in the Atlantic passenger service that he doesn't trust their evidence as much as he does the *Nautical Almanac*; so he examined the boat-deck carefully. Nothing there to show. The boats all had their covers intact. No stowaway had been in one of them. There was no canvas missing which in the wind might have looked like a soul whirling out into eternity. The dinner was postponed, the passengers assembled, all hands off duty were paraded, and the roll was called. Everybody present. All correct. Long before the roll was completed, because about eighteen hundred people were aboard, the dinner was spoiled, but the ship was on her course again. The missing soul, what there was of it, was abandoned to the deep. No boat was put out. Next day the captain heard there was a whisper in the ship—in the way captains have of hearing things, Captain Bennett—that he was a wretch who thought more of his programme than he did of one of God's own creatures. Three ladies in particular knew that he was a villain who did not believe they had seen a man fall into the sea."

"More like a ghost story than anything else," grumbled Captain Bennett.

"It is a ghost story," answered the doctor.

"But," asked Jimmy, "something must have been seen by those ladies?"

The doctor admitted it. "Yes, sir, I daresay. People do see things, then give names to them."

After they had solemnly considered the prospect of a world of intangibilities in which names and portents permuted in a dumb and dizzy flux, names and meanings differing for all who were looking on, Bennett spoke.

"Right you are, I give it to you, doctor. I won't argue. But thank God one thing with a name is all right—money. You can't deny that. You just let me have that, and you can keep the rest of the words, or what you call 'em. The only voyage I hanker after more than the usual charter is the one in the books, one of those treasure island hurroos. I'd sign on for that like a cabin boy with his first bolster."

"But if treasure is not the same as money . . ." the surgeon began.

"None of that, now. Of course it is. No good trying to pretend I don't know the ace of trumps when there's a name to it. Doctor, you can count money, which is treasure, and what more do you want?"

"We'll call it a go, captain. But I hope I'm with you when you count treasure and stow it. I'd like to see it done. But a chart for hidden bullion! That's enough to poison any desert island! I thought that was only a yarn for pirates and boys."

The surgeon rose. Jimmy looked round at him. A short fellow with a big bald head. A grey moustache. A sad but quizzical face. The surgeon paused with his hands on the back of his chair. He appeared to find inspiration in the seat of it.

67

"I've never heard of a chart for the things I want. I don't believe I can have it, unless I make it myself, and then the next man couldn't read it. If he did, he'd want something else. Morning, captain, I'll see you at the shipping office presently. Sign on at two-thirty, don't we?"

The master of the *Altair* was listening, and smiling ironically, while idly balancing his spoon on the edge of his cup. Then he, too, left the table, but without a word.

Colet soon followed. A clear decision had come to him to return to the office. There was no hurry, but he was going. Perhaps Perriam wasn't dead. And if he were, that was an inquisition he could face. Just see what would happen. Bound to be interesting. He went up to his bedroom. That surgeon was a good doctor. There was no name to him, but he was one of the fraternity. How surprised he would be if he knew that his demeanour and chance words had prompted a decision in a stranger about a quite irrelevant matter. Colet was passing an open door and glanced in. The *Altair*'s master was there, considering, with his hands in his pockets, a large example of Kuan-yin. Jimmy was brought up. "Hullo," he said to himself, and then would have gone on. But the man inside saw him. "That took my eye," Colet apologised. "It's a beauty. May I look?"

"Come in, come in. It is a good one?"

"I like it. I've never seen a better one. It's a beautiful figure. But only one or two men know this stuff."

"Are you interested in it?"

"Yes, but I don't know anything about it. It's different from Staffordshire ware, that's all."

The stranger shyly confessed that, when in London, he himself had paid furtive visits to the British Museum, he did not quite know why, to look at Chinese bowls. "There's something about them," he ventured.

"There is. They're the same as some music, I suppose. There's no reason in it, but it means something."

They approved each other, and showed it. They had confessed a common frailty. Colet handled the figure, while they speculated over her quality, and the nature of her attraction.

"We had better not look for reason in it," said the stranger. "For instance, just now she's a bit of a nuisance. I'm leaving here, but now I can't go to my ship till this afternoon. I've been called by 'phone to town. And there it is. I can't lug her about. I don't like trusting rough hands with her, but I shall have to risk it."

Jimmy was jolted by a thoughtless impulse. He might as well finish with a useless friendly act. Was it the word to say? "Where is your ship? Could I take it along? It would be safe with me. It's all one what time I get to the city to-day."

The sailor gave Jimmy a direct glance. Then he pouted at Kuan-yin. "That's very good of you. But it's too much to expect of a stranger."

"Not a stranger," said Jimmy. " I mean, I know her. I've got one—I had one—rather like it. No trouble to see that good thing is safe. If it would help of course. Is your ship far from here?"

"I should be grateful, sir, I must say. The steamer *Altair*. But could you really do it? I got the thing only three days ago, in a Limehouse pawnshop. I couldn't resist it. Now I'm suddenly shifted to this ship, and I shan't see home yet awhile."

Colet protested the simplicity of the task, if he could be trusted with it. His hurry was not great.

"It's very good of you. And I can't make any return. Sure you've the time for it? My ship is at Woolwich buoys. There will be a launch at the dockhead in half an hour. That would put you aboard, if you care to go. Could you wait aboard for me? If you would tell Mr. Sinclair, the chief officer, that you are a friend of mine, and that I shall be aboard pretty soon after lunch——! My name is Hale."

69

# CHAPTER VIII

MR. SINCLAIR, the chief officer of the *Altair*, was on the navigating bridge, with the boatswain and a few men, and his voice was raised above the importance of the job, which was but adjusting the weather-cloth. He moved about abruptly in dispraise. Something, the boatswain thought, had stung him that morning. His foxy hair was so boisterous that it strongly resented the imposition of his cap. There was reproach in his eye, and his darting energy was but the whooping of his exasperation. He had expected to get this ship, for he had earned the post; he had brought her home. But another master was coming to take charge. If there hadn't been a new baby this voyage, worse luck, they could have found another mate for her as well. "Bo'sun, why the hell! . . ." The boatswain indicated with a warning nod that a boat was at the gangway. Sinclair shot his head over the bridge-end, saw a man of his own age in a launch, nursing a package, and who was conning the ship with a bright appraising eye. Here was the old man, already looking for faults. Let him find 'em. Let the whole chromatic directorate run their indecorous noses over her. She was better than they had deserved, blast them. He flung down to the head of the ship's ladder, prepared for any complaint, and hoping he would get it. He faced the newcomer with a look as direct and doubting as that of a challenging bull-dog. "Well, what fault have you found so far?" But the thought was not spoken. This stranger did not look like a faultfinder. Sinclair mumbled something to the new master.

"Mr. Sinclair?" Then Jimmy explained. The red-haired

man, so radiantly contumacious, heard him in sceptical silence. Then abruptly turned. "Come this way," he said, over his shoulder.

Jimmy followed him along a covered alleyway, past three or four teak doors with brass handles, and another that was open. In the opening lolled a figure in a dirty singlet and dungarees, its face oddly patterned in coal-dust and sweat, eating an apple. It took an irreverently noisy bite as it watched them pass. Just beyond that door the mate seemed to save himself from falling from top to bottom of a perpendicular iron ladder with miraculous deftness, and Jimmy followed him down carefully, rung by rung; then along an iron deck; then through a door in the stern. There his guide, in the indistinction, disappeared. Jimmy heard a voice. "Here you are; in here. The captain's room. Better wait here."

Jimmy looked round. He placed Kuan-yin in the bunk. The mate stood for a second as if he were going to fire a question. He did not fire it, but vanished. Jimmy took a wicker-chair, which whined so loudly under his invasion that he thought it better for the silence if he did not move.

Eleven o'clock. New smells here. He couldn't wait long. Why wait at all? But he could not go at once. Not fair to disturb that carroty young man too soon. Must give him a chance to cool off. Might as well take the opportunity to think a bit. What right had he to be there? Say, then, that it was better to help to save a good piece of porcelain than to hurry to give the police a job of work. Perhaps the accidents of circumstances were not quite so accidental as they appeared. Perhaps they knew what they were about. Well, then they knew more than he did. If they knew so much, then they could take charge, and he would see what would happen. Apparently he had done that. It was all a muddle. A muddle to him. It was not much, after all, to be charged with Perriam's death; but it was of great importance now not to become involved again in that other life. That would be worse than murder. That would be a senseless existence. It wasn't worth a thought. That travail in London meant nothing but fodder for cattle. Cabbages for cows. Perriam alive wasn't as important as Kuan-yin.

All rot that! Reason could always justify fears and desires.

But what else was there to do? Couldn't run away to sea. That was ruled out. Too ignorant of life to know how to live independently. He was part of the protoplasmic reef of London, and now he was a detached polyp. There was a doubt whether it was possible to live alone. At the very next hint of destiny, one way or another, he would take it, anyhow, though it stranded the polyp high in the sun, and he dried up. The real difficulty was to catch destiny when it tipped the wink.

The room seemed to be listening to his thoughts. It was very quiet, but it had thoughts of its own. You could hear them, when your own thoughts stopped. The cabin seemed to be full of reminiscences. It knew a lot. It communicated with him through the chair; tremors, clicks of adjustment, a ventriloquial murmuring. Once he heard the mate's voice outside. That fellow did not seem much better yet. And then somebody in a white jacket burst into the cabin, opened his mouth when he saw the room was occupied, and left at once, closing the door with deferential gentleness. The distant trees, he could see through the port, had changed their position. She was swinging to the tide.

Silly to wait there. He was an intruder. Whatever place there was for him in the world it was not that room. He went outside. Mr. Sinclair hurried past him on deck. "One moment, please." He advised the chief officer what he had done with his charge, and that the contents of the parcel were eminently precious and delicate. Mr. Sinclair darted back to the alleyway without a word. "Steward!" he bawled. The man in the white jacket was there at once. "Parcel in the captain's room. Too good to be touched. Don't touch it. See?"

72

Then he turned to Colet, and his question was in his glance. "Anything more to say? I'm busy." Jimmy explained that he would not wait for the captain. He must go now.

"What?" ejaculated the sailor. "I thought you were a passenger or the ship's agent. Why didn't you speak? The launch has gone. The pilot's aboard. I've just had a telegram to say Captain Hale joins us at Plymouth. You'll have to go on to Gravesend now." He spoke as though it would not matter to him if Jimmy went farther still.

Jimmy made a little protest.

"There it is. I can't stop. I'm wanted above," Mr. Sinclair strode away.

The *Altair* was far from the shore. There was some inexplicable activity, and directing shouts. The ship began to tremble, and gave a warning bellow. She was under way. Jimmy half-wished he was going with her; a foolish wish; he did not even know where she was bound.

# CHAPTER IX

THE *Altair* went down on the first of the ebb at half-speed. Colet had not seen those shores since he came up this very reach more years ago than he could accurately count. It does not heighten the present morning light to count years you seem to have lost. But it was twilight, he knew, when he was there last. Not much use peering backwards to discern what has lapsed into an old twilight. All the people who were with him then were shades in a lost year. He could not recognise them. There was a vague woman in a pale dress beside him, whose face he could not see now, but he could feel her consoling fingers rumpling his hair. Here it all was. And an old man stood up there, who, somehow, accorded with the dark and the sound of the warning river. He remembered how the grave murmuring stirred him, while all was still. Who was that old fellow? His dim tall figure was still there. But nobody knew his name. He could hear only Mr. Sinclair's voice. No doubt about that. We live a dual existence. The people who talk to us in the present are unaware that we are not altogether with them. He was making two voyages now. If that chief officer were asked, he would give an emphatic opinion, which everybody would see was obviously right; but the truth isn't as easy as that.

He paced the deck, and watched two landscapes unfold, one in an evening without a date, and another that their pilot was watching. He felt that the actual was of less potency, in spite of the spring sun, than the obscure land from which the sun had gone, where the people were so merged in a fading year that nothing of them remained but

74

a gesture of affection and an absurdly solemn premonition about something he didn't know. It looked as if the doctor who talked at breakfast was right. There is no chart for what is of enduring importance to us, and nobody talks of what is of most importance to us. Infinity cannot be charted. There are only private symbols, but they affect us more than the loud fussiness of the day. Perhaps, in a time not yet, even that aggressive officer on the *Altair's* bridge would appear to be shadowy and significant to him. In what way? Mr. Sinclair's voice could be heard again. He was addressing somebody in the bows, and his voice was like a gun's. Jimmy saw some fun in that probability. It would not be easy to make an august memory of that red-headed man.

Something was happening. Of course, here was Gravesend. They had anchored. The day was still early. It would be easy to get back. The fellow in the white jacket approached him. "Mr. Sinclair would like to see you, sir. He's in the chart-room."

Jimmy went up. Sinclair held out his hand with an embarrassed smile. "I don't know your name. You'll excuse me if I've seemed inattentive. I've been rushed. The pilot will be leaving in ten minutes. He's talking to the chief engineer. You can push off with him."

He was assured that all was well. "Have you got an interesting voyage in front of you?"

"I haven't. I'd stay ashore if I could. I've been in this old thing too long. Four years and two sets of owners. It's time for a change, but she was turned round again so quickly this voyage that I didn't get a chance to do anything about it."

Mr. Sinclair now seemed slow and sad. He was opening and closing a pair of dividers. "Look here, I'm sorry I was so busy when you boarded us. No time for a drink, and all that. Things have gone in jumps the last day or two, and I never knew which way they'd jump. The owners, you know.

The blessed owners. But perhaps you don't know 'em. The present owners are worse than the last, and old Perriam was bad enough."

"What!" muttered Jimmy, suddenly shocked; "did he own her?"

"Under another name. Did you know him?"

"Yes. I worked for him. I was in his office."

Mr. Sinclair betrayed no interest. "You were?" He put down the dividers, and called to a sailor outside. "Go and see if the pilot is still with Mr. Gillespie." He pushed back a chart and perched himself on the table. "I saw in a paper that the old swine is dead. Found dead in his office. About time, too. What was the matter with him; heart? Couldn't have been. He hadn't got one. What was it?"

Jimmy took a steady look at his watch. "So far as I know, it was a punch on the jaw."

Mr. Sinclair looked up with amused interest. "No. It was a jolly good one then. Who hit him for us?"

"I did."

Mr. Sinclair threw up an astonished leg and laughed. He laughed with his head thrown back, loudly and with complete abandon to his enjoyment. He slapped his raised leg with his hand. He was wiping his eyes when he turned to Jimmy, who was speaking to him.

"Please tell me what the paper said about it."

"Eh? Oh, nothing much. I don't remember. Said he was dead. That's all. Found in his office, on the floor. Just dead. I say, what the devil are you doing here? It didn't say any one had hit him. I don't believe it did."

"Well, somebody did, and here he is, though God knows why."

A sailor came to the door, and announced that the pilot was ready to go. Mr. Sinclair slid off the table, hesitated, and snapped his fingers. "All right, Wilson. Tell him . . . tell him there's nobody for the shore."

76

He turned to Jimmy. "You'd better be in no hurry. You want time for this. No harm in running round to Plymouth with us. The skipper knows you, doesn't he? Nothing in it. A little loafing is all right. Besides," he grinned, "old Perriam. That old dear. I want to hear all about it."

# CHAPTER X

THE oil-lamp of the cabin, after a short sleep, would wake, and move uneasily in its gimbals. Its smoky glim was barely enough to fill the hollow with light, though the room was small, so the long shadow over the head of the settee might have been either a man or a hat and coat dangling from a peg; for, in sympathy with the movements of the swinging lamp, and the water in the bottle which sloped unnaturally first this way and then that, the limp coat came feebly to life now and then, and rubbed weakly over the cabin wall. It was reconciled to the perpendicular again when it found its tether would allow it no more freedom. There was no sound, except a suggestion that the night outside was a tide pouring headlong forever between the stars; but there was a tremor in the cabin, as of a dance of all its atoms, and a profound murmuring, which might have been the humming of an asteroid asleep with the speed of its rotation in space. An open book on a table beside the bunk, responsive to the dance of the atoms, was now projected over the edge, and was on the point of toppling over. The heavy brass handle of the door suddenly made frantic efforts to come off, and then the door opened, and the light flattened in a cold rush of night. The book fell. When the lamp flame stood upright in the quiet again, Sinclair was there, looking down on Colet. Jimmy continued asleep in his bunk with the calm abandon of the joys and woes of earth shown by the image of a crusader in his niche in a church. The sailor grinned, and was about to go, when the sleeper opened his eyes. The formidable figure he saw filling an unfamiliar and unescapable space, giant in its glistening oilskins, brought him up on the point of leaping out to meet the monstrous adversary of a dream.

"Eight bells," said the sailor, "and all's well. I just popped in to see how you were taking it."

Colet sank back in a release to ease. "Where are we now?"

"Mind your own business. Do you want this book? What a dirty light you've got, though. Won't it do any better? But this ship wasn't fixed for comfort; only for cargo and sailors."

# CHAPTER XI

THE steward had warned Colet that they were at Plymouth, and he was by the rail, watching a thin mist change into the hills of a Devon morning, when Sinclair came along.

"No hurry, but the old man is aboard. Give him time to find himself, then go to him. I've had a talk with him."

Captain Hale, in his shirt-sleeves, but wearing a bowler hat, was in his cabin advising the steward how he desired his property to be stowed. When Jimmy entered the room his step had to be stretched over a mound of clothes. The captain showed no surprise at his presence. "Come in, Mr. Colet. Sinclair has reported to me." He motioned the steward out of the cabin. "Come back in five minutes."

They talked, but the captain never took his eyes off a stack of shirts on the floor. Jimmy got an impression that somehow there was a difficulty with the laundry. They were discussing that. Some collars were missing? Even the neat pile of clean linen before him did not appear to interest the captain very much. Perhaps it was only old stuff which had gone astray; not much good. A grey and shy little man. The captain stooped and picked up a garment; turned it about as though in depreciating examination. Neither of them spoke for so long a spell that Jimmy was on the nervous point of bringing the encounter to a close and, going out to find Sinclair and a boat. The captain silently considered the garment in his hands

"It's irregular," he murmured at last, as if in dispraise of those pants. "A bit off the course. But I can log it, I suppose." He changed his regard to Colet, though not to his face; about as high as his knees. Merely comparing their pants?

"We leave as soon as our engineers are ready. They've uncoupled something below, but they won't be long. Well, what will you do then? Go on with us?"

"What? Yes, if I may."

"Well. It's your affair. I suppose it's in order. We'll know some day. Only thing to do is what seems best at the time. I'll see you at dinner."

That night at dinner hardly a general word went across the table. The captain was new to the ship, and he presided over the soup as though he were not sure that the others would care for the stuff. "Too much onion in this, steward. Remember that." Sinclair's stern interest was fixed where nothing could be seen. He was merely performing a duty in eating, and he picked up his cap from a sideboard and left the saloon as though glad to get out of it. The captain and the chief engineer then conversed in undertones of some technical matters. Jimmy wished to learn to where in the world the ship was bound, but he had to do without it.

Yet, when he got away from that confinement with strangers who were talking apart and confidentially of much which he did not understand and more that he did not hear, and was alone on deck, their destination, wherever it was, did not loom importantly. It was incidental. They were outward bound. Enough for one day; and one day at a time. He leaned on the lee-rail, amidships, watching a distant light. That was the last spark of the old interests. It was low down. It was a wonder that it could persist. Sometimes it did go out, but reappeared, to attach and remind them. Then a big warm presence bringing the smell of a cheroot was beside him. He did not hear it approach. He smelt it first. A dark night. It said nothing. Occasionally the cigar glowed. The chief engineer? They didn't know each other yet. That warm shadow also seemed to be contemplating the light. It remained there in solid ease for some time, but it did not speak. Then it stood up, and stretched. "Aye?" it soliloquised interrogatively; and then, as though in confirmation, "aye"; and that was all. Its place was empty.

So this, conjectured Jimmy, groping over his clammy door for its handle, is romance. There's no fuss about it. You wouldn't know it, unless you were told what it was. Altogether casual and insignificant; as if it were as silly as life itself.

# CHAPTER XII

GILLESPIE extolled the Scots. His hardihood left nothing else to talk about. The steward brisked about with the morning dishes. Jimmy, in a way that was new to him, noticed that the odour of the coffee had the effect of a clarion, of a hymn of praise. It smelt better than it tasted. The mornings were good. And this the Bay of Biscay, too! The seas were actually chanting. A stray beam of shine from the skylight swayed leisurely to and fro across the table-cloth; the water-bottle was in its track and answered the light by decorating the table linen with the spectrum. A rum thing, but as soon as you approached the matter of the resounding ballads and the tall tales, it was like this. On the whole, Colet thought he preferred it as it was. Look at Gillespie, that bold sea-man! Or Hale, whose downcast thoughts seemed absorbed into the emptiness of his plate! Easy-going and friendly. No deeps of evil and heroism there. Hale hardly ever spoke but his words then certainly hinted that he knew what he was talking about. Gillespie continued to admonish Sinclair about the Scots, and the chief officer was smiling derisively.

"Where would you have been without them? Answer that now. Talk of your Shakespeare! Aye, he wasn't so bad. Not so bad. But there's Burns. There's a man for ye. Have ye the like of him? And who did all that was worth doing, marine engines, the best ships, whisky, now?"

"And macadam, Gillespie. Don't forget that."

Jimmy had heard all this before. It was probably as constant at a ship's mess-table as bloaters. Gillespie's face was big and comforting, and its bronze made his grey eyes, and his crimped and wiry hair, oddly pale and noticeable; his back was as broad as the mahogany. Sinclair had confided to Colet that the chief engineer could smell in his sleep a minor fault in the engine-room and go to it by divination. Sinclair handsomely confessed now, pulling bread apart, that he would not so strongly object to the Scots if they could talk English.

"Man! I tell ye that Scotch is the original English, anyway."

"Of course, when we were hairy savages, living on heather tops. Before we learned better manners. I say, Gillespie. Didn't I ever tell you? There was a Scotchman, an Aberdonian, I sailed with once. He was an engineer, on his first voyage. I had to guess twice before I knew what it was he wished to tell me, but couldn't pronounce properly. Well, we were coaling out East, and this fellow-countryman of yours was at a hatch with the Chinese Number One. They were rowing. Pidgin-English and your kind of English. You never heard such a shocking noise. The work was getting all balled up. Nothing to do with me, of course, but I strolled along to hear what the trouble was. The young engineer tried to tell me, but the Chink broke in. He was so jolly wild. He pointed at your countryman. 'Look!' he said. 'No speakee English. No speakee Chinee. All same bloody Scotchman.'"

Sinclair went out of the room triumphant while Gillespie was considering a shot at him. The captain took no part in the discussion. "He's a lively young man," he remarked to the engineer. "You know, Gillespie, I'm told that I'm a Scot, or that I was."

Thus that day drew insensibly towards noon. The next day was like it, and the day after was separated but by another night. Time was alternate day and night. Their ship was enchanted in the centre of a vast and empty world. It was the dot and focus of a radiant vacuity; and it was a handhold when about them was nothing but stars and the dirge of the abyss. It laboured, it beat down without ceasing glassy upheavals into fields of hissing white, but it could never escape to that dark and distant line where the wall of heaven stood about them. They were alone. The romance of the sea had flown off, perhaps, on the wings of the clippers, and was lost. It was not there. But the sea and the sky were unaware of any loss. They were beautiful, but were aloof from the desires and anxieties of man. The deck was orange and crimson with rust. Even iron-rust, when it was seen in the right place, accorded with a mind in which perturbation was lessening. Jimmy had a word with Sinclair about that rust. Sinclair surveyed it, and advised Colet that it would do him more good to take a chipping hammer to it. What was more, it would have to be done. The black funnel and the yellow masts leaned this way and that, and sometimes swung in a half-circle.

A coast appeared, late one afternoon. It was illusive, but it must have been land. The shape of earth there, Colet saw, had the luminous indistinction of a pale blue flower in sunlight; those strips of orange would be its beaches. The sky over the inland hills of violet was a clear height of greenish ether. They were lost, very likely. They had strayed to a younger and brighter planet. An opposite coast formed with a scatter of white specks down by the sea. The captain stood with Colet on the starboard side of the bridge. "There's Tangier," said Hale.

Names. Bare names. They were no nearer the reality than ever. The only reality was their present ship and its men. Hale and that spellbound seaman inside the wheel-house were solid. They were there. But beyond them was the old vaporous abstraction. Perhaps an Odyssey could begin with every voyage of every ship. But how was a voyager to know that? What would be the alarming signal: "Here you start?" It must all depend on the spectator himself. Perhaps there is no adventurous morning light showing things anew for those who sleep on. But there is no knowing whether one is awake or asleep.

Captain Hale, having indicated the presence of Africa, remained in the same position, leaning on the weather dodger, with his thin brown hands clasped before him. His white shirt cuffs were linked with gold. A neat, precise, and sensible deacon. He was still regarding Tangier in apparent belief. Somebody was playing an accordion in the forecastle.

"How strange," commented the ship's master. "I don't think I've heard that tune since one night at the Queen's Palace of Varieties. You wouldn't know that music hall. Poplar High Street. I was a youngster then, in a barque in the South Dock. I heard Jenny Hill that night. Before your time, I think. No, you wouldn't know her. They called her the Vital Spark." Captain Hale was still considering the portentous loom of Africa, and seemed pleased with it.

Good Lord, thought Jimmy. Here we are, and the men together on the same ship are in different seas, and only appear to be together. They see different things. What would make this world common for us all?

"The Great Macdermott was on the programme that night," quietly continued Hale.

"We don't want to fight, but by jingo if we do?"

"Yes. You've got him. That's the fellow."

"It's a long time ago."

"Yesterday, or thereabouts, my boy. Just feel our revolutions."

Jimmy gave conscious attention to the incessant and energetic throbbing which was the only warning of their progress.

"She's doing her best," he reported

" She is," said Hale. "Well, that's how time goes." He turned to look at their wake. Jimmy turned. The track of their past diminished to infinity on the uneventful sea towards the declining sun.

# CHAPTER XIII

A LITTLE concentration with a chipping hammer will do more to the inexperienced back than to a rusty deck. Colet, not to be beaten, ached while he chipped, and the sun burned his neck. The rust was even drier than ledgers. How long to go to one bell? A flake struck his eye and he gave it a rest; he stretched his back. The sea, after the near red deck, expanded into an astonishing sapphire. An island was in sight in the blaze of day, a desert of tawny rock. It quivered under the sun and the lucent breeze. Where had that place come from? Conjured up? Sinclair, on his way aft, rebukingly active, descended an iron ladder to the deck with a rapid tattoo of his feet, but checked alongside Colet to peer at the island. One tiny house by the shore, a white cube, was all that showed in the desert.

"That's where she lives," confided Sinclair. "Circe waits for me there, but alone. No leopards. And especially no swine. Only jars of wine."

"Have you ever seen her?"

"On my first voyage. Yes, I think I saw her. Just a glimpse."

"But that line of white along the shore. That'll be the bones of sailors."

"Served 'em right. I'm the man. One day I shall land, and then she'll come down to the beach. No good looking to-day. You won't see her. She knows I'm passing the place. Not the time yet to stop. Farewell, Circe, my love!" Sinclair kissed his hand to the mirage.

Their ship touched earth again at Port Said. That was a solid abode of men, with the assured smells of historical contamination and well-established intercourse. No doubt about Port Said. It was an area of understandable life, noisy and lusty. It was ramshackle, insistent, predatory, and raucous. Goats reclined in its gutterways. Its crowds hinted indifference or hostility. Vendors of obscenities, purveyors of cosmopolitan lesions, enticed with the smirking confidence that the desires of their own species were well known to them. It swarmed with flies. Its Canal was a lucky way of escape.

But by Suez, one daybreak, Colet sat up in his bunk from sleep with the instant waking certainty that something was going to happen. The ship, too, he could feel, was waiting for it. She was still and reconciled. She was anchored. The cabin was as close and quiet as a crypt. A crypt; this might be the breathless resurrection day. There was no sign. It had not begun yet. The book he had been reading late into the night was just discernible, open on the floor, where it had fallen from his bunk. Something in his favour. It was the Bible. The book looked up at him. It counselled him nothing from that distance below. The ship, he thought, was abandoned; he was left aboard, to make the best of it on his own.

Colet glanced out of the cabin port. There he saw, though not without doubt, what must have been the usual stanchion. A loose rope was beside it hanging from above. The rope was as still as the iron. That appearance of waiting in resignation was more than strange. It was a warning. The queer thing was that London seemed of less consequence to him now than that book on the floor. Reading that book had been his last act. The bare shadow of London moved but once in his thought, as he sat up; but Billiter Avenue had gone. Of no importance. What was important now? Through the port, beyond the stanchion, the distance deepened as he looked. Light was coming. Land formed under it.

Syria, very likely. Somewhere hereabouts Moses used to roam with his aboriginal mob and his first laws done in stone. Perhaps this was the chosen region of earth, whenever it was decided to vouchsafe a new light. That silence and brooding obscurity would make a man contrite and willing to learn. Out there, something would soon begin. The eastern sky seemed to be indicating the dread judgment to come, but no sign was under it of the works of men. Or else all that work was in hiding. Men and their work guessed what was coming. They had crawled under the film of sin and night which the past had left on the earth. But the upstanding ship would be terribly conspicuous.

That stanchion was already plain. A level flush of reddish gold beyond made the earth shrink into a deeper dark, but the elevated iron of the ship from London, unable to escape, was brightly caught. Without the sound of a trumpet the eye of Heaven suddenly lifted and blazed. Bones and opinions were like glass. The earth was prostrate under that unremitting celestial stare.

And every man at breakfast that morning was dressed in white. Immaculate linen for a transcendent day, when the old things had passed! Colet surveyed his messmates in surprise. Were they all confident they would be approved, and had anticipated it in pure raiment? Captain Hale waved aside the bloater and bacon. No more grease. There was a stifling suggestion that furnace doors were somewhere open. "Not now," he said to the steward with the dishes. "This Gulf is the easier for a little fasting," he explained to his colleagues at the table.

"Man, never give in to the Red Sea," said Gillespie. "How would you care for yon engine-room now?" he asked Sinclair.

The chief officer was glum. He wiped his wet face. He glared malignantly at old Gillespie. "Engine-room! This is about the place where all that began, isn't it? Civilisation and engines. God seems to be savage about it now. On the bridge you'd think He was trying to burn out a mistake."

"It's no right. That's no the way to talk. Sun and rock and no wind. What would ye expect?"

"I tell you he is sorry he let us start it. This place is being paid out. That's what makes it so damned hot."

"Och. Get away, man!"

"It's your cursed engines and science, that's my idea, Mr. Engineer."

The captain smiled; he was not at breakfast; he was waiting for a message from the shore. "Don't let it worry you. We can't alter it. It's not Gillespie's fault."

"I think so, sir. If it wasn't for engines, we shouldn't be here."

"An' where would ye be? Piddling aroun' south with a bit canvas. I tell ye. The engineers are the men. Ye couldna do withoot them."

"I think," said Hale, "Sinclair is not really annoyed with the engines. He must find them handy at times. Perhaps he is is only thinking of the uses to which we put our knowledge. Is that it, Mr Sinclair?"

The chief officer had not seen this turn to his petulance. "Well, sir. No. I don't know. I was only hot."

The engineer presently left, still argumentative. "Hot! I never heard the like of it." The captain shook his head in amusement at his lieutenant. "Be careful, Mister. If you must get peevish, don't blaspheme science. Nobody will mind if you round on God. But leave the engines alone. They're sacred."

Sinclair looked round at the master in a little surprise. That elderly man was sitting with his eyes cast down, but he looked up in a friendly way at his junior. "You'll find it so," he said. "It's no good getting annoyed with the way of things. We might as well argue with the seasons. They change, when the turn comes. Some day—perhaps—even engines may not be sacred." He went out of the saloon, but came back to put his head in the door, "We get going in half an hour."

They went on. The ship came to sullen life, grumbling and stuffy, breathing cinders heavily all over them from a languid bulge of smoke. She had entered another region of earth, and was committed to another existence. Europe was far off, and out of mind; they were beset by another order, and must make the best of it with the little they knew. The shores near to them on either beam showed that Sinclair was right in one thing. Those coasts were burnt out. There the earth had finished with men. There was no more darkness in the high bergs of Africa. They were masses of radiant bronze and brass. The very sea was lumpish and resentful of the intrusion of keels. It did not want them to pass. At sunset it was a level of heavy lava, polished and opaque, where their ship was fixed centrally in a glow between fulgent metallic shores. Sounds had gone from that world, for no men were there, no rain, and no wind.

Off the island of Socotra they found some air, and their ship began to sway. They had crossed over; they were involved now in the hazard of a new probation. The waters opened to the East, to a legend that was fabulous in ancient cities when London was sedge and mud.

"It doesn't look as if the monsoon had broken, sir," said Sinclair to the captain. They were on the bridge. Socotra, a serrated confusion of the horizon, was far to starboard.

"No," said Hale. "I wish it had. We should know what to expect. The weather looks oily. I think we will have those hatch covers secured. Never know when it may break."

But Colet was trying to puzzle out Socotra from an obscurity of cloud, sea glint, and shadow. That presence, to him, was more insistent than a monsoon which was not there.

"I've heard of it often enough, and there it is. Have you ever been there, captain?"

Sinclair frowned to starboard as if that shape had no right on the seas. Hale took Colet's arm, and surveyed Socotra, with a smile.

"No, and I've never met a man who has. But there it always is, somehow. If you want to know about some of the things here, you'll get it from Sinbad."

# CHAPTER XIV

AT the saloon mess-table the guardians of the ship were allusive about her welfare. The set of a current had been adverse; she was seven miles astern of her estimated position. The signs in the heavens induced respectful references to the habits of the Arabian Gulf. The glass was briefly indicated; Colet surmised, while taking another piece of toast, that it was not happy in its divination. The high-pressure cylinder had taken to blowing through its packing; it was wheezy. "Man, yon's a sad waste o' power." And one of the deck-hands was sick. Fever, very likely, it was suggested.

"Or Rotterdam," Sinclair baldly hinted.

"Aye, the heat will bring it out," confirmed Gillespie, with luscious gravity. Then he exhibited some startling instances from the store of a long familiarity with sin. He indulged in illustrative cases with composure and fond irrelevance.

"I'll see this man," announced Hale, hastily rising while still the boding symptoms of another exemplary case were unfulfilled. Gillespie shook his paw in appreciative warning over sin.

Colet accompanied the captain on his way to the forecastle, and he noticed, because the master paused to inspect them, that the fore-hatches were laced over with cordage. The master disappeared within the dark aperture of the forecastle. Colet mounted the ladder to its deck. That was a noble outlook at the beginning of the day. It was dry and red-crusted, weather-stained, isolated as a vantage exposed to an immensity of light. It was solitude. It might have been as old as the sea itself, by the look of it. It was hoar with salt.

And the ship's head was alive. It was massive but buoyant. It seemed to inflate and to mount quickly and easily with enormous intakes of air; then, sighing through its hawse-pipes, it declined into the friendly rollers. If you looked over-side and down, the cutwater of the ship was deep and plain in the blue transparency, coming along with unvarying con-fidence like the brown nose of an exploring monster. When the ship's head plunged over a slope an acre of blinding foam spread around and swept astern, melting and sibilant.

Companies of flying-fish were surprised by that iron nose, and got up. They skittered obliquely over the bright polish of the inclines, and plumped abruptly into smooth slopes which opposed them. A family of four dolphins were there that morning. They were set in the clear glass just before the cutwater. They did not fly from it. Their bodies but revolved leisurely before it. The crescent valves in their heads could be seen sleepily opening and closing when they touched the surface, with the luxury of life in the cool fathoms. One after another idly they rolled belly up; they were merely revolving without progress, yet the fast-pursuing iron nose never reach-ed them. It was always just behind the family, which wove a lazy and gliding dance before the ship. Artfully leading them on, these familiars of the deep?

It was a fair world into which they were being led. It re-posed in an eternal radiant tranquillity. The Indian Ocean was as inviting as its name. There were clouds ahead, but they were fast to the skyline; they were as remote as the ghostly mountains and steeps of a land no man would ever reach. This world of the tropics was but an apparition of splendour. It was there by the chance of good fortune. It was seen only by the desiring mind. It was like the import of great music, for which there is no word. If you stood looking at it long enough, the bright dream would draw you out of your body.

The ship's head fell sideways into a deeper hollow, and Colet returned without warning to an iron deck. He was swung around on his handhold. The rail he struck was hard. Steady! Solid fountains burst loudly through the hawse-pipes. There was impetuosity in the lift of the ship's head . She got out of the smother in a hurry. By the look of it, more was coming. The rollers had seemed to be growing heavier. It was getting wet up there. Colet retreated. When he was mounting the ladder amidships a sharp lurch of the ship left him dangling by his hands. The boyish third officer on the deck above respectfully watched him while his feet sought the ladder again.

"A beam sea setting in, Mr. Colet. Makes her roll."

It was making her roll. But it was very agreeable. It shook off the weight of the heat. These were the first seas worth the lively name since the voyage began. It was like the real thing to see the decks getting wet, to be caught at a corner by a dollop of rollicking brine. Hullo, Sinclair! Colet mentioned this novelty as they met by the engine-room entrance. He spoke of it lightly, wiping some spray from his eyes. Sinclair showed amusement, but his gaze was elsewhere. They had to steady themselves, in their pause, by gripping the ironwork. The movements of the ship, to Colet's surprise, were exhilarating. They shifted him from an old centre of thought. The rhythm of the ship's compensations was the measure of easy and solid courage.

"I don't know," mused Colet, "but once, just once, I think I'd like to see all this when it was not play."

"Play?" exclaimed the sailor. "Play? If anybody else had said that, I'd tell him not to be a fool."

Colet made a dramatic appeal to the listening and jealous gods to forget his childish indiscretion. It was only his ignorance. It was born of his trust in his company. He reposed in the faith that the *Altair* was a sound old dear.

Sinclair grinned. "Perhaps you didn't catch what the old

man was mumbling at breakfast?" He poked his companion in the ribs. "You're coming along, my son. A bit too confident, that's all. When you're a sailor, you'll cross yourself if you hear some one talk as you did."

"I'm sure of it. What was it the captain said at breakfast?"

"Oh, nothing. He's a cautious old boy, I think. Wanted me to believe he doesn't like the look of it. But I can't smell anything in the wind. Seems all right. I don't see anything in this."

It was all right, though the draught which was upset by the rocking of the ship was languid, and the breath of an oven.

Night fell; the day was abolished abruptly. There were brief up-glarings of a desperate sun taken by an insurrection of darkness. He was put down. The authority of day was overturned. The ship alone of all the world below held with startled emphasis the memory of a brightness extinguished. For a few moments there was the pale wraith of a deck, vertiginous in its slant, with its fixtures bleak and exposed; and then the only lights were the stars concentrated low in patch of southern sky. In the south, the stars were the lights of a city without a name where there could be no land. They could see the frenzied glittering of its lamps. For the show of that city behaved only as would an hallucination in a region that was enthralled by the powers of darkness. Now its level was below them, and now it soared towards the meridian.

# CHAPTER XV

"COME now, will you?" said the captain.

Colet was glad of a change from that erratic dinner-table, and gestured his readiness. He was to be purser for the evening. He followed the master out of the saloon. As he reached its door the opening uprose, as though to frustrate his intent. He gripped the door-post. Whoa! He waited. The chance came. The deck took a slope the other way, and almost under control Colet shot through. The far side of the alleyway saved him, though harshly.

"She's lively," said the master. "Here we are." He steadied Colet into his room.

"I thought monsoons were friendly winds," Colet joked.

"There is no wind," he was told. "Not yet. Just a bit of a swell. Sit there. That way you won't feel it so much. There you are, if you would check the manifest for me with the stowage plan." He stood over Colet, and explained the documents. "I was not about when she was loaded, and we have a number of ports. You can help me here. It'll keep you from noticing her capers."

It was not easy to ignore her capers. They raised a number of doubts which jolted one's consideration from the job, yet could not be answered. Get on with the job then. Didn't know enough to answer them. He knew about as much as an ant in its hill under a blundering cow; and the astral cow blundering about now had enormous splay hooves. There was a boom, and an answering panic of crocks in the pantry. His consideration of his job was shifted, and he glanced at Hale, to see whether this was serious. The attention of the captain, however, rapt as at prayer, was devoted to his desk. Hale but cleared his throat, and turned over a sheet as though it were a token of a rosary.

They worked without a word for a time, and then Colet put a question to the master.

"Eh?" said Hale, turning leisurely. "No, that is probably a slip. Make a mark there."

The master remained, for a spell, thoughtful in that apposition to his amateur purser.

"It's an idea of mine that there's an intention to sell her out East, when we are cleared," he soliloquised. "Chinese owners, I expect. But don't discuss that outside. It's only a guess since I took her over. I go by this and that."

"Surely the owners would have told you?" Colet became bright. He was relieved to hear some cool and intelligent human sounds. It was enjoyable to encourage them.

Hale smiled wanly. "A ship's master is not so important as he used to be. Like the rest of the servants, he's on a length of string, and doesn't always know who is pulling it, nor why. But it's no good complaining of the way the world goes."

His thin hand went over his thin hair. Colet felt stir within him the warmth of a liking for that frail figure. It was insignificant, till its eye met yours. Then you guessed a hidden but constant glim. That man looked as though he had made his humble acceptance, but could not be deceived by the bluff of chance. He met Colet's eye then, and might have guessed that something had quickened in his junior.

"We are apt to make too much of our importance, Colet, when we don't like things, or they don't like us. But, you know, the best we can do is to keep our own doorstep clean. We can always manage that."

As if to try his faith, his own ship then treated him with indignity. She went over, and Hale, nearer her side, sank low, and was huddled into his chair. Colet overlooked the master from a higher position. Hale wrestled patiently with the arm of his seat to escape from his ungraceful posture.

"That was a big one. They racket things so."

The cabin itself was quiet. At times it complained a little, but in undertones. It seemed apart, an illuminated hollow where understandable and well-ordered objects were an assurance of continuity, while all without was dark confusion, besieging it, yet unable to do more than move it, never to disorder it. Its lamps burned steadily. Perhaps it was the master who gave it that air of sanity and composure while anarchy was at its walls. Hale, slight and elderly, with his deliberation which was not unlike weariness, was an augury of grey wisdom and the symbol of conscious control amid the welter of huge and heedless powers. Boom and crash, but the old man took no notice. The portrait of a stout matron, her arm round a little girl, regarded them sedately from a bulkhead. No other ornament was in the cabin, except the faded photograph of a sailing ship over the bunk. Colet's ribs were squeezed, first against one arm of his chair, then the other. That was another distraction; trying to keep still. The deck rose under them, and Colet dizzily wondered how high it intended to go; the grind of the propeller then grew loud in its monody, and even frantic. The cabin trembled. His seat sank under him, and his attention went another way, for the suggestion of empty gulf was sickening, and the propeller moaned in the very deeps. She heaved and tilted. The purser grabbed his escaping papers.

Something avalanched outside, and then continued a noisy career. What was that? Colet again looked at the captain for a sign. There was none. The master sat at his desk, turned from it a little now, scrutinising a document through his uplifted spectacles. His attention was wholly given to that.

Nothing in it. Don't be a fool. Look after your own doorstep. But a more violent lift, a louder explosion of a breaking sea, would set him calculating, as it began, the probable extent of a movement. How far would this one go? Worse than the last? Sometimes it was. Yet Hale released sheet after sheet, sometimes turning to his desk to make a note; he lit his pipe, and nothing could have been so reassuring as the leisure of its blue smoke. All was well. Colet resumed his clerkship, and half forgot beleaguerment by the unseen in an interval of comparative ease. The seas were lessening?

Certainly. That was only a minor jar; but when Colet would have made the cheerful comment aloud, he saw the captain had lowered his papers, and was listening attentively, as though waiting for another cryptic message from the night, gazing at the foot of the door of his cabin over the top of his glasses. Colet watched him for an interpretation. Hale only relaxed and sighed; and then, seeing that the purser was expectant, he spoke.

"Colet, it occurs to me that somewhere about now makes for me forty years of this. Yes. You see that barque there? She was my first, forty years agone this month. This job, when I'm through, will be my last. I was of half a mind not to take it. I've had my share, I think. But that child," Hale indicated the portrait, "she's in for her degree now. I thought I ought to make this trip. A little extra for her."

While he was communing a whispering began in the deck above. It increased to a heavy drumming.

"I thought so," Hale remarked, his ear cocked. "Rain. But no wind, and this swell. A cyclone in the north-east somewhere." He added the conclusion indifferently.

There was a knock at the cabin door. A man out of the dark stood there, a barefooted seaman in his dripping oilskins.

"Mr. Sinclair, sir. He wants you on the bridge."

"Anything wrong, Wilson?"

"I don't know, sir. The steering-gear, I think, sir."

"I'm coming."

99

Hale assembled his papers deftly, stowed them, and opened a cupboard. He hauled out oilskins and sea-boots. He was buttoning the stiff stuff across his throat, his head thrown back.

"Wait here, Colet," he said. "I thought I heard an unusual thump just now."

The captain, Colet imagined, was diminished by that armour for the weather. His face, framed by the sou'wester, looked womanish, as though he were in the wrong clothes. Hale glanced at the barometer, gave it a closer inspection on whatever it was it told him, and stumped out.

Colet waited. He continued his work, pausing now and then to listen for evidence. There were fewer noises. The ship itself appeared to be making no sound. The waters were nearer, or louder. Any one would think—had the engines stopped? He opened the door and put his head out. The steward was hurriedly balancing his way along the corridor.

"Anything the matter, steward?"

"Mr. Colet, the rudder's gone."

# CHAPTER XVI

THE steward departed, chary of words, as though he were on his way to get another rudder. He had no time to talk.

The violent rolling of the ship did not relent. That seemed senseless, when she was crippled. She ought to be let off, now she could not steer. Impossible to think, with that rolling.

Colet, to his great annoyance, found that his knees were shaking. He had not told them to. He did not want them to shake. He damned those quivering members of his body, and would have stiffened them, but that he was flung against a bulkhead, and so brought down some of the master's pipes from a rack. Something to do, anyway. He could recover tobacco pipes while others found a rudder. Better men had to look after the ship for those who attended to pipe-racks, while waiting.

They also serve, who only look after the tobacco pipes. If there was no wind when he first went into that room, something was howling now all right. It was no good waiting for the captain. Hale was not likely to return till—well, he wasn't likely to return. The best thing to do would be to go and find the men at the centre of things, because that cabin had precious little interest now. It was useless to wait there, at that time of night, when for all he knew they soon might be taking to the boats.

He heard a heavy concussion. The cabin shook. The papers on which he had been working fell to the floor. The boats! Colet watched the papers sprawling and scattering. They had lost their meaning. They were just as well where they were. But there would be no boats for the sea which could make that sound. The cabin reversed, and as it did so a tongue of water shot over the carpet straight for the papers. Colet dived for them and snatched them out of its way. Save the stationery!

He straightened them on the desk. With measured deliberation he sought carefully for the sheet on which he had been working. They were all in a mess, these sheets, but so was everything else. At least the ship's papers could be put in order. No more water seemed to be coming in. That was only a splash. Not foundering yet. He settled the papers into their sequence, and began again on them at the mark. The captain had said Wait.

It was the only thing to do, but that lad Casabianca deserved a better poem. It would be easy to wait on a deck diminishing in dissolution if one but knew the reason for it. But this was only an idiot joke, dutifully completing a ship's papers when the mysterious reason was trying to turn the ship over. Now the infernal water was under the desk. Reason! No more reason in it than there was in the hot gas which congealed to a mud ball, on which grew the truth, and crosses and nails for those who dared to mention it. What a joke; and nobody to get a laugh out of it!

Let her roll. He could not stop it. Time for a pipe. Not his affair. Funny, that a man should curse the stars in their courses, when he was beset. Same thing as a rat biting his trap, maybe. Best to call himself lucky. Lucky to have a job to do, if only a job of checking packages of pots and pans, when the heaven itself was cracking. "We are but little children meek." The tune of this hymn, for some uninvited cause, was running through his head. The movements of the ship kept it going. "Not born in any high estate." Couldn't very well call this estate puffed up. "What can we do for Jesus' sake?" Well, Jesus, I was checking this ship's manifest when I went down. Sorry it's wet.

What was the time? To his surprise, the clock said it was another morning again. The skipper's cabin was in a sorry state. Somebody was attempting the door, but the slant of the ship held it fast. The door rattled, and then Hale entered. He showed no surprise at finding the purser still busy. He took a towel and wiped his face. "I should drop that now," he remarked.

Colet told him he had just finished it. Hale looked at the clock, and thanked him. The purser modestly waited for the master to give a word on the business without, but Hale merely balanced himself patiently to the movements of his room, and sought for something in a drawer.

"By the way, Colet, you could turn in here. It would save you the run to your own place."

But Colet felt a sudden dislike of the suggestion of that isolation.

"Oh, thank you. But I'll make for my own cubby-hole. It'll do me good, to run for it."

That was all. Not a word about the rudder. And perhaps it would be better not to ask questions. Perhaps rudders were indelicate. By Hale's manner, too, it might be only a rather wet night. It would be nobler to assume the night was merely wet.

Hale led on to the head of the companion to the quarter-deck.

"Can't open the lower door," he explained. The master stood there, with his hand on the upper door, as though listening for some one who would let them out. "Now," he muttered, opened it on the instant, and they were both in the night.

The night engulfed them with a roar as though it saw them instantly. Colet was separated from Hale. There was no ship. There was but a pealing and a shouting. The darkness was full of driving water. It was hard to breathe. Hale had gone. Colet forgot which was the head and which the stern. A burst of spray raked past. Then he felt a grip on his arm, and a warm mouth sought his ear. Hale was saying something but his words were torn away.

"What?"

The skipper's voice was at once superior to the chaos: "We can do it."

Wanted a bit of doing. Like trying to walk a plank you couldn't see which was only there sometimes. It was a wonder it ever came back. My God, she was like a balloon, trying to sail out of it. But the water was up there too. Here was the ladder down to the deck. He had got on to its rungs when the warm mouth came near his ear again:

"Wait. Hold tight."

The thing under their feet heaved, but checked, as if this was too much for it. The night exploded over them and fell in broken thunder. Couldn't go through that.

"Go on," ordered invisible Hale. They reached the deck, and ran. Ran in short lengths. You can't keep running on a slope which changes direction abruptly in the dark. Together they got to the foot of the ladder to the bridge-deck, and Hale pushed Colet at it, the signal to mount quickly; but when he gripped the iron thing it came at him as though loose. He was pulling the ladder out of the ship. Nothing to stand on. Then the ship fell head first into nothing; the purser's face was dragged after the retreating ladder and struck it. Colet could hear the sea in behind him and clambered up; yet hesitated.

"Captain?"

The old man was in that below. No good shouting. The purser got down to the deck again, and groped, with the flood at his knees. He found Hale on his hands and knees, rising, and clutched him.

"Go on, go on," Hale shouted.

The captain came into Colet's cabin with him, and stayed there for a moment. He was smiling.

"You would never have believed that, would you, Colet?"

Colet, a little breathless, held to the edge of his bunk. He hinted that the violence seemed a bit unreasonable.

"No. There's sufficient cause. I've seen it before. We must wait for daylight."

When the master had gone, Colet considered his bunk. No. The settee to-night. No use turning in when things were happening all the time. But it needed very deliberate control to sit there, waiting for light to come, when the world was falling to pieces. Especially, when, the longer you waited, the louder grew the mania of the wind, and the more surprisingly delirious mounted the buoyancy of the ship. Could she stand it? She seemed terrified. Colet remembered a rabbit he had once seen leaping and convulsive in a wire noose. She was desperate, but she was done.

Colet surrendered limply to the anarchy. Once he rose and vomited. Well . . . not long to wait now . . . the day was about due. The wind did all the moaning that was necessary. That moan outside would do for all creation. No need to add to it. It was the antiphon of doom. And it didn't seem to matter now. Nothing more to do. A sea battered on his door, but Colet did not look up. He would rest rest while waiting.

# CHAPTER XVII

THE port-light was a grey round, and the lamp had paled. When Colet noticed that, he wondered how it had come about. He peered out from the port. He could see nothing but wan panic, and a long loose end of rope resting straight on the wind as rigid as an iron bar. This was called day. The deck looked as though no man had been on it for years; but Sinclair came into view, leaning and pulling up against the drive of morning. Coming to him? Colet got at the door to be ready for him. It felt as if it weighed tons. It fought.

"Fuh, Colet," he breathed. "You're not overside, eh?"

He tore his sou'wester off. His hot hair was extinguished and flattened.

"What a night."

Sinclair's appearance was almost that of a stranger. His face was bleached and seamed, his eyes were raw. They blinked sorely as he grinned. He plumped on to the couch and leaned back.

"She has had a time. Two boats look as if elephants had sat in them. The old man was right after all."

The grin remained on his face. He had forgotten to take it off. He was grinning at the window.

"Look at that rope. Hell. Look at it."

"Is Hale all right?"

"Eh? Yes, he's still up there."

Sinclair was regarding now in childish wonder a wound on his hand. "How did that come?" He dismissed his hand.

"The old man? Yes. Well, this ship's got a master. Colet, the old man's all right, if any one wants to know."

"How is it now?"

"Don't ask. She's taking it easier, though. Sitting in it like a duck. Shouldn't have thought it possible, but the old man was sure she would. Been rolling her bridge-ends under, too. Glad to see daylight."

Sinclair shut his eyes.

"I say, I think I'll take my ten minutes here. Handy, here."

He sought Colet again, with a grin.

"Nice job for this child presently, when it moderates. Coming with us? The rudder's broken at the couplings. You know that? Must get her under control. There's a boat to be got out. Wires from the steering chains to the rudder. That sort of thing. Fix it up. You'd better make for the bridge-house now, the old man says. Tell him where I am, won't you?"

The chief officer's head fell sideways; this time he was certainly asleep.

The purser adventured for the bridge-house. If you checked yourself from point to point, hand over hand, you were not hurled along. The wind was solid. The purser did not look at the seas, but some heights caught his eye as they fled past. They were aged. It was better not to look at them. Hale turned his head as Colet entered. He grimaced at him humorously. Was the old man enjoying it? A seaman was still at the useless wheel, as if apart, and in a trance, looking to futurity through the glass, and waiting. His jaws moved slightly, now and then, but that was all. Nobody else was there.

"Did you sleep, Colet? No sleep till morn, eh? Well, I think it moderates a bit. We shall be busy, soon. I want you with me in case. The lads are taking a rest now."

The master resumed his vigil. His head was turned to the world beyond. But that world had contracted. One could not see far, but the intimidated eye could see all that it wanted. The sky had closed down on them, and they were circumscribed by a sunless incertitude. In that grey vacancy shadows appeared which were too high to be of water, but those ghosts darkened and emerged as seas which saw the ship at once and came at her in towering velocity. As they shaped, each of them threatened that it was the one which would finish her, but the *Altair* heaved into the sky out of it in time. Yet another was always coming when one had gone. The desolate head of the ship, condemned to dreary unrest, streamed with gauzes of water. Its stanchions and rails were awry and tortured. A length of the bulwarks of the foredeck was ruptured and projected outwards raggedly. The deck ventilators had gone. One lay in the scuppers as if dead, but sometimes turned over and then back in a spasm of unexpected life.

That slight figure of the master, standing in profile, so watchful of vague and immense powers, and so undisturbed by their onrush, was like a token of quiet faith untouched by calamity and overthrow. There it was. He was looking it in the face. He did not move. He was timing the Indian Ocean, that little man. Colet felt he would as soon be there as elsewhere. Who did Hale remind him of as he stood like that? Somebody. Somebody in a dream? No, good Lord, he was like that dim figure of an old man when coming up Gallions Reach in an evening long ago; standing just like that, and muttering something of other worlds. Beyond the captain Colet saw a dire spectre loom and bear down on them, an immense sea, its pale head raving with speed and fury. Other worlds! This one? Colet could not help swallowing on a choking laugh. At that Hale turned on him quickly, and knew what the purser had seen.

"Laughing at it? They do look fairly terrifying, some of them."

The two men had made that signal to each other. Colet lightened, flippantly elate. Chanticleer crowing at spectres, sure of the morning? The steward pranced in with a can of hot coffee and some food. Wonderful fellow. How had he managed all that from the galley? He had saved the grub, but he was like a cat out of a ditch. Coffee was good. Calamity could not even blow off the fragrance of coffee. Stewards could dance through it, carrying coffee.

The three men in that bridge-house had no more to say to each other. They stumbled, made abrupt movements to steady themselves, kept their eyes on the world without. Hour after hour of onset and uplift; screens of white which keened and hid the ship, and passed; vaulting masses which strode over the bows; occasional gusts which careened her, held her over, and hid the sea with wool.

But it was lessening? The worse of it seemed to have gone. One could see farther. The ceiling had lifted. Hale was lighting his pipe when the engine-room signalled. The master listened at the black cup of the speaking-tube, and then put his mouth to it. His mouth and ear dodged about.

"No . . . not yet . . . we shall try soon . . . let you know . . . thank your men for me, Gillespie . . . not over yet, though . . . who? . . . badly? . . . where is he? . . . all right . . . . I'll do what I can . . . let you know."

"One of the greasers, Colet. Flung into the gear. Very nasty. He must stay there. We dare not bring him up yet."

He walked up and down the enclosure for a spell. He paused, and contemplated the outer world.

"We might," he said to himself. "Colet, would you tell Sinclair I want him?"

A bunch of the people of the ship presently dared the open. They appeared together in haste, as if they had suddenly agreed to submit no longer. They had come out to rebel. But how could they fight that? They were seen at once and attacked. They were expunged. When the cataract had gone they were still all there, hurried and desperate. They were minikin in a precarious wild, in a light as hopeless as nullity, their foothold a bare raft of disappearing iron. They could not do it. But they were hauling gear about, refractory stuff in league with the enemy, in an obsession that wires would bind cyclones. Sinclair was there. It was a losing game but he was playing it. His arm was flung out directing; he toppled over, but his arm continued pointing at the crisis from the deck—no time to get up—and his mouth was open, bawling, though he seemed to make no sound. It was a shadow show. A play of midgets who endeavoured with foolish efforts to frustrate the fate imposed on them by majesty. Well done, Sinclair. Nearly had you then.

They made for a boat as if they meant to use it. That ought to be stopped. That was carrying matters too far. They could not leave the ship. But the boat was manned and swung out—Sinclair, the third officer, the boatswain, and a seaman, were leaving them. They were determined about it. They were hanging outboard now, uncertain in a threatening void; their adversary was waiting for them below. Sometimes it swept along the topside of the ship, and then retired, for its next leap, to a sudden deep below the ship's wall. For a torturing moment the suspensory boat fell straight to disaster. It checked. It shot up on a roller, afloat. Colet was looking in astonishment straight at the faces of its men. The snoring ship heeled away from them. The boat dropped into a hollow. She sped to a crest higher than the funnel, and was poised for a moment on the foaming summit; she was lost. The seas opened, and she was seen close astern, askew on a slope.

When Colet next saw Sinclair that officer was climbing the ladder amidships, as happy and unexpected a token as an angelic visitor. The purser put his arm round his friend's shoulder.

"All right. Done it, Colet."

She was steering again.

"See that out there?" Sinclair thrust out his arm.

Something was to be seen in the murk. What was it? Smoke?

"Yes. It's a liner. She'll be passing us in an hour."

Colet went to his room in gratitude. He felt as though the sky had gone up to its friendly height. They were let off. They were getting out of it. The violence meant nothing now. His cabin seemed larger, more intimate. He was comforted by even the society of distant but brotherly smoke. They were not alone, either. He was thinking he would go out presently to watch their neighbour pass them when Sinclair entered, and something about Sinclair made him rise as though this were an important meeting.

"The liner's almost abeam. Go up with the old man, Colet. He's going to signal her. There's something not right— Gillespie says the furnace foot-plates are awash. That and our steering-gear together . . . he wants a tow, I expect. I'm going below now to find what I can."

There was light enough to see the signals of the stranger. It was impossible for Colet to make out what was passing between the two ships. The tumbling of their wounded steamer was accentuated, it was sickening, when things were happening, and you did not know what.

"Did you make out her last signal, Lycett?" asked the captain.

"Yes, sir, distinctly. He says he cannot tow. Got the mails. He asks whether you will abandon."

"No. Signal, no."

# CHAPTER XVIII

YOUNG LYCETT faintly hesitated over that signal; or so Colet imagined. Never before had he watched his fellows so closely. But the lad turned to the rack where rolled flags waited in their pigeon-holes to cue any fate that might come, and went out to his duty. There came another smear of bunting for them on the liner—too late; the light was not good enough. But a star began to wink at her bridge, and they all watched it till it ceased. Lycett returned to them.

"He says he will report us, sir."

The master nodded. "Of course."

That was ended. Nobody spoke. The seaman at the useless wheel was aloof. He had no part in this. He appeared not to have heard anything, not to be interested in what was passing. He was merely waiting for the wheel to show a better spirit, and he could wait for ever. He did not even turn his head to look at the departing liner. Only Lycett did that. The master had his hands spread on a desk, and was considering, so it appeared, a diagram before him. He had dismissed the liner. He had forgotten her already? And there she went. Colet, like young Lycett, watched her fade. She was already becoming unsubstantial; the upheavals and the twilight were taking her. Through a side-window Colet noticed a stoker below, clutching the bulwarks, his grimy flimsies shuddering in the wind, and he, too, was peering after the ship that was leaving them.

"Take over," said the captain to Lycett, and went out.

The boyish officer at that turned from the place on the seas where the promise of the other ship was dying, as if he had petulantly resolved not to look that way again, and instead stood gazing at the *Altair's* head uneasy in the surge, though not as if he saw it. He was silent. The man at the wheel might not have been there. What were the others doing? There was no sound but that of the swash and parade of the ocean. Lycett became aware of the diagram of the ship before him, and with a new interest began to examine it. He addressed the image at the wheel without lifting his head.

"Wilson, I say, do you think she is a bit by the head?"

"Yes."

"Oh, you have noticed it. How long since you first thought so?"

The image continued its fixed regard of nothing for a while, its jaws moving as though it were making its words. When they were ready, it spoke.

"About an hour."

The youngster bent closer to the diagram, and ended his inspection with a calculation on an old envelope he took from his pocket.

"Why, but in that case she won't last till morning."

Wilson eased his position slightly, and rubbed his mouth with the back of his hand. His voice was so deep and effortless that it sounded like the easy impersonal utterance of the room itself.

"She may. You can't tell."

He might have experienced a full life of such nights and occasions, and so could, if it were worth while, advise youth out of a privy knowledge which was part of the nature of ships and the sea.

"Something may be done," said Wilson.

Colet made as if he were about to leave them.

"Don't go, Mr. Colet," urged the officer in charge. "Wait here, will you, till somebody comes along."

Colet let go the handle of the door, went over to look at the diagram with Lycett, and endured the quiet, while listening to the seas, which were now invisible. The boy began to whistle a tune softly in a hesitating way.

What were the others doing? Sometimes Colet thought he felt the far thumping of human handiwork under their feet. Hale and Sinclair were there, anyhow, and old Gillespie and his men; it was comforting, that certitude. It warmed the world, that secure thought of its good men holding fast. And while his faith was sustained that they could save her, it was not altogether because he himself was there. The ship herself meant something. She had become important. That image at the wheel was admonishing; that figure might be, perchance, the secret familiar of their ship. It was more than human; it spoke out of the ship. Once the steamer plunged head foremost, and something gave in her body. They thrilled to it, as if it were the smothered parting of a piano wire in a house where all was quiet and suspect. Lycett glanced at Colet, and then at the helmsman.

"Was that a bulkhead, Wilson?"

"Couldn't say, sir."

Of course he could not. He was not going to give her away so easily. Colet winked at the boy, and began to pace their little prison; but paused and stretched his arms. No. Stop that. That worried the others. Better have a pipe.

"Are you allowed to smoke, Wilson?"

The seaman only smiled.

"Oh, he chews," said Lycett, and tapped a cigarette on the desk.

Lycett had just struck eight bells when Collins, the second officer, put his head in the door.

"Leave this. You can go below now, the lot of you. When you're wanted you'll know." He disappeared at once.

Colet roamed the deck amidships, accompanied only by the sough of the dark. Their own familiar and confident chant had ceased, that song which used to issue boldly from the open door of the engine-room casing as you passed it.

No message but an infrequent clanking came up from below. Her heart had stopped. A flare or two, while he waited for signs, passed deep under the gratings. They were busy, in the depth of her; but doing what?

There was no doubt about it; when one walked aft it was distinctly to walk uphill. Her head was heavy. He tried to convince himself that this was not so. But it was.

There were no stars. There was only the steady drive of the dark. She was responding to it as though she were tired, stumbling and sluggish. Now and then a sea mounted over her fore-deck. He looked at the shadows of some bent davits, with the swaying remnants of their falls, and heard a block mewling as it swung. That whining voice was the very trivialality of outer desolation. Creak. Whine. The captain's daughter was taking her degree. A bit extra for her. To-night, who was dining at the 'Gridiron'?

Morning came. Colet went out, when his port-light had shaped, and saw the crew, for the first time that voyage. The men were assembled on the after-deck, and they surprised him as much as would a miraculous visitation of quiet disinterested strangers. Most of them were squatting against the bulwarks, but a few stood gazing seaward, indifferently. It was a scene dim and unreal. The air was warm. Once clanking broke out below again, but did not last long. Neither the captain nor Sinclair were there. He could not see any of the engineers. Perhaps, though, they still hoped to pull her through. The cook appeared at his galley door above, and peremptorily called out that anybody who wanted anything could come for it. There was a cheer from the men, wavering but derisive, and they began to move up to the galley. They might have been ignorant, or they might have known they had plenty of time. The forward deck was level with the water; it could not rise; the head of the ship was a sunken warning. Its lowness prompted Colet at once to appraise the size of the heavy propulsions of the ocean; he looked beyond to see whether a sea higher than the rest was coming.

It was not coming yet. And the men were still murmuring about the galley. Nothing was in sight, but one could not see very far. The sun would be there soon. It was warm, but, when Collet was not thinking of it, he shivered. Yet the sky was rosy along the east. How long to wait?

There came the sun, broad to the ship. It saw them. Their case now was manifest to heaven. A seaman who was lying as though asleep by the coaming of a hatch below the galley rose to his feet, stumbled to the side, and began to shout at the sun. The man was in rags. His mates watched him in limp wonder. He raised his bare arms and raved at the bloody day.

"To hell with you—you're no good to us."

"Stop that man," commanded a voice. There stood the captain at the companion aft. Everybody turned that way.

"Stop him," cried Hale, and ran quickly forward. The watchers came to their senses; but the man had scrambled outboard and dropped. One of his mates leaped astride the bulwarks, but Hale got a firm hand on him, and looked over. They were all peering over.

"Useless," said Hale, still with his restraining hand on the seaman. "You come down. One's enough."

Colet was overlooking that from the amidships section. Some one's hand heartily slapped his shoulder.

"Nice morning, Colet," said Sinclair, and went pattering down to the main-deck, and passed through the men. Every one now listlessly eyed the conference of the master and his lieutenant. Gillespie came hurrying along to join them. While the rest had their eyes on the three, the deck lapsed. There could be no mistake about that jolt.

"Let's get a move on," muttered a seaman. The master did not appear to have noticed it. Then he moved one arm slightly, a gesture of abandonment, and they heard the end of the talk.

"Man, ye can do n'more," from Gillespie.

"The boats, Mr. Sinclair," said the master aloud.

Sinclair took the men's eyes with a glance. He swept his arm with a motion to gather. He strolled to the amidships ladder, and they after him. It was right to show her that they were not in a hurry to leave her. Gillespie briefly inspected his squad, which had gravitated around him, and jerked his head towards Sinclair.

"Job's finished, laddies. Awa' now."

She settled again while they took their stations, but the men kept their own gait. Colet sought the master, who was obscured by the activity at the ship's side.

"Ah, purser, I am just going aft for something I must have."

"I'll go with you."

"There's time. How good these fellows are!"

The captain, with a japanned dispatch box in his hand, appeared to know exactly where to find all that he wanted; he moved about his room with a methodical promptitude which gave Colet the impression that the foundering of a ship could be ordered to a common ritual. Hale opened a drawer of his clothes chest and took out a wrap.

"We must leave her, Colet. It's queer you should have brought her to this."

There lay Kuan-yin. The master glanced round his cabin; at his desk, at the barometer, and last, at his pictures.

"That's all. Time to go."

One of the two laden boats was waiting for them, close under a boom which had been rigged out, with a man rope.

"Now, my lad, off with you." Then the master hesitated.

"That greaser who was killed, Colet. I had meant to bear it in mind. I have a little packet of his in my cabin. His people might like it. Another minute."

"I'll wait."

"Get in, get in."

"No. . . ."

"The boat, sir." Hale flung out his arm.

"Come on," bawled some one from the sea.

The captain paused by the ship's side to con her. Then he called out seawards:

"Your boat, Collins, keep her away."

Colet eased off along the beam, and dropped from his hold as the lifeboat rose to him. He scrambled up to see what had become of Hale. There was no sign of him. Gillespie, in the stern of the boat, was angry with alarm.

"There's no time, there's no time." The engineer eagerly half-stood, as they fell away into a hollow, for a better view of that companion door within which the captain had vanished. It was unnaturally high and strangely tilted in a ship whose life seemed poised on a moment of time and the hesitation of a breath. It remained empty.

"Hale," shouted Gillespie; "Hale."

They waited. A sea lifted them swiftly and lightly, and Colet turned his head in measuring fear from the door aft to the head of the *Altair*. Her forecastle deck was isolated, a raft of wreckage flush with the swirls and foam. The seas were pouring solidly across her middle. Her funnel was bowed over the flood, and each dip of it to the declination of the ocean was, to the men in the boat, the prelude to the end. But it was her stern which rose and lowered her head.

"My God, she's going."

She gave a hollow rumbling groan, and to the silent awe of the watchers without a pause she went down. Colet saw the shape of the propeller over him and the bright sky through its frame. There was a confusion on the surface of the waters, which melted as a swell heaved over the place. The sea was bare.

# CHAPTER XIX

THE men in the boat continued to stare at the place where their ship had been as though they still saw her. They remained trance-like without a movement in an apparent refusal to believe their experience. They certainly heard Hale's voice there just now. The peaceful brightness of the vacant ocean was a mistake.

It was a stupid little noise in the shining immensity which woke Colet from his far absorption with what had gone, and brought him back to notice what new thing had taken its place. Lycett, beside him, was crying, but was trying to hide it. Mr. Collins, in the stern-sheets, had also withdrawn his gaze from the sea. He indicated something to a seaman, who spat on his palms, and made a few slow strokes with his oar. Nothing remained of the past but a spreading defilement of ash and oil.

Sinclair called across to them, and Collins held up a hand in understanding. Both craft set their lugs, and, in company, began to withdraw their occupants into another extension of life. Lycett's head was averted. He was watching the near water. An area of cinders drifted astern. He watched it go till the water was clear again. He sat looking for more cinders, but the sea continued to be pure, impersonal, and unconcerned. Colet crouched uncomfortably, without changing his position, as if this posture in an open boat were but briefly provisional, and he were waiting for a return to what was necessary and accustomed. The transition from one existence to the next had been so abrupt that he had not fully accepted the change. And big Gillespie crouching on the opposite bench, staring between his legs at the bottom-boards, was vague. It was hardly Gillespie, in that attitude and that place. Colet was still in a ship's cabin of another time, for the last minute of that room had survived its clock.

"That's all, Colet. Time to go." But he had not gone yet.

Through that immediate apparition Colet presently surmised, as in a dissolving view, a threatening incline of blue water above them, at a surprising height above them. It shut out the sky astern. Before he rightly knew it was there he was soaring on it giddily, and his hand, hanging over the side, was immersed. He hastily withdrew his hand, plucking it, the last bit of himself in that enchantment, out of one dangerous dream into the next. He was transferred. From the summit of that swell he looked round upon an ocean he had never seen before. It was a narrower place, but at its centre it was more intimate and overgrown. The water had touched his hand; it was in hurrying flux near to his eyes; and the seas had become steep, and ranged close round above their mast. They were imprisoned by waves. Their complete assurance of the company of the other boat was intermittent.

They thought they heard singing. They really heard it, when their neighbour was on a crest above them; chance fragments of a song blew over from windward. A quick ear in their own boat caught some odd notes and recognised them. That stoker in the bows began to respond in drawling sardonic sentiment, "I—don't—care—if you—don't love—me—I—don't—care—if you go—to—sea."

Wilson sat near Colet. He was triturating tobacco between his hands in a musing deliberation which hinted to Colet that there was plenty of this new time. When a movement of the boat threw him out of his balance, Wilson paused, patiently. No need to hurry.

The boat was rather crowded; there was a great variety of heads and caps forward. One fellow rejoiced to recognise a pal in the bows.

"'Ullo, Percy, I see you. Coming for a nice sail?"

There was a long silence; nothing was to be heard but the shrill swish and flight of the waters along the gunwale, and the creaking of the boat. When she mounted a sea and was exposed to the wind, she heeled and jammed into the broad round of the hill-top. Collins sat mute and observant, but occasionally made a request to a man:

"Keep watch by the halyards there."

Presently Gillespie spoke to him:

"You and Sinclair agreed about it?"

"Yes, the old man gave us our orders. The only thing to do. We ought to be picked up, on this course."

They heard, breaking another long interval of quiet, a plaintive voice in the crowd forward.

"Alf, 'ave you noticed where the gentlemen's room is in this ship?"

It grew hot, but there was no shelter from the glare. They must keep still, and ache. They could not ease away from the white fire. Colet, like his fellows, watched the seas. There was no more singing. They had begun already to peer beyond intently for the chance which would take them out of this huddled discomfort. Their narrow foothold was as lively as a bubble, flinching from every minor torment of the ascent and the dive. The inclines of the ocean were mesmeric with the horror of bulk whelming in unrest. The waters never paused. Respite was not there, and Colet found himself sighing for an outlook that would keep straight and still, and let him have his thoughts in peace. The sun continued its fire from a cloudless sky on the shelterless and silent boatful; but, whenever they were superior on a summit, and could see beyond the shifting and translucent parapets of their prison, only Sinclair and his crowd were in sight. And Sinclair's boat looked overladen and trifling. The inconsequence of their neighbour, when she was sighted below, as if fixed in a spacious hollow, was a warning to themselves;

they, too, were like that. Colet spied Sinclair's charge with relief, if it were but the top of her mast above an intervening ridge. All right, so far. Sinclair was still there.

Gillespie sat noting the pursuit of the following seas. He exclaimed to the helmsman:

"Look out, Collins. Here's a beauty coming."

Collins smiled, but kept his back to whatever was after them astern. The boat went squattering on the running hill till it found the wind at the top of it, and the hill was swinging ahead from under them. Not that time. Gillespie shook his head with dislike of it; but his eyes went again up their wake to look for the next attack.

The seas quivered in their mass with the original eagerness of that impulse which first sent them rolling round the globe. They would never stop. Their glassy inclines were fretted with lesser waves and hurrying cornices. They were flanged by outliers which deceived with hidden valleys, and the boat, rising briefly, dropped unexpectedly under the shadow of the superior headlong hill.

"Look out!" The startled watcher beside the steersman was compelled then to an involuntary shout of warning.

"It could be worse," said Collins. "She's not bad to steer, but it makes me sleepy. Here Wilson. Take a turn at it."

Collins then superintended the distribution of some rations. A little water, a very little water, and some biscuit went round.

"And listen, you men," he called out; "if you don't want to go balmy, leave the sea-water alone. Bear that in mind to-morrow. All loonies will be put overside."

"Good for you, sir. We'll watch it. But chase the cook along with the ham and eggs."

The sunset suffused with red and gold the transparent crests of the heights roving about them, and reflected in flashes from every transient facet of that region of crystal, where the foam glowed as runnels of coloured fire. Their little craft was transfigured. Its sail and boards were of a radiant and filmy substance too aerial to be scathed any more by the winds of earth. Its company were shining immortals, who had passed through their tribulation and were released at last from the labour and the wrecks where time is, and the lower seas of a troubled world.

"I doubt it will be a cold night," mused Gillespie, looking round on the brightness, "and my pants are wet now." A noisy shower of rubies swept over the crowd forward.

"That's it," said the engineer, "and wet shirts for the laddies."

The group aft, about Wilson, murmured a conversation, in which Wilson learned the name of the star which was in the general direction of their course, and how he should use it. They continued some speculations about the stars, whispering their attempts at mysteries, while the navigator gave names, haunting and occult names, to the glittering points of night.

"We shall have to keep this man awake," said Collins. "I was not quite all there all the time I was steering."

Their gossip went back to the ship. They guessed at where her plates had parted. They spoke of their old ship, but they did not name her master. Collins explained his hopes of the course they were on, and they wondered how long it would be before a ship was sighted. Frequently they glanced to the spark which showed where Sinclair was in the night. Then Gillespie was left to keep the steersman company, and to call Colet at midnight to sit with the second officer.

Colet tried to sleep, but he had no sooner forgotten the cramp and the cold than the boat kicked him awake again. He turned about, to try the other side, and so got a memory of Wilson's head bent forward, a presiding head, austere and calm, isolated in the gloom. A fellow at the other end was retching. The hours stood still. He thought he would never sleep; but then again the boat jolted him into full consciousness of the cold, and in surprise he saw over them the dark wing of the sail. He turned back again. The bench was hard and wet, and gave nowhere. He could feel the slight timber vibrating under his arm; she was as giddy as an air-ball. Impossible to sleep, while listening to the fall of waters in the dark. When Gillespie gently pressed his knee, he sat up abruptly as if he had been dreaming of a crisis. Collins was taking Wilson's place.

"Eight bells," said Gillespie, "and all's well. Change over."

Colet's teeth chattered on their own account. They got into full speed before they were checked. And nobody would have guessed that night itself could be so dark, when there was nothing in it but the sound of unseen waters in flight, and the thin protests of their frail security as it was hurled along through nothing.

Colet took a seat beside the steersman.

"Well, what have you got to say. Something good?" asked Collins. "Get any sleep?"

"Tell him about feather-beds," murmured a voice.

Then another voice piped up, with a quaver in it. "No. Tell him about all the pubs you know, sir. I know a nice warm little place kept by a widder."

"Shut up. You'd better go to sleep," said Collins.

"How can I sleep, sir? There's a bloke's boots in my mouth. Besides, she wants baling."

"Is there much water there?"

"Only enough for a drop of gin, as you might say, sir. It'll all soak in my shirt, the next time she heels."

Some one drawled a protest.

"It's a lie, Jim. You fellers on the lee side are as well orf as what we are. Our shirts 'ere got no more stowage."

"I don't wonder at it, Dave. It was Dave spoke, wasn't it? I know you, Dave, and I know that shirt of yourn. It's the same one, ain't it?"

There was a thumping on the boards forward.

"Put a stopper in it, aft. We're trying to forget it, up here."

"Then yore wasting yore perishing time, Alec, my lad. Only brass monkeys could forget it." She lurched, and a heavy shower fell across her, by the mast. The men up there groaned and swore. But they heard a laugh in the dark at the after end.

"Got that lot, Alec? Try to forget it."

# CHAPTER XX

THE interminable days merged for those open boats. Time lapsed into an uneventful fortitude, a thirsty desert, to which apathy could see no end. The sail of each boat was double-reefed and goose-winged, perhaps because Sinclair was afraid of running too far, or because he thought exhaustion would make his men careless. Smoke was sighted, one day. It was a smear which persisted for so long that the castaways thought they could make to windward till they were seen. They never lifted that steamer. And more than once a light had been glimpsed at night, when Collins' boat was on the back of a high sea.

"Light ahead!"

The men waited hopefully for the next lucky impulse which would lift them to a clear view towards the horizon. Yes.

"There it is. A light!"

But Mr. Collins had sighted it too. "That? That's a star."

The men huddled down again without another word.

"Better luck next time," their officer assured them. "Keep a good look-out. We're in the way of traffic."

It was strange. Colet, if he stood, was now easily thrown out of his balance by a movement of the boat. He was a little surprised by that. It was not, of course, that he was weak. He wasn't weak. He did not care much; that was all. But he ought not to fall over, though that would be the easiest thing to do. No good. Almost sure to knock against somebody. Pull yourself together, old son. Look at young Collins. Fine fellow, Collins; and he'd hardly had a word with him till after the ship went down. Never thought there was much in Collins. But that youngster's pasture, wherever it was, was the place for mettle. And Wilson, too. The whole lot of them. Not a murmur. There was something damned fine in this ordinary stuff.

If he could only keep seated he could last till domesday. He could steer that boat into the Styx, and save the passage money. Hullo, Charon, now watch a bit of real boat work. Beat that. He was only thirsty. Not hungry. It would be all right if that thick slime could be washed out of the mouth.

"You off biscuits?" asked Collins that morning. "So am I. I can't make anything of 'em, except to spit dust."

A few of the men lay as if dead on the bottom boards. If they were trodden on they did not move, and did not speak. You had to look at their faces again to make sure. The unshaven faces of the men were like those of destitute but bearded children. The purser sat considering vacancy, steering the boat. The way she was going, you kept the draught on your left jaw.

"We ought to see something any time," Collins soliloquised, a little querulously. "No need to worry."

The purser smiled, with his eye on the quivering luff of the sail. He felt resigned.

"I'm not worrying." That was the strange thing about it. He imagined his mind had never been clearer. It was like a steady light inside him. Nothing could blow that out. No wind could flicker it. Never knew before he had a mind. Sure of it now. He felt pale and lucid inside, but he did not want to move. He could look on, a sort of lamp, till the last wave of the sea had unrolled. The sea and sky could pass away, if they liked. They were passing away. They had got more distant, and less impressive. They could no longer daunt with their show of grandeur and dominance, and so they were going. Their game was up. But this old boat, she could go on till they had sighted Helicon. They might beat to windward round the Last Hope. Something like seafaring, something like life, when you knew you could hold on till the dark was encircled. Get right round it. One more drink, and he could sit there till the sail was a film, the men were ghosts, and they had the Pleiades close abeam. He gave her a touch, and she nicely missed an ugly one.

"Purser, you might have been doing this all your life," the officer told him.

Colet reflected. "I think I have," he said. Quite true; all the life he had had. Collins glanced at him, with a trace of alarm.

"I say, Colet. Don't you go light-headed, like some of 'em."

"I'm all right."

"I wish it would rain."

"A drop would about save the worst cases. Lycett's bad."

"Yes. I can't do any more, can I?"

"Collins, you're fine. We're lucky."

"I wonder how Sinclair's bunch is getting on?"

There she was, just on the round of a sea, a tiny model. They sighted her together.

"About the same, of course."

"Well, we'll hear when we're picked up. I say, Colet, it wouldn't do to give the fellows more water, would it?"

"No. Not the way we've reckoned it. Wouldn't do. We must wait."

"Yes. Take our chance. Colet . . . talking of drink. Lord. I was going to talk about it, but I won't."

"No. Keep off the drink, Collins."

"I know. My mouth's coated with gum."

The quivering of the sail had a strange effect. It was like a ceaseless glittering. It was like sun-points on a milldam on a drowsy summer afternoon, when you could just hear the rumbling of the mill. Colet took his eyes off that hypnotising movement, and glanced to windward. A mass of smooth

128

glass was about to pass under them, and deep in its body he saw a long phantom, a suspended monster, that writhed once, and faded. It had gone under the boat.

The steersman's eyes went back to the sail. Collins was still talking, but his voice was only like the muttering of the mill. The men were very still. Somebody ought to cover up Lycett's face. The sun was too bright.

"Wilson," he said, "cover up Lycett's face." But he did not hear his own voice in that silence. It was impossible to break that silence. Wilson did not move. The seaman sat like a statue. He was the Sphinx, his hands on his knees, staring like that.

Nobody moved. Nobody. They couldn't. They would never move again. They were dead. There was only a deep humming. That was the world. It was droning in space. That was the sound of its sleep. They were floating off. All their weight had gone. Their boat was under them, and so plain you could still see it. There it was, that shadow inside the sea, but it was fading, fading. The old world was sinking under them. That was why they could hear it. It was dwindling and droning away. Wilson was watching the world leave them, and it was all right. You could trust Wilson. They were getting near that star now. Light ahead! The star was coming their way, and it was growing, growing round, like the sun, growing bigger every minute: so bright that it was a white blaze, the white centre of eternity with time streaming from it in spears. That was God. His face was going to show in that white light. They must keep looking. . . .

"Colet!"

"What's that?"

"Were you asleep?"

"Not me . . . I dunno."

"The sun's cruel hot. I wish a squall would come along. Some rain. . . . Those men look pretty sick."

They sat with their heads close together, their tousled hair

129

grizzled with dry salt. They looked aged, with grey beards. Only the boat retained youth and eagerness. She was as buoyant as ever. They could find nothing more to say. Collins sighed, and stood up. He looked to Sinclair's charge, a mile away to windward. His eyes circled round, and suddenly his hand gripped hard the steersman's shoulder.

"Coming up astern! Colet, a ship."

His voice was raised and confident.

"Sail-ho!"

The dead figures stirred. They came to life. Some of them rose, clutching the gunwale, crouching with a grip on the thwarts, or clasping the mast. They were staring aft.

"All over, boys. Here she comes."

"It's a liner, sir," said Wilson.

"Of course it is. That's what we want. Share round what's in the breaker, Wilson. She can't miss us."

Sinclair had seen it too. His boat had luffed. Colet did not remember afterwards very much of what followed. Collins took the helm. She was black, the liner, with a long row of round ports, circles of gold. She was enormous, when she stopped. She was bigger than the sea; she blotted it out. Her upper works were white, and she hardly moved, though the waters were dancing beneath her. There was some one shouting from her bridge. Along her rail was a row of still figures, regarding them silently, from a great height. Colet sat in dazed astonishment. Women in white dresses were looking down at them.

# CHAPTER XXI

THE liner's deck was a neat road, a disciplined promenade, and the seams of its scoured woodwork ran so far and straight that they were as incredible as plain truth. It had garden seats. The extraordinary thing about that deck was that it was too solid and steady. Colet could only flop loose feet upon it. It was funny, trying to walk on a steady deck. The feet didn't know it was steady.

"Purser, I can't move," complained Collins, in a whisper. "I can't walk."

A beneficence had come unexpectedly out of the blue, just as the apparitions of monsters had loomed beside the boat in the body of the sea, and as the hopeful lights of ships, in night watches, had declined into setting stars. But it had come. It enfolded them. They were in luck. Colet was tucked into a cabin, a luxurious place, not yet to be believed, but quite solid, for all that, and there he lay in the surrender of release, while yet his body was responsive to the soaring lightness of that boat. His body still had a ghostly apprehension of the swift lift and the descent. Couldn't forget that. Never forget that; nor the swaying ridges of the great seas overshadowing them at dusk. Hale's last words: "That's all, Colet. Time to go." And Wilson's head at daybreak, watching; watching without a movement the march of the seas as if he knew all about them, but doubted the loyalty of their inferior nature. Nothing to do now but to snuff up the smell of cool linen again, and forget a book while listening to the soporific whirr of the electric fan. The surgeon would then come in, easy and bland.

"Morning, doctor. How's the rest? How's Lycett?"

"That's how you feel, is it. All is well with the child."

"And Sinclair, our chief officer? You've seen him, too?"

"Ah, the red-headed pirate. Couldn't help seeing him. He's picking up. He just told me to go to hell."

"Gillespie?"

"Don't know him. Oh, you mean the dear old Glasgow Highlander who keeps on asking for a long whisky and soda? Unless his anxiety exhausts him first, he'll smell whisky again, some day."

"Don't be hard on him. He's all right."

"So the engineers say. But he hates me. You all do, you know. I've never seen such a crew. Some of the women here are nervous. It's as much as I can do to keep them out of your cabins."

"They're not coming, are they?"

"Not unless you don't do what I tell you."

The youthful but white-haired surgeon, tall, deliberate, and gracious, who in his white uniform could have been a functionary, immaculate and revered, in a sphere where all was pure and noble, one morning took Colet, shrunk within a borrowed suit, which made him feel like an awkward mortal who had blundered into the abode of the blest, to the smoke-room. There was Sinclair, with some strangers about him. Sinclair came to meet him. He was much amused by something in Colet's appearance. He held him off at arm's length, and laughed.

"You look holy, purser. You look as if you were just coming out of the wilderness after turning down the devil. Come and have a pick-me-up."

The strangers made room for him, adjusting wicker chairs about one of the tables with an air of quickly providing for a welcome guest who was really invisible to them. Colet noticed that they observed him cautiously only when they supposed they were unobserved. They continued their conversation as though he had not come. They did not want to embarrass him by showing they were aware of his unusual presence. The shyness of Englishmen was so delicate and polite, he thought, and so encouraging, that a nervous kitten might be deluded into thinking that it had the room to itself, until it was trodden on. They evidently knew nothing about the rescue of any castaways. They had never heard of it. Luckily for him, no boats had been picked up in mid-ocean, so there was no need, if challenged, to confess to an episode which probably had never happened. They talked of rubber, of one or two important men who ought to be shot, of one or two unimportant women who had provided the ship, that voyage, with a little welcome unexpectedness, and of a fellow-passenger whose luck at cards was evidence of the existence of the devil. But presently, when the conversation became various with subjects discreet between pairs of these strangers, the man next to Colet tapped out his pipe and leaned over to him, as though with a chance private thought.

"Feeling all right now?"

"Fine."

That was as far as it went. The stranger began to refill a beautiful briar with some rich tobacco which moved Colet with a sudden yearning. But the stranger was unaware of it. He lovingly loaded that ripe bowl, and Colet watched the rite with the happy knowledge that he had come back to the sun, that sights and smells were good, and that there were pleasant things to be done.

"What happens to you, may I ask, after an occasion of this sort? What do you do?"

"I've no idea. Sent home, I suppose."

"But an official has to worry about it, presumably. They ought not to land you at Rangoon and just leave it at that."

"Rangoon?"

"Where we're going. You knew that?"

"No. I forgot to ask."

The stranger was amused. "I guess you're right. Any old place would do for me, after an outing like yours."

"Do you know Rangoon?"

"Pretty well. All round from that purgatory to Bangkok."

"The names sound very attractive."

"They do? How one forgets!" His amusement was faint but provocative. "Yes, I suppose they sound attractive. Must have sounded so to me once. Must have."

"And now they don't. That's the worst of disillusionment. The real thing goes."

"Eh? I'm not disillusioned. I'm busy. I heard you all right, didn't I? Didn't you say the real thing goes when we know the reality? Now, what on earth do you mean by that?"

"Well . . . of course it means nothing. Only a little doubt about the nature of the reality, perhaps."

"You'll feel stronger presently. We understand reality well enough, when we bark our shins on it. Now, I say that's the fun of it, seeing what things are in good time, and treating them as they deserve; don't you?"

"I expect you are right."

"Sure of it. Like testing a piece of rock. That's my job. Most people would call it road metalling. Good enough for them. But if you know what to do with it, it might mean—it might mean kissing your hand to those places with names you think so attractive, and getting that deer park at home."

Colet laughed. "Have you come across that magic lump of road metalling yet?"

"Not so far. Only something a bit like it. Enough to keep me going on. Can't have the park yet, but I could buy a fawn—one or two nice little fawns."

"Perhaps the fun is in the search, not in finding."

"Say that again. It sounds interesting. Though I'd like to hear you say it after you'd ploughed through Siamese forests in the rains, punctured from head to foot by ticks and leeches, and no more to show for it than enough to buy quinine for the next bout of 'the shakes.' "

"I think I'd say it then. The hunt's the game. The quarry doesn't matter so much."

The stranger swerved in his chair to inspect Colet. He frowned at him comically, and his scrutiny was met with a candid conviction of good cheer. This stranger was a man some years older than himself, with a hard but amiable countenance, eyes that were mocking him now in good nature, and a little moustache which might have been cast in iron. There was a scar on his chin, and Colet judged that very likely it had been well earned. That chin would take some breaking, though. The man would take some breaking.

"I don't see it. Though if you're not looking for much perhaps you're right. I'm looking for important metal that goes by troy weight; or by the ton, if it runs to it. When I find it I'm very loving. If I don't find it I'm not happy at all. Your abstractions wouldn't turn my scales with a martyr's crown as make-weight."

"Well . . . I wonder whether we wouldn't look twice at the scales, if we know what was in them? Though of all possible things the last I want is martyrdom. It's too lonely."

"Here, your talk is quite Christian. I'm afraid to listen to it. Let's have a merry drink and forget it."

They waited while a steward, with no sign of emotion but the deepest respect, listened in turn and without a comment to the trivial wishes of that circle of men.

"So you don't know what you'll do at Rangoon?"

"Not in the least. I'm a destitute seaman."

"Um."

"Eh? I said I am a destitute seaman."

"I heard you. I only made the noise of a thought. You don't know any one at Rangoon?"

"Nobody. Never been there."

"Well, I do know Rangoon, and any one destitute there

would be about as happy as a hungry dog in a stone yard."

An elderly neighbour leaned towards them with a gentle contradiction. He had heard Rangoon mentioned, and he and the stranger began a blithe dispute about their destination which left that port uncertain between a dream city of Oriental delights, and a worthy abode of rectangular commercial ideals, in their satisfactory concrete, surrounded by quarters for ministrant coolies. Sinclair extricated Colet, and they began to pace the deck, and gossip of what had been. Colet learned that the end of his voyage was now but a matter of days.

The surgeon, on his next visit, was perfunctory.

"I only call because I'm very dutiful. You are fit for treasons, stratagems, and spoils. Only be quite sure," he added, "that the spoils come safely in at the end. By the way, that passenger you were talking to yesterday, Mr. Norrie. He's coming here. There's a book he wants you to look at. And here he is. I'm off to find your friend the engineer."

Norrie took the settee.

"I heard the doctor give you my name. It really is my name. And I have brought you a book. As good an excuse as any for walking uninvited into another man's cabin."

Colet regarded the book politely. It was not exactly technical, but it appeared to be a serious address to geologists and surveyors, should the thought ever occur to them of exploring the chances Siam held in secret. It was loaded with maps. They bore such legends as Chlorite and Hornblende rocks; Gold Sands; Gem Gravels; Sandstone. What was most attractive about it was its amateurish drawings of temples, boats, camps, and natives. While he turned the pages with respect, looking for something he might say for this kindness, he did, for a moment, become lost in a brief description of a place named Wat Chinareth . . . "far in the jungle, when the eye has become accustomed to green for weeks, the wonderful yellow-red of the tiles of the temple roof, picked off with green borders, and light-red lower buildings of the cloisters, were most striking . . . the entrance to the tower was in its day very prettily panelled and gilded; now, alas, bats and cobwebs are legion."

"Don't look for entertainment in it," he was advised. "Look for facts, Mr. Colet. But not now. I have an idea, but you may not care for it. You'll find in that book some faint hints of the barbarism of my own life, when poking about for a good substitute for that deer-park. I'm a prospector, that's what; but I will say for myself that I was passed through the turnstiles of the Royal School of Mines. I won't flatter you by suggesting that you could be my expert assistant. Field geology is not learned in a day. But, if you're at a loose end, it would be pleasant if you could come along with me."

Colet got up on his elbow in his bunk, and considered Norrie, but not his suggestion. His visitor gave no hint of a barbaric life. His dress was only a little less punctilious than the surgeon's uniform. His intonation was that of one in authority. Colet twisted the point of his beard.

"But—but—of course, I shall be glad to read this book. It's travel, anyhow. All the same, I can't see where I could come in."

"Naturally. You've never done it. If you had, you'd refuse. If you can believe me, I'm trying to beguile you into a most damnable passage. For my own sake, of course. Don't make a mistake about that. I don't like getting fever in the forest on my lonesome. It's beginning to frighten me. Then there are the natives. They're sometimes so volatile. Two could manage them better than one. If they make trouble, you might get it, and not me. That's one advantage of a partner."

His manner conveyed that he was explaining but the melancholy truth.

"Don't let me persuade you. I want you to come, but not if you don't feel like it."

He began to fill that briar slowly, and once he rubbed it on his cheek, as though caressing it. Colet considered the man, and thought of road metalling, levelled and hard. But there must be something in a fellow who could choose such a pipe, and treat it like that. Not easy to read that man, but easy to read his pipe. Go by the pipe, and jump for it?

Norrie began to form leisurely clouds, and to watch them unfold; and at his ease, in a reminiscent way, to insult the Orient attractively because he had nothing better to do just then.

Colet fumbled in a jacket pocket.

"Before you go any further, for the love of Heaven hand me your tobacco-pouch."

"Oh, you smoke, do you? I thought you didn't. That was a count against you."

"I don't know when last I had a pipe." He held his nose over the smoke of his bowl. "Now, if you talk to me, I think I'd agree to go with you either to perdition or the pearly gates."

"Then I shan't say any more about it; not yet. Neither of those two places is in my prospectus."

"No? Well, the very smell of your mixture warns me that it must be one or the other, and there's no telling which."

"Odd; I thought it was a better tobacco than that. I like to listen to you. That's why I've come in. But don't forget I'm a metallurgist. My only anodynes are the pipe and drink."

"Is doubt about the nature of things an anodyne?"

Norrie was sadly emphatic. "Rather. That, or an infection. It's debilitating. It's worse than dysentery. It takes away a man's inside. When I want something, I don't doubt whether I ought to have it or not. The only doubt is, can I get it?

That's the miserable doubt, can I get it? Usually I can't. No doubt about that."

Norrie, Colet thought, was a man worth looking at, large and satisfactorily indolent, but with quick and wary eyes which usually looked down his nose when he was talking, as if his converse was self-communion which you overheard. There was nobody else for him to look at, of course; nobody who mattered so much as himself, anyhow. But the man was kindly; the purring, perhaps, of one of the larger carnivora when it was well fed. Now and then, when he had a question, a sly glance went with it, instant but casual, and you knew your answer would have to be precise; no use to hedge; but, if you hedged, then at least he would sympathise with so human a failing. His taut moustache was dark, but its hint of cruelty was forgotten in his abundant hair, which was careless of definition, and allowed a few tumbles of grey waves to stray over his brow. His eyes and hair gave an assurance that he was often playfully human, while his long thin nose reminded Colet of a knife that would be always prompt to the usual bidding of that firm mouth with its lurking derision of scruples.

"Now, Colet, I've been talking of the jungle, not the pearly gates. I don't like the jungle, but it happens to be a verifiable fact. And please don't dwell on the thought of per-dition. It makes me uncomfortable. Think of valuable deposits, which are much better. They might come in this life. Mine is a business notion. It isn't metaphysical. Leave metaphysics to the senile, who take to thin joys because they can't have babies. What I'm looking for is something a bank manager would respect; and yet it might come to nothing but quinine and another shot at the game later. Let me press the button for your steward. Let's have something to make us hopeful and foolish."

# CHAPTER XXII

THEY arrived at Rangoon before the day had begun; and though that city had a name which had the appeal ·of a call of the oboe, yet Colet discovered that he was in no hurry to leave his cabin. Something had gone out of him. He could feel no magic in the Gulf of Martaban. He rebuked himself for that. He could not be fully alive, to be in Burma, and yet not to have the sense of a strange occasion. He might be still in Billiter Avenue. But perhaps the ship and the open boat had given to him all he could accept, for a while. There is a limit. Burma could not be much after the old *Altair*; and her modest little master was more significant than all the pagodas and lotus ponds.

Norrie strolled in, to remind him that there were lodgings to be found, that he was concerned with a wreck over which officials would be nosey, and that there was work to be done.

"You are coming with me now, and you'll know it. Here's Burma, but you won't find any lotus about me, except after I've fed."

"I was just thinking of that pond weed. How is it I don't feel very interested? And on the Irrawaddy, for the first time. Do you think I'm ill?"

"Not a bit," Norrie told him. "It shows your sound health. It's just your blighting divination. You smelt the spicy breeze of this open counterfeit afar off. That's all. You'll smell it stronger presently."

Off the two of them went. And Rangoon was not the expected vision of the Orient, nor was it fully of the West. It was an industrial western city which had got mislaid to sprawl in fatigue in the tropics. Languor and warehouses. Its white people were too hot and bored to get it replaced. They wanted to do it, but they had no will and energy for that. The brown folk had been drawn into the city, but had learned that it was not of their sort. They were enduring the orderly and stagnant heat till they had the means of escape.

In a hotel bedroom hot and dim, where the electric light was needed though it was morning, Colet looked at the grey mosquito curtains of the bed and asked, involuntarily, how long they would have to stay there.

" Well, until the proper person within the meaning of the act has discovered to what extent you are stained criminally. You've gone and lost your ship, you know. As a seaman you are suspect, naturally. A man of your intelligence isn't a seaman for nothing, either. It's against nature. After I've bailed you out, you can make for Penang."

"What shall I do there?"

"I don't know. They do funny things there. But I'll tell you carefully, at the proper time, what I want you to do there."

Norrie surveyed him plaintively.

"I don't like your style, now I come to think of it. You can't go about with me like that. My friends would think I'd given up mining, and was going after locusts and wild honey with a sacred crank who would look more picturesque in goatskins. It would never do. You don't know how particular we are in the tropics. Come along."

And Norrie, though he affected to be indolent, was casually familiar with the devious city; he wasted no time in his search for what was wanted. The stores, to Colet's surprise, would have been appropriate in the Brompton Road, and his companion was no better than a shrewd and ironic housewife who had been wearied by the ways of the keepers of shops, yet had to meet them as penance for existence, and so converted them into an opportunity for foolish amusement. He knew too much of the secret motives for the trifling devices of commerce. He sported in a feline way with the disarming candour of salesmen, leading them on with unsmiling humbug till they were sure their skill was happy. Colet began to see that with Norrie he would be protected from the guile of the worldly, because to his companion that was only the cunning of children, simple and endearing. It was enough to make a diverting interlude when not engaged in the really serious task of beguiling the greater powers.

Colet was released early from the quiet questioning of officials whose knowledge of ships, he realised with a little alarm, would have been infernal, had it been applied with the intent to put gyves on the wicked. They knew too much about ships. He learned, in that brief cross-examination, that no enterprise on earth is under so many jealous eyes as a ship on the high seas. And when, immediately after that episode was closed, the little coaster *Nibong* put out from Rangoon for Penang, and he was its only white passenger, Sinclair said farewell. As the coaster's syren warned that she was about to depart, Colet had a suspicion that he would have been glad to be returning to London instead, with his old shipmate. Penang had but a minor inducement, and Norrie, though engaging, was new and unpredictable. It was not easy to know for certain which possessions were better worth cherishing, but at least he was reluctant to let Sinclair go. And Sinclair seemed reluctant to go. He was cheered by that. There could be genuine dubiety over the implications of what, in a hurry, people often called good luck, but his friend Sinclair, he was admonished to see, did not enjoy this inevitable break from a chance messmate; there was little to be said about such a trifle of human understanding and nothing about it at all to Sinclair, but it was of happier augury than the most hopeful hint of valuable deposits in Siam, or wherever they were.

Sinclair marched stiffly away in that brisk manner, and

he did not look back. Sinclair had gone; but chance had added Sinclair to his store of riches, anyhow, though no bank manager would look at that credit. Perhaps additions to good fortune were always so, imponderable, unaccountable, and of no use to any one. Yet they were positive. His knowledge of Sinclair and that bunch of men of his old ship gave to an aimless and sprawling world the assurance of anonymous courage and faith waiting in the sordid muddle for a signal, ready when it came. There were men like that. You could never tell where they were. They were only the crowd. There was nothing to distinguish them. They had no names. They were nobodies. But, when they were wanted, there they were; and when they had finished their task they disappeared, leaving no sign, except in the heart. Without the certainty of that artless and profitless fidelity of simple souls the great ocean would be as silly as the welter of doom undesigned, and the shining importance of the august affairs of the flourishing cities worth no more homage than the brickbats of Babylon. Those people gave to God any countenance by which He could be known.

The informal little steamer, the quiet, the radiant day, and the seclusion compelled by his difference from that crowd of noisy native passengers on the deck below, brought him back to a central loneliness. They were off. He began to hear from himself again. His brief glimpse of the East at Rangoon had not been disturbing only because he had gone about in the shadow of Norrie. But he remembered that Rangoon's slow flux of multitudinous people, like the movement in a nightmare, had been appalling with its reminder of a sightless ooze, without more distinction between fear and laughter in it than there is in the flat expanse of a grey river descending for ever to be lost in the deep. A slow pour of viscid life, just like the tide home-going over London Bridge for the trains, moving to a compulsion which was as dark in its nature as a starless patch in the clear sky of night.

What was there? Nobody would ever know. If you gazed too long at that abyss of night you would cover your eyes to hide your thoughts. It would not bear looking at. That mob below him on the fore-deck was as alien as anything nameless could be. It was a separated puddle, still slowly eddying with the original impulse.

A woman's voice in it brought his vague survey of the mixture of moving and noisy colours to a focus. A diminutive brown creature in a green sheath, with a silver stud in her nose, was wandering about and calling a name—it sounded like a name. She was seeking somebody in the mob, which took no notice of her, and she appeared to be anxious. She was as though the light of understanding had been let into that ship. She had separated from the agglomerate, and had a personal voice. Then she stopped below his rail. She was bending over a yellow bundle. A child was asleep there in a patch of shadow, with a face as pale and still as a flower upturned to the moon, and its frail hands curled as loosely as fallen petals. Of course, the dark patch in the sky is that only because we cannot do any better with it; not near enough to it; not our place in the sky. That child was as Sinclair, and the woman as himself. There is no such thing as humanity. There are men and women.

The day glowed and was lazy; it was a blue intensity loosened with a tincture of gold. No land was in sight. Yet, with a sea dreaming in so virtuous a sleep that peace itself would have thought that here was its home, a traveller did not look for land. The sky was gracious, brooding in solicitude over their little company of chattering innocents. Their modicum of a steamer—for her size checked Colet with the idea, when he boarded her, that she was venturesome—was enjoying herself as freely as though she knew nothing ever darkened that favoured region.

Colet began to feel, after the first day, that he had drifted into another sphere. He watched a company of brown people squatting by a hatch, whose happy stoicism and doll-like figures were appropriate to ancient tranquillity and unchanging skies. They did not know harshness. They made on stringed instruments improbable music of a tenuous appeal which was heard by a part of his mind of which he knew nothing. It was music in accord with that aromatic fore-deck. That was a smell he did not know, any more than the music, but if they were foreign they were known to a dream that was mislaid somewhere in his memory.

The *Nibong* had many ports of call. Each place appeared unexpectedly, as though by chance. The ports had rare names. A legend, as it were, would precipitate as a silent appearance, and remain by the ship for an hour. If he came out from his cabin to look at it again, it had gone. It had melted into the sky. He began to suppose that this voyage was one without purpose, as vague as the drowsy afternoons. The course of their toy ship was set to nothing more than a fancy generated like the music, fixed by the whimsicality of a song. They paid calls to get settings for the music: Moulmein, Martaban, Tavoy, Mergui. It did not matter where they went. The company on the fore-deck changed from place to place, but its colours were the same, and music was always there.

They had a coast to port, after Moulmein; it was that, or a perennial enchantment. Probably it was but the promise of a kingdom, the auspice of a happier time. It was not the spectacle of solid earth. Beyond the indeterminate green where the foliage met the sea there were heights. They might have been mountains, but when you were not watching them their violet outlines changed. When next they were seen they had risen into stupendous ranges of cobalt and bitumen, too massive for clouds, too high for mountains; and that meridian range was hollowed, as lightning glared and quivered in its body, by profound gulfs, abysms seen for an incredible instant, and then gone. The clouds and the far

K

mountains were of the same nature as the constellation of islands through which the *Nibong* was threading. Norrie, when Colet was leaving him, had an afterthought. He mentioned a place called Mergui.

"Look out for the Mergui Islands. Be careful. Unless it blows hard you'll want to land on one of them. If you do you'll forget all that I've told you, and I shan't see you again."

Here the islands were. But nobody, of course, ever had landed on them. They were unknown to man, except as fond reflections. They were as silent as unspoken thoughts. They were versatile. The thoughts changed. The next was better than the last. As the *Nibong* cruised through the vision Colet saw faceted stones interrupting that polished level of lapis-lazuli, small mounds of emerald on the mirror, bergs of white marble, glimpses of retirements with coral thresholds leading to palms and a forested mountain under a spell. A canoe or two was seen, but they melted round promontories. The secrets were undisclosed. The shades which haunted that seclusion faded when men approached from the outer world.

Colet was told, later, that they were nearing Penang. It was time, he thought, to do that, and to touch reality. The ship should not cruise off the map for too long, or they might never get on to it again. Now, at last, she was close to a proper shore, a high coast solid and brilliant as it looked to the setting sun. There were great ships, and the level light discovered pale houses recessed within the green of the hills. But as he found it, even as he reached it, it went. The sea was transfigured to a shining expanse of carnelian, and the very air was the rosy glow of a heatless fire. Penang and its sea assumed another nature as he watched. Its only affinity to earth was a faint odour of pepper, and the sound of a gong.

## CHAPTER XXIII

IF he had landed on the further side of the moon he could not have been more in the dark. Those letters with which Norrie had armed him—chits, Norrie called them—they were all very well, but in a way they made the darkness of Penang a bit more questionable; not darker, but more eccentric. One of the letters was to a house called Senang. That suggested the local variety of Clovelly or Bella Vista. To ask for it might be like asking a London policeman for a prayer-meeting. Not worth risking it. One of Norrie's little jokes, possibly. His fun could be esoteric. His allusions were oblique. And there was another chit to a Mr. Ah Loi. But not likely. Not after dark. Much rather see this Ah Loi first in the daytime. A Chinese friend of Norrie's should be guardedly approached, in a morning light preferably.

He warned off a loitering Chinaman who attempted to grab his bag. The man did not go away, but stood there watching him, in fierce reproach. Still, if he attempted to carry that bag himself he would sweat till it guttered from his eyebrows. He was sticky already. The night was close. Night in a tropical city, to a stranger new from northern mud, was like the hearth-rug to a fish free from the aquarium. It was not according to custom. He watched men trotting past drawing passengers in light go-carts. One of these carts swept close to him, and stopped, its man picked up the bag as though he had come for that, and Colet climbed up after it. The man glided off in silence at a long easy lope. Colet called out to his man that he wanted an hotel, but the beggar swung on without taking any notice; didn't know what he was talking about, naturally; but of course that fellow had guessed the right thing to do for a newcomer.

Colet saw that Penang was a city varied and curious enough to mislead a wayfarer easily to an interesting predicament. Its bazaars were involved, continuous, and their wares problematical. Yet it could not matter what was sold by shops illuminated with paper lanterns and advertised by scarlet banners covered with cabalistic symbols. The maze of people moved as would the characters of a ballet with an incomprehensible rhythm, or of a charade of which the secret would never be guessed. They had their ardours in pursuits not to be known by him. Somehow his orbit had coincided with theirs. He felt as absurdly conspicuous there, on his high perch, as though he had chanced on the stage where actors in a privily illuminated masquerade were rehearsing the Lord knew what. It had nothing to do with him, and yet there he was. Luckily, nobody there had an idea he had barged into them. He might have been watching the mystery while protected by the gift of invisibility. He was unseen.

Or else—had these figures agreed to allow him to deceive himself? For occasionally he thought that by some weakening of his protective magic he became faintly and transiently visible. Once a monstrously tall ogre with a black beard parted to hook its inordinate length behind the ears, a sentinel who once might have turned a dark and discerning eye on intruding Sinbad, appeared to have seen him. Yes, certainly that Sikh policeman saw him.

They came, beyond the last bazaar, to the design of a palm crown blacked high on the stars. It stood over a grotesque cornice, and under the framing eaves was the golden hollow of a room open to the night. Within that room three girls, three pale sibyls swathed in filmy tissue, sat absorbed in contemplation of the runes. Colet did not descend, though the Chinaman lowered the shafts of the jinrickshaw as though here his service ended. The scene was too much like a picture story without a name to prompt anything more than a puzzled stare. One of the sibyls, whose pale face was not like Europe, but moonlight, and to whom, Colet fancied, had been delegated the announcement of whatever oracle had been resolved for a visiting stranger, languorously rose, looked towards him with eyes which entreated a release from a weird, and spoke at the window in a discreet and mild version of English. And Colet's Chinaman, though he did not understand that language, knew at once Colet's peremptory order. He knew he had made a mistake. He picked up his shafts and loped from the shade of that grove, leaving a tinkle of merriment behind.

Soon he was at a standstill again beside another conjuration of a welcome in the shades, and its light showed several frail idols in embroidered silk, with faces of chalk, their foreheads hidden in black fringes, oblique eyes which had no thoughts, and lips that were little crimson buttons. They resembled, for a moment, the illustration to a beautiful fable of Cathay, but Colet's loud voice shattered the spell before his man had ever lowered the shafts. The coolie turned about, with wondering disapproval, wiped his shaven crown with his disengaged hand, and tried again. This time he took longer, and when he halted it was before an Indian enticement, some with studs in their ascetic nostrils, their slight bodies bedight for the gaze of idling rajahs.

And then the 'rickshaw man knew he was right. He did not hesitate. With definition and relief he concluded his journey; and his astonishment was obvious when Colet leaped from the go-cart with savage energy. The Chinaman's recoil was that of innocence surprisingly attacked. Colet could see, by the light from the room, that his man was now at the end of his resources, and was obviously worried; the fellow was protesting that he had done all he could. Colet pointed to the glow of the city behind them, and made emphatic indicatory noises. The man seemed to understand. He must have guessed that, somehow, he was at fault, though for no reason that he could ever know. He turned about, dolefully.

Colet, with his face to those lights, though now disturbed, sustained his faith that Penang somewhere must have a different roof to offer; and down by the water-front, within a short distance of the quay where the adventure had begun, there it was. The hotel, except that its servants in their white uniforms were of the East, and that the building was adjusted, as well as was possible, to a temperature not altogether within the control of its management, might have been on the Riviera. As far as it could, it excluded the tropics. The hotel used its ingenuity to suggest that it was not where it was, looking out over the heated dark which brooded, with lightning glimmering in its roof, above the Strait of Malacca. When the bluish glare was vivid, then sleeping palms appeared in the foreground like tracings in ink on burnished metal.

# CHAPTER XXIV

THERE was no difficulty, after all, in discovering a Mr. Ah Loi. The hotel people knew of him. Even a 'rickshaw man, when challenged, made almost satisfactory signs of intelligence. Colet viewed him suspiciously, speculating whether this was the genie of the night before, still hanging about in the hope of improved bewitchery. But Penang, on his first morning in Malaya, was superior to all the trickery of mortals. It was as fair as though this were the original daylight of the earth. The morning was certainly heated by a sun with pristine strength, but the air was perfumed, and it sparkled. He thought the sapphire between them and the island of Sumatra was younger, after all, than the tales of Marco Polo and the ancient voyagers. One junk was suspended in it, the first to explore that blue. As he rode through the bazaars and by the shrubberies beyond he was joyously confident that he was equal to the wiles of any Chinaman.

His man, this time, knew where to go, and turned in at a gateway flanked by a pair of porcelain beasts that were not dragons and ought not to have been dogs. Beyond a garden was a large pinkish house, not unlike a temple.

Its door was open, but the house, he was afraid, was deserted. Its interior smelt of teak, or some unusual wood. There was not a sound, except that of an insect making a dry whispering in the garden. The hall subdued its English visitor with its severe integrity, for its sombre panels receded in almost a bare perspective. It was relieved by only a few white silk hangings bearing delicate images of Buddha, water fowl, bamboos, and flowers. The tiled floor was muted with old rugs which made Colet forget, as he looked at them, why he had called. And he had called with the unthinking courage of a fellow bringing a bill of exchange. The fine texture and quiet of this interior began to reduce his confidence with the challenge of another order of things. There was no bell; should he clap his hands?

Apparently his thought had been heard, for a genie in a blue tunic approached him, and kowtowed in perfect gravity though it did not speak. It led him to an inner room and left him.

What at once was seen there, and nothing else, was a bowl of pale jade that appeared to give the silence a faint light, as though it were a lamp. It was honourably isolated and elevated, as though it were the significance of a poet. It was then that Colet noticed that the backs of his hands were not only moist with sweat, but a little hairy. He did not care to approach that luminous fragility; he looked about and saw by his side some shelves of books. They were as unusual as the bowl; perhaps they were even stranger, in that place. They were of European mathematics, philosophy, and theology, and though a chance collection of books on such subjects is placed, usually, where it will not be in the way, the names on the backs of those volumes betrayed a knowledge of the latest mental enterprises of the Occident which shook Colet's confidence in the range of his own reading.

"You are interested in philosophy, Mr. Colet?"

How had that voice got there? Mr. Ah Loi was behind him. Interested in philosophy! Ah Loi had a friendly smile. He was a smile, but not much more than that; an interrogatory appraisement, tolerant and cheerful. His face was rather like his bowl of jade, delicate, pale, and bright. Colet would have preferred to wipe his hot large hands before taking the one which his host offered to him. This was confusing.

"It interested me to see those books here."

"Why, Mr. Colet? Are they out of place?"

There it was. Colet knew his first words had been as hairy as his hands.

Ah Loi was not old. He was not young. His years were merely a clarity of the spirit. He spoke English as though his home overlooked an Oxford precinct. Behind him, no doubt the *portière* through which he had entered the room, were crimson silk hangings; they dropped in heavy folds from the high ceiling and were waved on the floor. They were lettered in gold with Chinese characters, and embroidered figures of men and dragons were ambushed in their coils. The slight figure of Ah Loi, in his western suit of linen, cool and friendly, with that draping of old China for his background, was as noticeable as a gentle word. Of course, Colet thought, this blessed Chinaman had those European books here to learn what the rude children were doing, when out of sight.

"The truth is, Mr. Ah Loi, I only looked at these books because I had not the courage to go closer to your fine bowl there."

"That? That bowl? Come and handle it. Such things are made to be touched, as well as looked at. The touch should know as much as the eye."

Colet nerved himself and turned the bowl about. He realised that its frailty was but simplicity and strength, which were unctuous and cool. Ah Loi took it, and replaced it.

"Sometimes," said the Chinaman, "I have wondered whether Western culture turned into chimney smoke because of a neglected sense of touch. You see, you must pause and weigh it, when you handle an object. You have time to change your mind."

The man in the blue tunic was there again, and Ah Loi spoke to him. The servant brought in bottles, ice, and a syphon.

"You will have a stengah, Mr. Colet?"

"I don't know what that is."

"Then you are certainly new to this country. It is a small

153

whisky and soda, the half of a tonic, as you say. A Malay word. It means half. But you English use it, besides for whisky, for a person of mixed blood."

"Thank you. But no stengah for me, if you please. Not now."

"You have been in Penang only five minutes." Ah Loi was amused. "Wait till Norrie comes," he added. "At one time we Chinamen, who find it not easy to understand, kept champagne for our English guests. We heard so much about champagne that we thought it must be the same as your happiness. But now it is whisky. Well, let us talk about Norrie. He is our friend. You know him very well?"

"No. Only a little."

"A little of him is good."

"I met him on the voyage out."

"He is going to Pahang?"

"I don't know quite what he intends to do."

Ah Loi looked at his bowl.

"Nobody knows that. But he is going round to the other side of the peninsula, and he will know why. I like Norrie. He would have been the same as a Cantonese. Yet he is a Londoner."

"He has no place, then?"

"Yes. It is all his place. It is all one. He knows."

"Well, Mr. Ah Loi, I should like to know. What is it one has to know?"

"I think perhaps you know too. But the best things have no name."

"Not even such as that bowl? What about that?"

"Of course not. That is but a sign."

"Then we cannot talk about them."

"Oh yes. We do little else, when we are together, but they are not named. What shall we say, shall we say they are the communion? Come and see my porcelain. You will stay to tiffin?"

Colet, for an hour, received glimpses into a past which heartened him with a confirmation of his nebulous and shifting faith. Even a glaze for porcelain could persist, like the thought of an anonymous benevolence. Once he expressed a poignant concern for the safety of these lovely shapes and colours. Ah Loi did not altogether sympathise with him.

"They may all go, some day. There are accidental fires, and men riot. The world is rough, and it is careless. The world is abundant. But you see, Mr. Colet, these things have been done, and so they cannot be lost. They have been added, and they cannot be taken out of the sum. Tell me why it was your Shakespeare did not think it worth the trouble to preserve his poetry? I think that is the strangest thing about Shakespeare. That is why he is the most significant poet. Perhaps that indifference is his greatest gift to us."

The Englishman supposed that they were alone in the house, but Mrs. Ah Loi met them at tiffin, and Colet's memory of precious rarities went in a new confusion. She was not a Malay, though slender in a green sarong and a white muslin tunic. The gold buttons of her tunic were her only adornment. She was hardly Chinese, and certainly not English, even with that abundance of brown hair. The simple cordiality and assurance of her greeting meant that she was well used to visitors. She accepted Colet as though he were a frequent guest, but that made her fastidious hand no easier to grasp. She spoke to her husband with a droll mimicry of indifference. Where had he been all the morning? There had been stengahs, of course, and before midday, too. Colet saw that her banter disclosed a glint of serious intent. Ah Loi assured her that not a cork had been disturbed. She then gave Colet an innocent glance, not of disbelief, but of surprise. Ah Loi convinced her.

"Mr. Colet has not been long in Penang. He got here only last night. Give him a little more time, my love."

"Yes, but is he not a friend of Mr. Norrie?" She pronounced the vowels of the name with a comically slow precision. Ah Loi avoided a mention of Norrie.

"We have been talking of Kuan-yin and much else."

"It is pleasant to talk of her; but Mr. Colet, he does not know her."

"Oh, but he does."

"He is a collector?" There was a shade of anticipated disappointment in her voice.

"Oh no. He admires."

"Then I shall like you, Mr. Colet."

The more attractive a woman is, the more the resolution needed to look at her; their laughter was freedom to Colet for a candid glance at beauty that was unusual and debateable. Others might not like it. Beauty may cause a little fear. Her dark eyes were large for so small a face, and their soft uncritical light gave Colet a suspicion that she could penetrate to the thoughts at the back of his head. Her eyes, which only seemed slow because their lids were a trifle sleepy, did not rest on one's face, though they looked at it. She listened, but not so much to what you said as to your reservations; or else she pondered childishly, finding it difficult to understand. (Don't deceive yourself, Colet thought; she understands very well.) Her face was wide for that delicate chin. But then, of course, her brow had to find room for those eyes. Only the rather high cheek-bones were faintly tinctured with colour. She would have been a rarity in the court of Kubla. The nose was the more diminished by the bold curves of her lips, which really looked like the Orient.

Colet began to speak of Norrie, but Mr. Ah Loi smiled uneasily, moving an object or two about the table.

"My wife does not like him. Norrie is a little different for each of us."

"A little? Mr. Norrie is evil," she said.

Her husband protested ardently.

"No, no. He is not that. I know what you mean. He is naughty, but he is not evil."

"Yet you tell me he understands."

"Yes, and for me, that saves him. He is a sad man, for he knows too much, but he had accepted so very little. He is a little amused by all the gods. I am sorry for Norrie."

"I like him, too, when I am talking to him," she confessed. "But not after. Then I remember that he knows, yet smiles. He is only polite to you," she advised her husband, "but he smiles when he goes away."

"I know he does." Ah Loi admitted it. "I know him. Yes. There is no ultimate value, for him. Think of that. It has been killed by his science, which is—what is it?—the formulation of dirt. He must pay for that, of course. But he does not understand the penalty."

"Then he doesn't understand after all," she challenged.

"Well, no, not the last things. We must lose all the first good things if we do not understand the last. It is sad not to have ears to hear, especially if one hears so well as Norrie."

# CHAPTER XXV

In his Penang bedroom, alone with what he did not know of the tropics, Colet guessed he was inappropriate to that variety of dark. It was not only a covert dark. Its nature was foreign. It was unlike the nights of the north. The boards of the room were bare, and they were a deep red. The room was too large and high for one small glim, and it contained but a wardrobe, a table, a chair, and a bed enclosed in a muslin box. It resembled a large meat safe, that bed. At a glance by lamp-light the gauze did not quite hide the fact that there was a body in his bed; but he saw it was a bolster lying fore and aft, the uninvited Dutch wife. It was there for some reason well known in the locality, of course, but it was a silly mitigation.

The hot night came close up to you. It tried to keep you from moving. It was an obstructing presence, mum and unseen, but heavy. Yet it was full of a sly stirring, though always behind you. Something was going on in it. Nothing there when you looked round. He went to the wardrobe, and the opening of its door surprised whatever was hanging about in that. A crack flashed in a zigzag across the back of the cupboard. He imagined he heard the movement, but when he looked closer there was no doubt the wood was all right. The crack had gone. Nothing in the cupboard. Nothing he could see.

He went to the table and began to write. His moist hands made the paper damp, and then the ink spread into blots; but if you tried to write while poising the hand, to give it air, then the paper became sportive under the pen. It was so ominously quiet that he heard a tiny voice at his ear. A mosquito was about. But that solitary beast had got at his bare foot. He held the light over the floor, and saw a dusky flight of gnats undulating about his ankles. Nothing for it but the inside of the meat safe.

Then a creature harsh and green, a sort of gaunt and membraneous moth, if it was a moth and not a heartless joke, plumped on his writing-pad. He immediately surrendered the pad, as that thing wanted it. What name among the bugbears had this beastly object? Its green wings were like a petticoat of leaves about its waist. There was a phantasmal head at the end of a stalk-like neck. It had a chin. It turned its cadaverous face lugubriously towards him, and waved its hands in dispraise. He didn't like it. It didn't like him, either. Its long thin arms, which wearily motioned him to keep off, had grappling hooks for hands. One of the Little People maybe; the Malayan sort. Not from the fairy rings and the daisies pied, but out of the jungle. When he moved it flew away to a corner of his ambiguous resting-place.

Better see where this thing went. As he lifted the lamp, shadows from the ceiling came down the walls to go with him. There the thing was, on the floor. Its grappling hooks were raised, as though in the act of malevolent prayer. But it took no notice of him. It had no time for him. It had other business. That triangular face was watching something else, straight before it. He followed its gaze. A shaggy spider, as large as a straddling mouse, with minute eyes like twin starboard lights, was observing the mantid. Colet was glad he was not either of them, glad that he was only the mystified audience of this show. The two horrors sat staring at each other, each waiting for midnight to strike, or else for the other to make the first move. Human life was not the only problem of life. The chimeras on the floor knew that; each of them knew something that is not in Plato. They did not move. Their apprehensions must have been tense enough to snap. Colet moved, and their thoughts snapped. He did not see what happened. There was a mingling of green and black, or else the mantid leaped forward and was caught in the spider's mouth.

An usual bedroom. Dreams were there before you slept. A place of torment for Cimmerian eccentricities, a cockpit for boggarts and kobolds. He was sure now that something was in that cupboard, and he wondered, while the floorboards were clear for the journey, how long it would take to get under the mosquito netting once the lamp was blown out. A loud voice addressed him from the wood beams of the ceiling; a clear whistling cluck. He could make out a brief slender shadow up there which was cast by no visible object; and, anyhow, it was too small for so much loud confidence. It was motionless. It was a mistake, that reptilian mark. It was a stain in the wood. The voice spoke again aloft, chee-chak, chee-chak; not an unpleasant sound; rather like shameless and noisy kissing. The little shadow writhed forward a yard, as though the lamp had been shifted quietly, and that prompted similar shadows to move above, though the lamp remained still; abrupt divergent wriggles of creatures upside down. The ceiling was populated with lizards; one fell to the floor, rather solidly. That smack knocked the stuffing out of it. No. It was off—going to get into his bed, perhaps. A close night.

Did any one ever manage to sleep through a tropic night? Not likely. You turned over, and then found that that side was hotter than the other. You turned over again. Not a sound. The lizards had ceased to kiss aloud, now the light was out. But a swift slithering passed over the boards beneath the bed. The silence was the heat. The heat was muffled. The silence was soft and hot, but heavy. It could not be pushed away. The darkness outside the curtains was waiting. For what? He was waiting too, for sleep, but it was no good waiting for that when the unseen was waiting for something else. The idea of that bolster beside him was to keep him cool, but it was an imbecile lump. He pushed it off with petulance.

That spider. There it was. It was looking at him out of a tunnel. Its eyes were as big as the headlights of a locomotive about to emerge. To emerge at any moment. Its hairy legs filled the tunnel. Its hunched legs made the tunnel dark. He could not move because he could not breathe. He was being held down for that brute. It was coming out. It put a hairy foot on his mouth. Faugh! That released him. Touched him off. The bolster was in his face. It was night still, not morning. Daylight was slow about it.

When next he woke the day was nearly there. The night had thinned; everything in the room could be seen in it, even through the mosquito curtain. It was cool at last, but the silence had not been broken.

Now it had gone. A bird was fluting in the garden, trying to remember a morning song. Strange, he felt rather like singing himself, though sleep had been only an intermittent nightmare. In that cool grey light the bare room was merely bare. That reminiscent bird had not yet got the tune right, but he kept at it on his lonesome, a meditative and conscientious little fellow. Quietly trying it over before any one was about, to be ready for the sun.

Colet opened the shutters of the verandah, and stepped out. The garden below was asleep. Only its familiar spirit was awake, tuning up before sunrise. The garden was still in the mirk. The trees were night itself settling out of the sky, descending to the earth, spreading there unequally while being absorbed. The bathroom was the first door to the left along the verandah. The liquid fluting of that bird was bathing for the mind. It made it fresh and glad. The bathroom tiles were delicious to walk over; another touch or two and they would have been cold. In a corner was an

161

earthenware cistern, with a brass dipper on its ledge. A lizard was stuck to the wall, upside down, a flesh-coloured creature with eager and prominent eyes. It raised its head to watch him. Almost indecent to strip before such an expectant gaze; but it went off, shocked, in a flash, when it saw what he was like. You held the full dipper as high as you could, and tried to imagine you would shrink from the fall of the water. The water was felt, but no more. There was no shock. The water was as soft as new milk.

By his chair on the verandah, when he came out, somebody had left biscuits and tea. These Chinese boys moved about as though they were disembodied spirits, and unless you were watching they were never more than wraiths in the very act of vanishing. At that moment he was sure that a Malayan sunrise, with some tea just after you had bathed, was not to be exchanged for a halo and a harp. This corner of the earth had leisured and regal scope, and its jubilant light, with the musky smell of its lush growth, was good enough for the pleasaunce of an archangel, only he might be upset by a sight of Aphrodite. The crowns of the dominant palms, and the filigree of the upper foliage of the shrubbery, were black against lambent gold, and that tide of fire was plainly welling rapidly to flood the garden. The colours below were already bright; the orange and ruby crotons were separated, and the blossoms on the vines. The sun was so quick that he could be seen moving up behind the screen; he was blazing over the top before the first moment of coolness and calm was forgotten. Wasps arrived with him, to blunder about the joists of the verandah, and they were not ordinary wasps, and knew it. The seething had begun again.

This morning he was leaving with Norrie for the other side of the peninsula. What was to come of that was as speculative as being born, for Malaya was to him what the latencies are about a child playing hop-scotch, and Norrie was as debatable as poker or immortality. It was as good as just coming into the world. The liveliness of Penang that morning was the celebration of nativity, the perennial birthday, old earth a cherub again and having another cut at it. Their 'rickshaws had to stop to allow a Chinese wedding to pass. That was the way to do it. No bare certificate of legitimacy, with a registrar's stamp, for these people, not even for the additional third wife. The regiment of forerunners of the joy were in scarlet, hats and all, as exceptional as the oncoming of an Olympian circus. They cleared the way for musicians in pale blue robes, with stringed instruments wailing bliss. The bride, if it was the bride, was a large doll with dark hypnotic eyes in a face of porcelain, a capricious crown holding her head firm on her neck, and her turquoise silk dress a call to extravagance for the poor in spirit and the homespun.

Norrie was damning his coolie for pausing to watch the procession. He wanted to get aboard; but it was unfair to expect a man to dodge a bit of luck like that. It isn't a Malay morning every day of the year. Now if all cities were as Penang, then there would be no reason to regret Ithaca and the young days of Ulysses. Our birthright would be as plain as a sign given by the gods. To think this coast had been here always, waiting for whoever doubted the earth was planned for asphalt and regrets, while there he used to be, clanking his chains west of Aldgate Pump, dutiful as an old soldier grateful for the workhouse and skilly. Colet went up the gangway, and saw the leisurely smoke from the funnel of his small coasting steamer as though it were the beckoning of the original Argo.

# CHAPTER XXVI

NORRIE was taciturn. He had hardly spoken that morning. It was noticeable, too, to his companion, that he was very generous in the confined space of that cabin for two with the broad of his back, which was in no hurry to get out of the way. He was a little testy over the refractory angles of events. Sometimes it was an angle of Colet's. His white jacket was showing the damp smutch of the heat. He peeled it off and flung it down, and then the cabin became mordant with an alien smell. Colet was aware of a distinct and opposite being, weighty and offensively otherwise, to which all his sympathy did not naturally flow.

Not all, but some, for the leisurely presence of Norrie was a warrant of literal meaning. Norrie was a cunning centre of gravity, never overset in the drift of light chances. You could hold on to him. He accepted and named events, often not vouchsafing them a glance, with melancholy understanding, as though he had known them before Homer. He dismissed occasions which perplexed Colet with droll epithets, though sadly tolerant and broody. All the same, then he was in the way.

They continued to stow their properties for the voyage. Neither spoke. Back to back, they kept impeding each other, forgetfully. Colet wondered whether men were not better apart; might not admire each other more if they were not in contact. Ought to have separate cubicles. Each man had a different aura. What did Norrie think of his? The aura was worse on a close morning. Better to be alone.

They bumped again, and Norrie put out a hand to steady himself. Colet felt aggrieved; it was all Norrie's fault.

"Don't mind me, Colet. And don't hit me. I'm simply intolerable most mornings. I couldn't be civil to the sweetest young thing in the morning."

He stretched, wiped his face, looked round.

"Now, where's that blessed bag with my maps? Where is it?"

"What's it like? If it's maps, we must find it."

"I should just think we must. It's got some whisky in it, and I simply can't drink trade poison. I wouldn't change it for all the commercial substitutes in the ship."

"This it?"

"That's right. Put it in my bunk. We shall want it. No other way to shorten this voyage."

"Need we shorten it? But you've done it before."

"And before that. In and out of the mangrove swamps. When I die, I shall be shoved into a mangrove swamp with an empty bottle, to sweat for ever, and nobody to talk to but the sort of people you meet at a ship's saloon table. You júst think of that. It would make a man virtuous, even if he had a long time to live."

Norrie reclined on the settee.

"I wonder whether Ah Loi telegraphed for berths on the Singapore steamer. We shall have to change there. But of course he did."

"He certainly did, if he said he would. I like your friend the Chinaman."

" That shows your good taste. That Chink reduces most Europeans to the texture of clay pots. He's rather too rare, for my taste. Strictly speaking, he oughtn't to have a body. He's only a subtle appreciation of refinements. Yet he seems to enjoy life. Did you see his wife?"

"She was at table."

"She was? Then you really were honoured. She won't always eat before me. I'm too coarse. You've never seen anything like her, so don't say you have. I mean alive, and walking about."

"No. Not in great numbers. I felt large and cumbersome."

"She doesn't know it, but I'd go without food just to look at her. I'd be as good as gold. She doesn't know I've got the heart of a poet under a most unlikely outside."

"What is she?"

"I should call her a masterpiece. But the best people out here, they say she is a stengah. That's what they would do, you know. Her mother was Siamese. There are little bodies in Siam who would make you forget almost anything important. Her father was a Scotchman, and he must have been a forgetful Burns with red hair. I feel almost like a bishop when I look at her. Good job you are not an artist, or you'd be blethering now."

"That couple surely are not typical here."

"What an idea. They wouldn't be typical in Chelsea. Nothing good is typical. It's a surprise. I don't know where my cork-screw is. Where is yours?"

"I haven't got one. I haven't got even a stepladder."

"Now, what a traveller. He hasn't got a cork-screw. I wonder you've got a shirt. Press the button for a boy. There it is, just behind you."

Colet went outside. The island of Penang was already a place apart, and they were leaving fishing stakes, sampans, steamers, and junks behind them. He did not always know what the queer objects signified, those marks of strange human handiwork on another order of nature, but he was satisfied that they were amiable. The waters of the Malacca Strait were the reflections of an upper light, desultory with its display, as though the celestial operator had time to waste, and wanted to see what would happen to the human stage when oriels, seldom used, were opened in the supernal. Norrie was in a hurry to get round to the coast of the China Sea, but there was no need to hurry along this coast on his account.

There were a score of superior passengers at the saloon

table. The table was full. Norrie insisted that Colet should sit beside him. He was to talk eagerly whenever the man on the other side showed the least sign of affability.

"I can't stand it. It isn't natural. If that planter once begins with his insufferable rubber, I shall have to kill him with the water-bottle, or else sit with the Malays on deck and eat bananas and dried fish."

Colet thought the deck passengers would be an attractive alternative.

"I'll squat there with you, if you insist. It's fun, that crowd on the deck aft."

"You've made a nice start. You do like it?"

"Never seen anything better."

"That's the way to look at it, when you must. But there's no hurry for it. You'll smell lots of ripe fish presently, heightened by durians."

"Let 'em come in their due season. Though I've never met durians."

"You will. They're as sure as death. It's a fruit, but you'd think it was a gas escape in a mortuary. Our pleasures are before us, and yet you think I'm too particular now over trifles, like cork-screws and chatty fellow-passengers."

"I was down on the deck this morning. Not easy to keep away from it. I'd give a good deal to know what goes on inside those people."

"The devil you would. All right, Colet, but don't learn it while you're with me. There's an odd chance you would get a real inkling of it. You seem built in that wasteful way."

Norrie, leaning on the ship's rail, considered the blue heights and opalescent cloud masses of Malaya.

"No, it's no good. It's rather different. They begin their ideas at another mark, where we have too much gumption to begin. I do my best not to see it. It's disturbing. Dammit, you and I might be wrong after all, and then where should we be? We might have to scrap home and altar, and I can't bear the thought of it. God bless Clapham Junction. You be careful. The Oriental is dangerous, once you begin to monkey with his notions."

They got well down the coast. The same things occurred daily, and were getting usual. The loading of the steamer at one of the small ports was nearly completed. Norrie was asleep in the cabin. On the leeward side a few empty sampans and prahus were rocking slowly. The shore was about two miles away, and their port of call a mangrove creek, by the look of it, inhabited only by crocodiles. The hills inland were no more than the lurking masses of a thunderstorm in reserve for the evening. They were distant, whether clouds or mountains, and a warning which need not be heeded before noon. The sea about the estuary was shallow, a level of opaque olive-green, and only the lighters, and the coolies in them who had nothing now to do but to smoke and watch the life of the steamer while waiting for a tow, were an assurance that this anchorage was merited by a veritable and inhabited shore.

From the bridge of the steamer Colet and another saloon passenger watched a derrick manœuvring the last piece of freight, a motor-car. It was too awkward for the hold, and its bulk made the restricted foredeck of the coaster appear to be dangerously encumbered. Colet remarked to the man beside him that the car was an incongruous interjection. It had no real part in the drama of Chinese, Malays, and Hindus on that deck.

His companion, a young man who had been prompt with knowledge, made his monocle comfortable to regard with kindly amusement that lively huddle of chromatic humanity.

"Oh, hasn't it a part? That car is as much a part of the East now as the natives. We're here now, you know."

Colet ventured to regret that aspect of our presence.

"You must have seen a lot of it?"

"Oh, rather." The young man freely acknowledged it.

"All round this coast and the islands." He indicated with a generous gesture all that was beyond, in the east. "Travelling here for two years now."

"Fun?"

"No. Hardware."

That tickled him. The monocled stranger asked for some news of London. Stood Leicester Square where it did? He hoped to learn that before the year was out.

Colet was trying to imagine the Orient in the terms of a captivating prospect for hardware. That was not easy. But this commercial traveller was bright and explicit, if his confidence had not lost all the jaunty indiscretion of youth. His judicious monocle and accent, well maintained in excellent simulation of what was authentic, perhaps made an advance with ironmongery among palm groves the less noticeable. Still, the young man quite evidently knew something of the East. He confessed to a familiarity with Malay. He knew these people.

Colet felt his inferiority. "I must learn to talk with them."

"It's really easy to learn their language. And they're jolly nice people. I get along fine with them."

He adventured into some personal history allusively, but with oiled enjoyment. There was a Malay girl, an apt pupil of love. He sweetened his narrative with a touch of sentiment. He tried to picture the girl for Colet, and Colet realised that she was a female. But she married a chief; only another addition to that populous household. An elderly chief. A friend of his, too. Then the girl ran away from her new home. She came back, in fact, to him. The young man could not help showing how much he appreciated this demonstration of affection; nevertheless, he was frightened.

"So would you have been, if you knew these people."

"What did you do?"

"Why, you see, that raja kept a regiment of young men about him. No joke. One of them was the girl's brother.

Real hot stuff. If the chief had nodded—no need to say anything—I should have looked a pretty mess one morning, take it from me."

When the delectable morsel of girlhood appeared again at his bungalow, therefore, the Englishman, seeking safety, went to the lion's den. The best thing to do. He went straight to the raja and said the girl had come to him that morning. But the old man, who knew girls, waived this one aside royally. Too trivial for a dispute between friends. Nothing in it. Colet gathered, too, that the episode was now entirely closed. His fellow-traveller had given up the girl. All right now. One should not keep them too long. They grow fond of you, and it doesn't do.

"There—you see that fellow there?" His companion nudged Colet. He indicated a Malay squatting on his hams, among other native passengers, his back to the bulwarks. Colet remarked him.

"Well, he's very like that girl's brother."

It was a scowling figure notably attired in a bright sarong and jacket, and a black velvet cap.

"They look fine people, don't they?"

That one was a picturesque example, from what could be seen of him; and while still idly noted so handsome a presentment of a folk strange to him, Colet unlearned much that he had accepted of the East. Not much to-day in all that. It had all become ordinary. The natives, he was advised, were not difficult to understand. They admired the English. They would do anything for us, take it from him. Orang puteh, white men, they call the English, and orang blanda, yellow men, the Dutch. That shows you, doesn't it? These Malays know gentlemen when they see them. When once you were used to their funny little ways the rest was easy. They were only strange until you had lived with them and could talk their language. It was a good thing to take one of their girls. Some of them were very pretty. The girl could soon

170

teach you a lot. Take it from him, a man like himself got to know more of the guts of things, out there, than all the interfering officials who were so touchy over this and that.

A group of Chinamen below stood bent in appreciation of some cocks, each in its own wicker cage. The cocks stridently challenged each other. One cage was carelessly handled, and the gladiator hustled out. A bystander grabbed at it, but it flustered to the topside of the ship, and another indiscreet clutch at its tail sent it protesting into the sea. For an instant it was a frantic bunch of feathers there, and then an unseen body from below swirled the water ponderously and the cock had gone.

Colet was shocked. This was not in accord with what was familiar. The penalty had come so suddenly, just when he had allowed the motor-car, in spite of its size and appearance, to displace some old conceptions, to occupy with the certainty of a late solid engine the ancient mystery of the East. Yet nobody else seemed affected by the incident. The Chinamen stared indifferently at the place where the water had swirled, but the others might not have been aware that anything had happened. His companion made a humorous reference to the incident, but returned with soft pleasure to some more intimate words on the pleasantries of native ways. Colet, with a divided mind, listened while his eyes still rested absently on the Malay below who had been used to illustrate a little colourful drama of no value except to show to a stranger the delights and simplicity of the things he did not know.

What his fellow-passenger was telling him Colet did not clearly hear, but the narrator was at least cheerful and pert. The heat made one slack. A Chinese cooly was passing the crouching Malay, who rose, and was seized with a sudden convulsion. The Chinaman fell. Colet noticed in disbelief that the man's head was off. Colet did not move. He had not decided yet that the head was dead, for a little cigarette smoke still moved from its nostrils.

The crowd below, which for a pause as long as Colet's incredulity had remained still, began to swirl, as had the sea just before. The Malay was running. Several men vaulted into the water. As though it were not real, Colet watched that trotting figure cut down two more men who also were uncertain of its reality, and then disappear into the forecastle. The deck below was now empty, but for several figures in ungainly postures. There were noises in the forecastle. Colet stared at the dark and empty rectangle of its entrance, fixed his attention to those sounds. The Malay came within that frame, cool and leisured, his blade in his hand, the appearance once more of the principal actor in a play, and stared sullenly at his sole audience of two white men in the gallery. With his gaze on them he trotted for the bridge ladder. Colet discovered, as the man began to run, that now he was alone, and that his two hands which gripped the rail did not know they ought to let go. He desired to run, but was held to the spot by himself. How run from a dream?

A gun-shot released Colet's grip. There below him was the tall figure of an engineer, standing at the foot of the ladder in singlet and trousers, his uniform cap on the back of his head. He was pointing a revolver at the Malay. The gun clicked with a silly inconsequence as the coloured figure reached the ladder, and the engineer crumpled. When Colet got to his cabin door the eyes of the Malay on the ladder stared up at him from the deck planking, and were coming higher. The door shook while he was making it fast, and then the face of the man darkened the open port window. The shadow passed. Colet stood holding the handle of the door till the silence told him his arm was aching with an unnecessary effort.

"What are you standing there for? Do open that door. I'm breathing steam." Norrie was sitting up, looking sleepy.

"Can't open it. There's a johnny outside knifing everybody."

"Keep the devil out, then. Is it locked?"

"Yes. It's fast all right, now."

"I should close the port. He might throw something in."

Norrie got up, and made the port fast, and then sat listening, on the couch. He stretched himself again.

"Lucky you got here first. Why doesn't someone shoot him?"

Colet looked round for a weapon. There was only the water-bottle. The ship was very quiet. It might have been deserted. Were they left aboard with that lunatic?

"Norrie, have you got a gun?"

"Several, in that trunk under the bunk. But no ammunition, of course. But he'll be downed by some one. Don't worry. They're slow about it, though."

Once cries broke out in the after-part of the ship. Once feet pattered rapidly past their cabin. Once there was a challenge in a strange language, but nobody answered it. Something warm trickled down his nose. He put his hand to his face quickly. Sweat.

How much more of this? Norrie was a cool customer. Colet peered out of the port. There was nothing to be seen; only the usual patch of deck and the rail. But heading for the ship was a steam launch. He watched its progress. It was bringing four Malay policemen with rifles, and a white officer. The launch reached them and got under the ship, out of sight.

Nothing could be heard. Two of the little noiseless policemen, with their officer, went by the cabin. Then they heard the white man's voice calling some orders at the head of the ladder. They opened the door and went out. All the police were there, and were beginning to descend to the fore-deck. The men advanced cautiously towards the empty forecastle entrance, and one of the policemen chanted to that vacant door words which sounded like taunts. There came the Malay again. He was still cool and leisured, and answered the taunting with dignity. The police halted. The white officer talked quietly to that figure in the doorway and signed for him to drop his parang. But the fellow jumped for the police, toppled into a sliding heap, and was still.

# CHAPTER XXVII

ONE day on the China Sea side, well up the coast from Singapore, they reached a hut. It was night, and it rained. Here they would begin their inland journey. It was somewhere near a beach. It had no other description. When coming up from the landing-place Colet had no faith that any roof could have resisted that abrupt smash of rain, even if a roof once had graced that outlandish shore, which did not seem likely. Yet Norrie moved as though he used to believe it, and knew of no reason yet to give up the idea. There was a sleeping-place, cavernous and bare, partly discovered by a mournful lamp; and one of its shadows, and a large one, did not behave normally like the rest. The lamp set it going. It gyrated ceaselessly amid the stationary shadows. Colet was satisfied that it was a bat. It might have been a black cloth circulated about by silent magic.

Then came morning, and the morning when they were to start for the interior of the land. Colet, on the verandah of the house, with the packs for travel about him, did not share Norrie's annoyance over the delay. Any later time would do to start from there. Don't let a good thing go too soon. It was folly to hurry from a place like Kuala something or other. By the map, these coastal hamlets were nearly always kualas, or river mouths, and he was not quite sure which one this was. But Norrie knew. There was Norrie now, outside the chief's house, gossiping with a bunch of men as though he had lived in that kampong for years. Perhaps he had. A character of that place. If anything, Norrie knew too much—more than was good for him. He seemed to be amusing those informal Malays, who somehow gave themselves an air of distinction and good mettle, though Norrie was a head taller. They certainly accepted Norrie as an equal. The village headman was smiling knowingly. Now and then one of the men in the group would glance his way, as though he too had been accepted. A quiet and understanding people. Norrie himself could not hurry them, though from the ease of his manner he did not appear to be attempting it. Women, slight and limber, who walked slowly in a way you had to watch, strolled past the group of gossiping men, but pretended to be unaware even of Norrie's prevailing shape.

Why fidget over a delay in getting out of that village? It was not likely to come twice in a lifetime. Let's have the full taste of it, at leisure. We resurrect from the dead only in odd moments—might as well let the moment live itself out. Wasteful to hurry over a sudden flavour of the richness of the earth, as though it were the invasion of a licentious and inappropriate thought. It would take about a week for him to make sure that he was really there. He had had no time to ascertain that. The fact then seemed doubtful. In an unusual fancy dress which anticipated, when its wearer did not, an unaccustomed mode of living, Colet was uncertain of his own identity. This was just a bit absurd. He was only a self-conscious character in an unusual theatrical setting—round about Drury Lane—and the limelight was too bright. A mass of rigid metallic fronds shadowed the house, and formed motionless crenated black patterns on the road. There was a glimpse of the China Sea at the end of the street, a name which suited it. Too much like the China Sea. One could have guessed its name. The Chinese shopkeepers opposite were waiting for custom beside wares which would have been useless, without descriptions, in a museum. Not easy to believe all this. The sun now was full on the street, and Colet began to wonder how he would shape, marching in that white intensity. But he could sit and look at it for ever.

Norrie left the men and strolled over to Colet, affecting a complete faith in the outcome of eternity.

"No carriers yet. We've got to pay for that entertainment on the ship coming round. We were expected by the last steamer."

"Shall we get away this morning?"

"We may, as you don't happen to be able to tell them all about the amok. It's such a juicy story. They don't often get one, and they're so sorry you can't tell 'em about it. All. Every crimson wound."

"So am I."

"They can't bear to lose us so soon. That's what it is. We've brought bright news—all about a butchery. They've no newspapers. Don't you think we ought to be kind to them?"

"You could make it better for them than it was, Norrie. Let yourself go. You couldn't make it worse than it was. Give it a little art."

"I haven't got the cosy love for it. The story would be prettier if your friend the ass in the eyeglass was one of the coloured exhibits. But it is tame without him."

"Queer. I've been watching them. These villagers don't seem to be made of the stuff which goes off with a bang, like that Malay on the ship. They're sane enough."

"Of course they are. So are you. So was he. We're all fine, till some button is touched. That Malay was all right. He only wanted to commit suicide, but his God said no to it. So what's the poor beggar to do? Only one thing in reason, Colet. You can see that yourself. Make others do the dirty work. But don't let us talk about it any more. It's such a fine morning. If we begin to chin over the springs of human conduct we should be here when Gabriel tootled, and so intent with enjoyment that we shouldn't hear him. We'll surprise God Himself on the Judgment Day. He thinks He knows us, but does He, Colet, does He?"

The sun was lord of that country when at last they got going. Beyond the village they entered level rice-fields, and moved towards a dark escarpment of trees, low with distance, which in that torrid light suggested the unapproachable. Norrie led the way, solidly, at an enduring gait; the Malay carriers followed him, and Colet marched at the end of the line, behind the Chinese cook. They had to walk indirectly across that half-dried marsh, one step behind the other arduously along the ridges which parcelled the expanse into square aqueous areas. Some of the ridges were as hard as rock, and others sank under them into a black sludge with a stink of its own. Colet occasionally glanced in hope towards the trees. They took their time over getting higher and plainer. A buffalo bull ahead, broad and black as a rhinoceros, with horns as lengthy as a ship's yard, snorted at Norrie. Colet heard him, and knew that he must pass the same way. He would be the beast's last opportunity. The bull had its nose up, waiting, sunk to its belly in mud, just aside from the ridge along which they were looking for a sound patch for each step. If that brute attacked he was done. It snorted again when Colet was level with its nose, and heaved its bulk impatiently. Colet saw the bubbles stir in the mire about it, and realised what moral control is required, at times, for even so simple an act as putting your foot in the right place with care.

The cliff of trees rose over them. There was a clear deep stream bridged by a fallen trunk. When Colet removed his strict attention from a difficult poise over that greasy bole he saw that the rest of the party, even the Chinaman, had disappeared. There was a portal of two great tree trunks, and gloom beyond it. He saw it was the gate to the stuff of the legends. That must be the door through which the party had gone. He entered it, too, and at once relished the coolness of the forest. The track ascended. It was sandy. The twilight was green. Once he was assured by a glimpse of a man ahead that he was not alone in the silence, for the quiet had quickened his pace; the anxious thought had moved him that he would be comforted there by a contiguous human

M

creature. He foresaw that solitude in the jungle might plumb to an unexpected deep in the soul. Only fellowship would keep him buoyed above that dark pit. Well, he would go anywhere with Norrie, over any pit, perhaps into it.

The track was often unmistakable; usually it was compulsory; there could be no divergence. A riot of green cordage as repellent as flourishing cusps, antlers, spines and bodkins, was piled between the trees on either hand; hooked fronds were suspended to catch in the neck and the helmet; the track was reduced to a loose tunnel meandering through edged foliage. Sometimes a prone giant had to be mounted, for it had fallen across the path, a tree that was a hilly jungle in itself, to be climbed, its vegetation forced, and a descent discovered through its bastions to the other side. Roots like low easy walls, or coiled like pythons, made a maze of the track. It descended into a morass where, apparently, monsters had floundered, leaving wallows and pits which compelled Colet into the trees to find a way; and there he paused, while avoiding the taloned raffle, to pick a sound out of the heavy quiet to get the direction of his friends. Nothing moved there but themselves, except flies which hovered and flashed wherever a beam of sunlight fell through a hole in the roof. They waded across streams, and picked leeches off their bodies; as if clothes were meant to be kept constantly wet, and bodies were the normal feeding-ground for worms. Colet compelled his mind to fight against the desire for cleanliness and dryness, and to regard without surprise a bloated and pendant black parasite taking the blood from a white limb. But he was surprised, nevertheless. That worm was the emblem of a world which was new, potent, inimical, and besieging; and not very particular. It waited silently, without respite, for its chances. You couldn't be always on your guard. It had you, whenever you were not. Colet became wary even of trifles. They stung.

The sun was going when they sighted areca palms ahead. Colet already knew that glad sign. The slender mast of the betel-nut palm, with its cluster of stalked nobs just below its graceful crown, was the sign that fellow-creatures were near. The brown thatches of huts appeared, like haven to sea-farers. Nobody was about, but huge shadows rose from the ground as they arrived, and then went walloping loudly among the frail structures, a black torrent of buffalo. Colet felt so limp then that he would not have cared if they had been elephants, so long as they left the house props intact.

A brown little man came out to the verandah of one dwelling to see what all this was about. Like the others, that house stood on stilts, well above the earth, and now, as night was at hand, with a stowage of darkness already underneath it. The old fellow, in a tartan sarong, descended the ladder of his home to them as coolly as though such visits were usual. He conversed with Norrie in a gentle voice which was part of the quietude. Their carriers had disappeared. Except for two children above them on the verandah of the chief's place, nobody in that hamlet had the curiosity to note this invasion of its solitude. Perhaps the huts stood there to serve as chance sanctuary for wayfarers caught by night in the forest. Or, perhaps, except for that one home, the huts were abandoned, and the old man and the children were alone in the forest.

They went up the ladder of rough beams, its steps slippery with clay, and catchy in their spacing for legs care-less through travel. Norrie and Colet reclined on mats of grass, mats which did something towards levelling the floor of separated boughs. They put themselves at ease in native dress. Other men joined the chief; they betrayed no surprise to find white men there. Now and then a newcomer hailed Norrie with mild jocularity. There was a brass lamp on the floor, and brass dishes with fruit about it. The figures mur-mured to each other. Somewhere, perhaps in the rafters, Colet thought he heard the subdued whispering of women and children. He relished the picture of those men, with their apocryphal background. It was as unconformable as the chiaroscuro of a book belonging to another age. Yet he felt more at home than ever he did at the Gridiron in Soho. He knew only a few words of their speech, but he understood that it could be trusted. They did not move their heads, and scarcely their lips, as they spoke, which was soberly, as men would at night in a house with the wild at its door. Colet, through interstices of one of the walls, could watch sections of palm fronds motionless in moonlight. These fellows had a lot to say to Norrie. If one of them retired but slightly from the lamp, then the shadow almost absorbed him. Several of the men were only bright eyes; or they showed the ridge of a cheek-bone when the head turned, and the feeble glow put a polish on bronze skin. But even the figures in the obscurity were not more strange than the smell of the quiet place, a smell faint, but zealous and nameless.

Norrie, later, was appealed to sombrely by the Malays. They wanted his wise confirmation. Anyhow, he was assuring them, that was plain enough, of his warm agreement that a conclusion of theirs was just and right. His wary and skittish eye, his ironical mouth, his expression of intelligence too drowsy and good-natured to contradict anybody, for he was comfortable, stirred a little curiosity in Colet, who divined this phase in his companion more readily than would these simple folk.

"Now, what's this you are telling them? What's the game?"

"Game? Not at all, my son. It's about a mystery. I love mysteries, and treat them with proper respect. I wish you could have picked up the yarn that the penghulu had been telling me. It's a true story. All these men know it is true."

Norrie addressed himself to the penghulu; the chief answered him with gentle explicitness; and Norrie turned again to Colet, grave as the deep shadows and the brooding night. The Malays were watching the two travellers sadly but closely.

"It was only last week, Colet. You are now as near as that to the old original once upon a time. You've marched all the way back in one day. It only shows you what a fraud time is. You'll learn something, before we've done with you; but don't you grin, don't look at all superior, or the magic will pass, and so may you. Keep your face as confiding as if I were flattering your sound moral character. There's been a tiger about this patch. These men were too artful, just now, to call him that. They don't want to hear him again, so they gave him polite and allusive names. You can't be too careful here.

" But they knew he was a tiger, and more. He took their buffalo and chickens. Any tiger might do that, but soon they had doubts about the sort of tiger this one was. They heard him after dark, for he was an insolent thing, and used to prowl under where you are sitting, night after night. They sat and listened to him snarling. They don't mind tigers; not very much; they don't mind tigers who keep their place, and eat pigs and deer. But they do dislike what is more than a tiger when all good people are indoors. Are you listening? These foresters are watching you. They know more about tigers than we ever shall. If you think I am trying to be funny you don't know me. There is more in the forest about us than these people would care to whisper, at this time of night. There's a woman they know of, for one thing. She is only a lovely head trailing a length of entrails, and it is the end of you to meet her; and there are voices where nobody will ever be seen; and there was this tiger.

"He was only heard; they never saw him; only his pug marks were seen, but they were plain enough. And he was never heard snarling except when a certain old Malay peddler, a fellow from Sumatra, was in the neighbourhood. First they lost two buffalo, and he had the nerve to eat them where these people could hear him enjoying himself. But the buffalo grew wary after that, and bunched, and he didn't dare to touch them. Then the chickens went. That was when snarling was heard under this house, after dark, and a tiger's tracks were found in the morning. One day, though, after the peddler had gone beyond the village, they could hear him, being sick. Somebody had to pass that place afterwards, and, you would hardly believe it, but he saw feathers where that fellow had vomited.

"Well, you ought not to shoot a man, of course, but a tiger is not a man, is it? Especially when it robs you of cattle and chickens, and might take to cannibalism when the fowls were finished. That sort of thing can't go on. So these men got a gun, rigged it to the proper bait, and put it where a tiger, in the boldness of his confidence, was likely to find it. The end of the story shows that all the suspicions of these people pointed to the truth of the matter. That night they sat here talking, just as we are now, and they heard the brute snarling again. Nobody dared go out. He was certainly hungry. He insulted these people. Once he sprang on to the verandah here, and shook the flooring. Tigers are heavy brutes. He kept sniffing at the door. The penghulu says he could smell the thing. Presently they heard the gun go off, and the tiger roared; it had got him; and then they thought they could sleep. When daylight came they went to the trap, and sure enough there he was. The gun had shot the peddler. There can be no doubt, after that, as the penghulu says, that some men can turn themselves into tigers when they want to. The village buffalo have returned to their old habits. They know things are all right again. And do you think you will hear snarling under you to-night? No, Colet, the reason has gone."

Colet nodded his head in sad confession of the dubious nature of things. He glanced at the Malays, as a comrade should to those with him in the midst of dark powers; for the Malays were waiting, watchful, expectant of his full understanding. All wise men know these things are true. Over Norrie's head, high in the gloom of the opposite wall, was a glimpse of moonlit things without, a panel of luminous silver, with the grotesque black shape of a leaf set in it, like the profile of a leering mask.

## CHAPTER XXVIII

THEY had wandered beyond the verifications of the map, which for some time had been little better than the nearest a cartographer could do with what was mainly hearsay. When the country about a camp gave them no hope of gain it was easy to build a house elsewhere; four corner props, some palm leaves laid on cross beams, and a floor of boughs raised well above the ground. A constant fire dried the gear, for the rain, though terse as a rule, made no mistake about it while it was speaking; the fire kept the fanatical leeches at bay, and discouraged the curiosity of night prowlers. Norrie was cleaning his gun. This was one of the mornings when, bent and patient, he sat at a small task suitable for meditation, occasionally pausing to consider the ground before him. His thoughts at such times he did not always avow; they were, usually, but the prelude to packing, and another departure; taking with them again, so far, no more than the hope of a luckier site.

Colet was getting used to it. He had never known what morning was till he saw the dawn from a camp by the side of a jungle stream, a brief inauguration of the earth. He could wake at night now, hear the snarling moan of the tiger on the hill, rise to give the fire a plentiful feed, and forget it. He could work all day and not pass a word to his companion. And that was a good thing. He and Norrie did not have to speak, unless it was necessary, nor even look at each other. There might be a comment from Norrie, late at night, after he put aside the book he had been reading, and began to watch the firelight convulsive on a tree trunk, making the tree move in and out of the forest.

"Listen, Colet."

Colet would listen. The hush was that at the world's end. No. There was something beneath the silence. Perhaps the sap rising in the trees; the breathing of creatures; the pulse of the forest. But all was dark, the darkness over which had never been pronounced the call to light. The collapse of a little ash in the fire was notable. One looked at it instantly.

"Listen to what?"

Norrie smiled.

"To what we can't hear. Suppose we heard begin the Andante from the Fifth Symphony—out in the trees beyond our light. Or if a choir suddenly exploded with 'Worthy is the Lamb.' What about it? The leopards would change their spots with fright. And what would you make of it? You'd think it was the Last Day and your number was up."

Sometimes you considered Norrie as though you had never met him before. He knew that, though, and before you could recognise him he was behind the door.

Now he was cleaning his gun. The Chinaman was squatting by the stream below, washing the dishes. They could hear the Malays cutting firewood. All the immobility of the forest was but the whirr of a grasshopper. The gun was put aside.

"How long have we been on this pitch?"

"I dunno." Collet went into the shelter to find a date. "Eight days."

"Nothing here but signs. Good signs, too. All the bright promises of earth, Colet. Isn't she kind to her children? But they lead nowhere."

"But if they were not meant for promises! They may not have been. Not meant for signs at all. What could you expect them to lead to more than they have?"

"Dear old Colet. There he goes. But I'll tell him again. I want to give the moths and rust a chance to corrupt something that belongs to me. I'll moth 'em, if they come near it."

"I don't feel that way about it. But look here. If you do lift the lid off a hoard, watch me do the Highland fling with the accordant triumphant noises."

"I know. You are like that. But it's not the right spirit. It's simply devilish. It's only your damned playful sympathy. You'd have been a nice Christian all complete with another touch of dreary misfortune. Colet, it makes me doubt you. You'll come to no good end. You really won't. I'm inclined to think that you might even fold your hands like a pale martyr, or a skinned rabbit, some day, and let the other fellow have the girl. It's wicked, you know. It's unfair to the poor darling. Don't you ever love your neighbour as yourself, unless you want him to know what a fool you are."

"I should like to hear your own answer to that."

"Then you'll have to wait till I'm perfectly safe."

"No point in it, then."

"Oh, there will be, though. There will be. That is the point. It's the right time to embrace the sad victims of fate when you have got nothing better to do. No point in being another victim."

He waited a minute, and then picked up his gun again.

"I wouldn't have the nerve to look at the world unless I were sure of a cushioned corner in it. It would be a terror of a hole. There's no sense in it unless we put it there, so don't you try to find it. Just think of humanity messing up its planet with progress—shoving things about, piling 'em up, and especially getting cock-eyed with deep religious conviction when making its worst muck of its place. It's enough to bring down on us the Olympian sanitary inspector. I want a clear space in that jolly old riot. Then I shan't mind the Gadarene rush so much. It might be comic to watch it then, something to pass the time; but I've no fancy to be among the hooves."

"Well, by God, Norrie, I never thought of it before. But you're afraid."

185

"I am, when it comes down to it. You've given it a name. When I look at life in the eyes, in the hope of finding reason in it, my little inside turns pale. Cast your mind back to the Thames embankment and its outcasts at midnight, and get the horrors. Here, we'll be off. Let's go and do a little healthy gravel washing."

A shallow stream so clear that its bed of quartz granules appeared to be under glass, came down in an easy glide from a valley head. It coiled about the lower buttresses of the forest. Only in brief stretches of quieter water was its surface open to the sky. The trees enclosed it, and muffled its voice, which was the only one there in the heat of the day. To Colet its bed was but unusually clean and white. The angular grains were displayed by the clarity of the water. Yet for his companion the stones had various names and implications. They were more than stones. Norrie must have known a lot. If he could find in the eternal forest an outlook from a ridge, he could guess the nature of a distant valley by the tone of its foliage, which all appeared to be of a sombre green; an ocean of rounded billows. He could read a spread of gravel in his palm as though it were a page of a book. Show him a lump of local mud in a new place at night and he would tell you what you would see in the morning, with instances of detail according to his humour; what vegetation would be infernal there, whether they would still be as hungry as they were then, and whether the inflammatory patches on their feet would improve or suppurate.

"It's the nose, Colet. Only the nose. It's my gross selfishness. I'm so uncomfortable when in ignorance that even an unseen novelty anywhere near will make my nose twitch till I find it. That's what unwholesome curiosity does for a man. That's the result of being a dirt washer . . . but there's a lot in dirt. It tells you what the bedrock may be. Haven't you ever watched our Chinaman? Doesn't he ever make your soul curl up at the corners?"

"Johnny? He's only a shadow. There's nothing the matter with him. He never even speaks—only makes a guggle or two."

"That's all he can do. If he wasn't so careful with the stuff I'd be afraid he'd drop some of his opium into the grub. But he loves that more than he hates us. I should like to see a section of the bedrock of that Chink under the microscope. Have you seen him putting little saucers of rice under one of the trees? A devil there he knows about, and we don't. He keep crackers, to frighten the goblins. A section of his faith would prove unusual, under polarised light. Or of yours, Colet, or of yours. A bit of the bottom of your mind, ground thin, would fascinate me all the evening, with a lens of high power."

"But not me. Nothing there to give me an appetite. That predilection of yours for Beethoven—did you find it in the dirt?"

"Quite right. All my fault. I asked for it. Now we'll conclude our little inquiry into origins. When a fellow like you grows metaphysical I get lost. But you wouldn't. Mystics can see anything in a fog, just anything, if only it's thick enough. The thicker the better. But I loathe fogs. I can't see so well in a fog."

"Well, perhaps it wouldn't be unfair to ask now whether we may look for gold here. Is there any?"

"That's better. And there is. But Colet, where does it come from? That's what beats me. I wish I was a mystic, or had second sight, or inspiration, or the devil's own luck. Anything to take me where science can't. The truth is, there's bright little signs of happiness everywhere in this country. They lure us on like the portrait of a charmer whose favours were all distributed long ago, though we don't know it. Oh, Colet, to think of it."

They stooped to the stream, whirled the gravel in pans, and when neither perspiration nor another storm could saturate them more would examine the pinch of yellow dust that was all their reward. The metal had a strange loveliness, under the lens. To Colet it did not seem inadequate. For Norrie was near, with his droll comments. There was the apparition of the forest about them, silent and still; you had to touch a leathery leaf of it, to make sure of it, when stretching the back after intent diligence with the stream. Colet would pause in the washing now and then, checked by the only movement, a visiting butterfly, designed and coloured like joy, a flicker of silent mirth in the face of the wild. The butterflies did not object to a close inspection when they settled on a damp hummock of white sand under his nose; if he touched them they merely circused a little, and then came to the same spot, made themselves comfortable, and laid out their wings for inspection again.

Norrie declined to eat, when they sat by a tree, at midday. If he spoke, it was captiously. Once or twice his companion looked at him, surprised by a word that was venomous. Here was a corner beyond the hubbub, in a light like glory, and Norrie addressing Heaven, for his want of luck, as though it were the face of a dirty urchin who had soiled his property. Anything the matter with him? His hands were hanging listless over his knees, and he was brooding. His hands seemed queer. The fingers were lemon-colour, and the nails blue. Then Norrie peered over at him, and his jaw was chattering.

Colet became solicitous.

"Anything wrong, old chap?"

"I wondered what was coming. We'll get back. I've got a touch of fever. Cold. It's damned cold."

# CHAPTER XXIX

NORRIE sank into his hammock, and remained, still and yellow, with his eyes shut, as though dead. The camp that evening suggested a depth in solitude which was more remote than Colet had ever known. The four Malays were apart, conferring together, unheard, almost merged in the wilderness. The Chinaman was nothing; his face always was expressionless and averted. And Norrie, in a sense, had left them. He was with Norrie, but Norrie was not with him. It was lucky he had got that dose of quinine into the poor old fellow before he became light-headed.

What was he muttering about? Nothing more to be done for him. The natives didn't seem to care; they only glanced casually at the lumpy hammock, and then forgot it. The day, the last of it, was in the tree-tops across the stream, and under that lane of upper gold was the unknown, and night already filling its hollows. The cicadas abruptly began their sunset ovation. They knew the signal; the signal was the light on the tree with a dead top. The gaunt antlers became flames, and the jungle instantly was a din, though it never stirred. There ought to be a movement, surely a leaf should shake, when pandemonium broke loose: buzzing of circular saws, hissing of steam, shrill whistling, the husky stridulating of dry membranes, the humming of wires, the verberating of notes inaudible; the exultant celebration of another life in a place not his. It was like triumph over mortal men.

Norrie called out, but when Colet went to him the sick man was moribund, with his eyes closed. The light died. The uproar in the woods instantly ceased. Night put out both day and the pæan. The darkness and the silence were the same. Colet sat down on a packing box by the hammock, to wait. This was going to be a night of it. He touched Norrie's face; it was indifferent; it was hot and dry. What happened to men with malaria?

The silence stretched out into illimitable leagues of nothing, to a depth where it could never be stirred. The air became cooler, and he packed up Norrie. The Chinaman stretched on the floor. He was only a loose rag on the beams. The Malays were in their own hut. The fire was alive. Only the fire was alive. The hammock had not moved for a long time. All right? Norrie was still hot, anyhow. Colet took his seat again, and waited.

It was queer to watch the feet of the trees. The firelight shaped them. They moved in and out of the forest. Sometimes they vanished. They had retreated into the woods. When a lump collapsed in the fire the flames started again, and the feet of the trees moved in and out of the skirts of the darkness in a noiseless but massive dance. . . .

What was that? He must have been dreaming. Perhaps Norrie had called out. No; the hammock hadn't moved. Norrie was the same as before. The shadow of the Chink was still like a loose heap of rags. He had not stirred. There was only night, and a hush as though something were lying in wait. Queer. He grinned himself into confidence. This was a rum situation; like being a child at midnight lost in the Tower dungeons.

The fire had gone down since he saw it last. About time he made it up. Wanted some resolution to get up and do it, though. You had to move from where you were. What would happen if one moved? Would that set anything going? It felt as if some diabolical business was hanging about. Certainly he heard a sound. It was like the dominant prelude of a Handel march, the music Norrie had told him to listen for, one night. But it was a long way from the croak of a frog in the jungle to Handel. Good God!

Loud in the night he heard the blast of a trumpet. Just beyond the fire. That was no dream. The Chinaman was sitting up. Colet hesitated, rose, and went to peer aside from the hindering of the firelight. He would have felt better if he had known what was there. He could see only a shadow was out of its place beyond. He could make out two white marks like the branches of a tree. But a swamp was there. No tree there. Then he heard a whisper in Malay: "Gajah."

So it was. The shadow was an elephant; what was plain was the gleam of the firelight on its tusks. A flame shifted in the fire, and the beast's ears then spread out; its trunk was curled over its head. The flame incensed that huge front. It squealed, and advanced a little, squashing and lumbering.

No good trying to shoot dead such a bulk at night. It would have the flimsy show flattened in a rush. He went over to the sick man, helplessly, but Norrie was not interested in anything on earth, not even wild elephants. Colet stood by the hammock while the brute raged and trampled about. He would have to stand there. That beast was trying to make up his mind to come on. Better keep quiet, out of sight, and chance it. Trying to make up its mind, and evidently doing it. Colet snatched up a flaming brand in desperation, and flung it at the uproar. It backed, but worked itself into a worse passion. This couldn't last.

The Chink had gone. There were no Malays. The burning sticks wouldn't last long. The beast began to threaten with agile little rushes. Surprisingly quick and light, yet the place shook. What could you do with a man in a hammock? Colet's eyes were on the huge and noisy shadow, and so he swore when the unseen Chinaman unexpectedly clutched his arm. The fellow was voluble, and had something in his hand. The Chink went to the fire, touched the object with a brand, and flung it at the invader. The spark leaped into a tangle of erratic explosions, and the elephant at once became a series of rapidly diminishing crashes in the forest. Colet began to laugh, but stopped. He recognised that his laughter was pitched in too high a key. A blessed cracker—one of those the Chink used for keeping off devils. The Chinaman stood there with his head solemnly bent, listening to the sounds of an elephantine panic retreating out of hearing. Then he curled up again on the floor without a word.

## CHAPTER XXX

THE high cliffs of trees around their hut so overhung that the sun never found them till near noon. It was like being at the bottom of a well. Daylight fell to the stream beside the hut as a few long shining rods which leaned on upper shadows and rested on the bottom of the rivulet. The hut was foundered in the forest. None of them ventured far from it alone. In the cool of the morning the calling of birds gave clear depth to the surrounding obscurity. One bird was a tolling bell, and another was a blacksmith at an anvil. There was another who was an idle boy learning to whistle, but who never got the phrase right. But he persevered. No bird was seen. Nothing ever moved there, except themselves.

The leisurely bird was still learning to whistle. It had nothing else to do. Nor had Colet, but to listen to it. Norrie mimicked the bird, and corrected it. A good effort, for Norrie.

"The little beggar always falls off the tune just before the end. I think I make a noise jolly well. Did you notice it?"

"I did." Colet cheered the attempt, though his amusement was not quite assured. He was dubious. There was Norrie, but reduced to a framework. His face was not of the colour of life, so when he smiled it was anything but a smile. His sardonic nose was pinched, and with his light-grey eyes, understanding but bleak, and his rumpled grey hair, now too plentiful for his face, he suggested a crested predatory bird.

"My whistle was about as thin as me."

N

"Let's have it again. We could do with a cheerful noise."

"Don't shovel out any pity on me, Colet. After a bout of this sort we excite pity, but not enough for a shovel. I'll walk your legs off in a day or two. You won't lose me yet, so you needn't abandon yourself to hope."

He made to pass Colet; but paused, rested his hand on Colet's shoulder, weighed on it perhaps rather too long, and went on. Old Norrie was strange; you couldn't tell then whether he was sentimental, or only gave way at the knees. He did that sort of thing. He simulated humanity, for a lark, or else he pretended that satire was the best he could do.

But as Norrie said, he soon had them going again. There were new activities. He began to lead them another dance. They left the hut for whoever might want it. Colet had got used to that floor of rough boughs with its roof of brown fronds. He knew the individual bits of the floor, the beam that rolled if you put your foot on it, the catchy knot by Norrie's hammock, the depression in which he preferred to spread his own sleeping mat. The only bare dry earth he had seen for three humid months was under that floor. Actually, the patch of ground under the hut was dusty; the dust was an experience when you crawled under for a knife which had slipped through. Their fire would go out to-day. Without a light there, and nobody near, that hut would be worse than the jungle. It would deepen the quietude. He turned, the end man, to see the abandoned camp for the last time. The bare thought of solitude in the old shanty gave Colet a presentiment of the horrors. One would want hardened nerves to face only oneself, in the wilderness.

The regions through which they travelled suggested that they were the first men to see it. They were under an earlier spell of the earth; it was not merely a new country. The sunlight was younger, and sounds were clearer and without fear. Its life, which was its forest, was haunting with its magnitude and extravagant outpouring. It was mute, except at sunset and evening, when it praised the sun, the only god which had yet come to it. When day came, and just as day was departing, the creatures of the woods broke out with that racket which was the sudden release of the pent vehemence of spirits that were without name or shape.

The sun was well down towards the roof of the jungle when they emerged from the twilight of the woods. They were in an open space by a greater river. The men began to build another shelter. It was a relief to see the open sky. Here was full daylight, and the sight could range to distant prospects. Colet wondered how Norrie, still absurdly thin, and bleached by fever and the forest, had maintained so evenly that day's long hike; even the patient Malays showed they had had enough of it, and they were made of bronze. The Chinaman, of course, wasn't human. His own body felt as if every length of elastic in it had been stretched; pulled out and snapped all day long. Now he was at ease, fatigued but contented. Norrie was a wonder. He would have given stout Cortez enough for the day, and then have shown even a conquistadore, in an evening talk, that there were things he did not know as surprising as the prospect to be seen from a peak in Darien. But in these latter days good men were not conquerors, but navvies, or prospectors, or engineers, or chief mates. Nobody knew them but one or two pals.

The river was low, a shining network about reefs of smooth granite boulders. A beach of white sand under the sombre forest had the shape and pallor of a crescent moon. The water could be heard; it was just audible; but its voice was subdued and stealthy. And it was the only sound, except the occasional slashing of the parangs of the Malays, and that noise was as though the sanctity of an inviolable concealment were being riven. The slash of a heavy knife across that quiet was not quite right. The trees beyond the water, however, took no notice of it. Were they an illusion, or only dumb with astonishment? The front of the jungle opposite ascended into high cupolas and pinnacles, and was draped from its cornice to its base with a dense mesh of vines, green curtains in voluminous folds which sheeted the heights. One palm leaned out from it, its head over the river, as in an attempt at escape, which was checked, from the silent confusion. The sheen of lightning wavering round the coasts of clouds that were the colour of calamity moved and changed the hues of the sunset. The old clearing in which they stood was heavy with the scent of flowers. Over the forest, beyond the corner round which the river came down to them, was the hull of a towering berg, its flat summit dark with trees, but its walls bare and gleaming, as though of white marble. The last of the sun fired the clouds; the isolated hill became a beacon; and at that signal the cicadas and the legion of hidden creatures broke out with their celebrant jubilation. Colet had to raise his voice a little when he spoke to his companion.

"There are others here beside ourselves. We are not the first."

"So our men say," mused Norrie. "They want to go back."

"Anything wrong? They have seemed moody to-day."

"Enough to make them. They tell me this land is full of hantus, things that ought not to be about; souls not stowed safely away in Gehenna."

"It looks rather like it, now you've mentioned it. Shall I let off a few crackers, to keep them from crowding us?"

"No good. Something more elaborate than we could think of is wanted. The tobacco is in your pack. You notice how soon the fire is going?"

"They're not afraid of the people of the woods?"

"No people there. Not the right sort. Nobody lives here. But long ago a prosperous lot of Chinese miners had this clearing. They did rather well, too."

"God rest their Chinese souls. They're not here now."

"They are. Our Malays say they are. They did too well. The raja got to hear of it—something he could get for nothing, being a raja, so naturally he asked for it. The Chinamen forgot where they were, though. They told the raja to take a carrot. I think that was what it was. And anyhow, Malays don't regard the Chinese as men. Why should they? Chinamen have a different religion. So the Malays had nothing to argue about, except their honour. When a talk among themselves about honour had sufficiently excited them, they went on an enjoyable and successful outing, without warning, and the country has been like this ever since, except for the hantus. It does seem lonely, doesn't it? The Malays know those Chinamen are still hanging around, though a bit changed in nature; and if I told you all the story you wouldn't wonder at it. But the end of the yarn is better if heard in daylight. . . . Did you see that lump over there, that high rock with the trees on top? We'll have a look at that in the morning. If we have to be turned aside by spooks, we'll try to learn why they are so stuffy about it."

## CHAPTER XXXI

THE berg rose out of the level forest by the river, and to Colet it was anomalous. It was an isolated mass of white limestone, a lofty island in the ocean of jungle. Its pale cliffs fell sheer to the green billows. Its summit was flat, but was so near to the clouds that its trees were but a dark undulating strip. Its walls, when glimpsed from below through breaks in the roof of the forest, appeared to overhang, but there were scarves and girdles of green on their bare ribs. An eagle soaring athwart its loftier crags was a drifting mote. Stalactites were pendent before the black port-holes of caves in upper stories, like corbels over the outlooks of a castle of the sagas. If the number of those dark apertures meant anything, then the berg was hollow, was honeycombed with cavities. This enormity was not inviting, even in a morning light; not in such a land as that. The unexplored dungeons of such a castle might hide anything.

But Norrie judged it with a casual and professional eye. It was curious, but only geologically. He had seen such lumps before, of course. It was only what was left of an earlier skin of Malaya, a fragment of that country's prehistoric hide. Time and the weather had peeled off all the rest. Unnatural? Well, look at it; was it not there? So how could it be unnatural? What he wanted to do was to get at it.

That was not easy, near and great as it was. The climbing palms, the rotans, flourished about it. Their taloned cables were coiled over the low ground in barriers unfriendly to the haste and impatience of men. Colet, bleeding and perspiring, had forgotten the rock by the time they had reached it. A little journey in that kind of undergrowth, crouching and crawling, while following the sound of a Malay's parang, leaves room in the mind for but one interest. He crawled into a little clear space beside Norrie and two of the men. The island stood over them. They were at the base of a wall, and almost under a high Gothic porch, the entrance to the retreat, by the look of it, of midnight. Norrie but briefly inspected this rude resemblance of architecture, and was as indifferent to the sinister suggestions of the interior. He was not now discussing the ways of humanity, and so he appeared very cheerful. He declared that he loved caves, and insides that were convoluted and obscure. He was preparing to go in; he was testing some electric torches with a brisk assiduity which had its back to the forbidding fantasies of geological structure. The Malays, so they said, preferred to wait without. Their interest was spent. They went down on their hams and began to roll cigarettes while watching the tuans preparing to disappear on a foolish quest.

The threshold of the cave was of dry sand strewn with fallen rock. The day, venturing within as far as it could, hinted at fretted columns and aisles receding till the last shapes became what Colet chose to see there. The berg was hollow. Its recesses were capricious, and the disturbance of a rock by the invaders awoke echoes in lofty transepts and high vaultings unseen. That sharp sound brought down the dark in flying atoms. Myriads of bats fell like night whirling in shreds. The gloom moved with a screaming rush. Norrie, though, went on as if unaware of it, except that he broke out against the smell of the little beasts. It certainly was lairish, that stench; not to be forgotten.

"Keep close," said Norrie; "but if you lose me, keep still."

It was not easy to keep close to such erratic activity in the dark. Norrie, intently inspecting the floor at times, developed an insatiable curiosity and energy. He said little. He kept going. He might have forgotten that such a preferable enjoyment as daylight was now well behind them.

"Come here," he said at last. He stood then, relaxed and indifferent, as though here they would turn back, and with his lamp illuminated black sand at his feet. He idly scraped the ground with his foot.

"Know what that is?"

"Sand."

"Cassiterite."

"What's that?"

"Haven't you brought that Highland fling with you? I'm showing you what we came for."

"This stuff?"

"It's as ripe as a freehold in Piccadilly. The floor of this hill is tin. It only wants spades."

Norrie stooped, and poked the grains about with his fingers.

It only wanted spades. Colet felt a little hungry. It was near midday. Besides, Norrie himself was just scooping the sand as if he were a child at the seaside. Norrie twisted round, and turned up his torch to Colet's face.

"I say, Colet, blast you, you haven't got the expression of a lucky man. But you might try to behave like one. Sing something agreeable."

"Me? Hang it, you're not setting a lively example. I thought it was dirt."

"So it is. So it is. There's acres of it. Well, we've found it. Let's go and get something to eat."

# CHAPTER XXXII

Now they had found it, now they stood firmly upon the security which most men desire but usually fail to reach, their camp-fire, somehow, burned with less of its old companionable light. This was the end of the hunt. Norrie had explained, rather seriously, with hardly a lift of his usual buoyancy, what the law of averages, or something mathematical, had calculated against the chance of good luck coming to men on a rummage like theirs. This good luck, nevertheless, had coincided with their track in space; and to some extent, it appeared, that was not wholly because of blind chance; it had happened, too, because of a little artful designing by knowledge and intelligence. Norrie, with that, then looked round the camp, not perhaps as if his interest in life had gone, but as if that particular day and place had failed in savour for him.

"We shall get used to this scene, Colet. A sort of home."

Colet followed his friend's glance. The immense front of the forest on the opposite bank was still majestic and illegible. It was the same forest? Well, when he saw it first it had seemed outside time. Once he had seen it as a symbol of that which does not pass with the episodes of passing men; it was superior to days and nights. The cry of the tiger in the night, while he was sleepless, watching the stars, not knowing what was to happen on the morrow, was only a disturbing but relevant note in a great passage. Yet something hardly definable had happened to his view of it all. Good fortune had changed it. Perhaps the forest itself was no different; maybe he was not exactly the same man, and so could not see things as he did before. What was lost?

It was extraordinary, but the discovery of the hoard afforded them less to talk about than had such a trivial matter as the song of an unknown bird. Yet now the song of the bird passed unremarked. Tin did not prompt Norrie, now he had plenty of it, to a pleasing similitude of his old relish of Malay fables, which have no market value, though they can keep a camp-fire bright till late. The assurance of much tin induced in Norrie even a certain correctitude. He could no longer abjure their Chinaman with his accustomed histrionic abandon. He was direct, and saved time.

Colet, reviewing it all, while Norrie was diligently drawing a map, rebuked himself. He ought to feel excited. No good. He didn't. What does not excite the interest cannot be made to do so by any deliberate concentration of reason. If intelligent discontent is the beginning of progress, is it also the end of happiness? Of all the frauds of the sensational drama, this joy on access of riches, this elation on the discovery of the treasure chest, as though it were wealth, was the silliest. There was nothing in it. More seemed to be lost than was gained. That was hardly fair of the law of compensation. One's light was not turned up, but down. Colet had hinted to Norrie that there was not so much blithe interest in these abundant and exclusive details of business, this strict adherence to the mining law of the country, as there used to be in his sparkling nonsense. Norrie's eyebrows moved in surprise at a consequence of good fortune which he had not remarked. Then he assumed a show of his drollery.

"Of course, I'm purged of dross. Fever and the tin have done it. I'm pure now. I've got salvation, I feel almost kind. Too kind to be lighthearted."

Almost impious to say damn the tin, but Colet had that desire.

It was night, and Norrie, still at his work, not present enough in the body to notice that his pipe was out, sat beside a lamp. An apparition formed by the camp-fire.

"Sorry to disturb you. May I come in?"

Norrie scrambled to his feet in quick alarm, but before he was upright he had recovered himself. A glance had satisfied him.

"Come along in."

The stranger entered, and sat on a box between the friends, looking in appeal from one to the other, as would a child that had been naughty, but was sick. This elderly and bearded man, with the tired, but open and wondering eyes, was sick. His wrecked shirt held to but one shoulder, and its neglect of the other exposed an ugly boil on the upper arm. Only his grizzled beard filled the hollows of his cheeks. He took off a soiled helmet, and arranged it on the floor with what might have been an amusing care for the battered relic, or it was the hesitancy of a man who was preoccupied. His delicate cranium was bald, except for a monk-like but untidy tonsure.

"I was very glad to see your camp-fire. My Malay guide, an exceptionally good man, was lost. Is the river here the Sungei Buloh?"

"No," said Norrie, "you've taken the wrong turning. The Buloh is five miles down stream. What are you making for?"

"Mount Berching. I shall cross the divide into Perak about there. My name, by the way, is Parsell."

Norrie, astonished, had taken his pipe out of his mouth, and had held it away for an intent inspection of their visitor. Now he put his pipe beside him and leaned forward, with his hands clasped.

"Parsell the ethnologist, the author of the 'Mon-Khmer Influence in South-eastern Asia?'"

The veteran gnome looked quite pleased.

"You know my name, then? Curious, curious!"

Norrie was clearly perplexed. He sang out for the China-man, and gave him some instructions. He stroked his nose. He looked with wariness at Colet, as if for a cue.

"No need to ask you, sir, what you are doing here. Didn't you mention Gunong Berching?"

"I am making for that point."

To Colet it was plain that if Norrie had addressed him in the matter of that mountain, it would have been in a few choice words to demolish a folly.

"Do you think you can manage it, Mr. Parsell?"

"Of course I can; why not? That is part of my plan."

"A good plan. But here, what with the want of food, and the floods and fevers, we have to alter our plans occasion-ally. It is rough going to Berching, and I should fancy that beyond it the going would be worse. Hardly anything is known about it."

"Very likely, very likely." Mr. Parsell spoke with decision, and a hint of asperity. He was unwell and a little crabbed. Nor did he promise to be the kind of man who would listen at any time to the warnings of common sense, not when he was mounted on his hobby.

Norrie, tactfully, tried to draw from him confessions about his supplies, his guide, his men, and the time he had estimated would be necessary for the journey. But these to Mr. Parsell were only negligible details, of small account compared with the pursuit of truth. He was vague about them; he himself was barely concerned. The Chinaman came to them with dishes, Norrie polished his pipe thoughtfully, and Mr. Parsell addressed himself to food in an attitude of abstraction which allowed him but fitfully to acknowledge the nearness of nourishment. Indeed he would pause with entire detachment, fork held loaded and upright but for-gotten, to seek, with the cool and disarming inconsequence of a barrister who knew his case, a betrayal of their own notions of the natives they had met. Had they seen any Sekais or Semangs?

Norrie humoured him. More than once Mr. Parsell sat round to look at Norrie squarely and with the unaffected curiosity of a pundit who is surprised by a suspicion that a layman may be not so ignorant as in fairness could be assumed. Yet, when the subject was not his own, he was, despite his bald head, a ragged and helpless infant one would have been prompted to nurse and cherish, if one had known but the way to hold it. The lifted appeal of his fearless but innocent blue eyes moved the paternal instinct in a man. It was not safe for him to be about.

Then, with talk and food, his nervous energy flagged; would they excuse him? He thought he would rest. He would have to make an early start in the morning. Norrie led him to the hammock, which would be easier for his bad shoulder than the floor, and tended him as carefully as though their guest were a wilful but royal orphan. When Mr. Parsell was out of the way, Norrie stood, for a time, staring into the night; then he turned to Colet with a wry smile.

"We shall have to stop this," he whispered. "There's enough hantus here."

## CHAPTER XXXIII

MR. PARSELL did not make an early start. He found their
Malays and the situation of the camp too attractive. The awe
of the Malays for this eager and energetic little man, who
mystified them with his ease among their secrets, was manifest; no doubt they thought he was mad, and the favoured of
God. He knew things which were hidden even from Tuan
Norrie, and wizards should be carefully reconciled. Norrie
watched the play about the hut of his men with amused concern.

"Colet, he knows more about those fellows than they
know themselves. He has scared them. He isn't aware of it,
but he could order them to heel like dogs. I wish I could."

"You've heard of the old boy before, Norrie?"

"But naturally. Who hasn't? I knew his work before I
could play dominoes. And we meet him here at last. That's
how the surprises are sorted for us."

"What about this journey of his? Can it be done?"

"Yes. Almost anything can be done, by the right people.
What do you think?"

"That he won't go far."

"No, he won't. Not if I can stop it. We can't afford to
lose men like Parsell."

"You won't stop that man."

"Then he will die. You or I might manage that traverse,
with any luck, but Parsell—it would be as reasonable to
expect a kitten with a brick to come home after being
dropped in the river. He'd never be heard of again."

"You won't stop him."

"You don't think he can be frightened into going back with us?"

"Frightened? I say Norrie, did you see his eyes? When they are fixed on what he thinks may be the truth he wouldn't see Apollyon in his path."

"Eh?" Norrie became alert, and turned to his friend, frowning, as if a new thought troubled him. He shook his head sadly. "Colet, you think so? But of course you do. There are such fools in the world. I rather fancy you're another, and that's how you know."

Colet lit his pipe. Norrie, devising with resourcefulness fancies in the macabre which pictured that region as the portal to every horror of the soul, wondered whether a selection would be useful when arguing with Parsell, to warn him off. Colet smiled, but did not answer. At the end of the recital he explained that, as far as he could see, the only way to head off a man like Parsell was to give him an injection. That man would not go forward only if he could not move. Then, indifferently, he asked some questions of Gunong Berching and the country beyond; but Norrie ignored them.

"It's no good talking about it. You know what this land is like. It has nothing to do with the case. It's like talking of walking the waves. The man can't do it. He simply can't."

Mr. Parsell came towards them quickly and nervously, his head thrust forward.

"You see," said Norrie; "he doesn't know even enough to regulate his speed in this climate. He oughtn't to have been allowed out."

"How interesting your men are, gentlemen. Most useful to me." Mr. Parsell chuckled with a little vanity. "They will be wondering how I knew what part of the country they came from, and I'd never seen them before. Simple, simple. They tell you themselves, but don't know it. Perhaps you have guessed it already, but they dislike this locality. What they had to say about it was a little mine to me. You'll excuse me, but I think you will lose them soon. You ought to know that."

"I know it, Mr. Parsell. We're turning back here. We're returning to the coast. You will find our company helpful, if you would care to travel with us."

"My dear sir. My dear sir. I go on, of course. My work is far from finished."

There was a brief silence, and then Colet turned to him, with deference.

"I don't think you understand, sir, what lies ahead. There are very few natives above this point. The main range of the peninsula will have to be crossed, and that has not been done from here. On the other side of it you will be in the unknown till you get to the middle reaches of the Perak river. What we fear is, sir, that you will die."

"Young man, it is very good of you. But I have considered that."

"Sorry, sir, but you speak as if that did not matter."

Mr. Parsell made a gesture, glanced round as though for a more interesting subject, and walked away to the hut.

"Well, Norrie, this ethnologist's strong point isn't humour, is it?"

"Of course it isn't. It never is with these fanatics. In the Middle Ages he'd have been a holy martyr, but now he is only a scientist, offering his life for a ha'porth of facts."

"What are we to do?"

"What is there to do? Damn the man. Why did he turn up? Isn't life complicated enough? We can't go doddering across Malaya behind an inspired crackpot following the Holy Grail, can we? Got something else to do. I wish he hadn't come. There's quite enough worries in life, without wondering what one ought to do."

# CHAPTER XXXIV

THE two partners were sitting together, pulling on their marching boots. They were returning east, to the China Sea coast, and Mr. Parsell would set out for an Indian Ocean beach. Their Chinaman placed beside them their breakfast. Parsell was over with the Malays. He preferred their circle. The last Colet had seen of him the night before was his back against the firelight of the men's hut, with the Malays about him. The men knew he was different. An odd character; his simplicity had an importunity which compelled you to defer your own affairs, as though it were the appeal of an innocence which, so you guessed, knew more than its blue eyes rumoured. To Colet then the man was an intimidation which could not be ignored, however much he pretended that it was not really there. Something would have to be done. Parsell certainly had recovered. The respite of a few days, and Norrie's careful feeding, had so changed the man that occasionally he had intervals of jocosity, elfish phases of erudition which, when the other two men had recovered from their start, caused them to laugh a little awkwardly. Norrie, though, said the benefit would only help Parsell into a further and deeper slough; but the idea that he could be persuaded out of his alarming project was abandoned. It was not worth trying. It was an immovable resolution. The man was going.

Norrie stretched his legs; looked round.

"Colet, not a word from you all the morning. Some worm feeding on your bearded damask? Not worrying over the ill we can't prevent?"

o

"No. No. Not now. I've just given that up. I've been thinking it over. Now there's no option, I think. It seems to me I ought to go with him."

Norrie drew his legs up. He tapped with his foot for a time before speaking again.

"Say it once more; perhaps I got it wrong."

"I'm going with him. Put it like that."

"Not coming my way?"

"I wish I could."

Norrie did not move. He smiled, for a spell, at the fire. Then he rose, kicked a box out of his way, walked a little distance, and stood with his back to the hut, considering the forest. Colet went over to him.

"What else is there for me to do? You help me out of this."

"You could let old destiny takes its course."

"I don't know destiny when I see it. What is it like?"

Norrie did not answer that. The forest appeared to absorb his attention.

"Is there anything else for me to do? He can't be allowed to go alone. It is impossible for you to go. I'm free."

"So is he free, free not to go."

"I don't think he is. He's obsessed."

"And you are free."

"Of course. I know what I'm doing."

"Nothing to argue about?"

"Not that I can see."

"Who made you his keeper?"

Colet waited, without an answer. The men were beginning to pack. In the woods the bird that whistled like an idle boy was having no success with the tune. The dissolving of the mist uncovered areas of the distant forested hill-tops to the young sun; green islands were floating high in the blue. Norrie was contemplating that daily miracle of the morning, the late descent from heaven of the hilltops to join the earth. Then he addressed the hill-tops:

"Of all the blether. Of all the sacred, predestined and inevitable Gothamites. Isn't one enough? What is he going to do? Leave his luck, turn the other way, and toddle after a crank searching for what people won't look at when it is found."

"That isn't it."

"Then what the devil is it?"

Colet had no answer. Norrie strode farther away, but after a while he turned about as though some of his heat had gone, and faced Colet.

"I might have expected this. I suppose you're bound to follow your selfish conscience, which is thinking only of its own comfort?"

"I suppose so."

"Your sort always do. They're an infernal nuisance to the world. No good talking sense to a noble conscience. That will find all the reasons there are for pleasing itself. You're as bad as the old fool himself. But don't forget I've got my follies. As it happens, I prefer you to the other loony's books. And do you know that when you go this morning that will be the last of you? Your enemies will never see you again."

"Leave that to me. I'll bear it in mind."

"I know. But it won't be enough. You'll learn that a pure intention is of no special value in a cataract. It won't even keep off amœbic dysentery or blow-flies. You'll never get that man over the range—and if you do you'll regret it. Let him be. He'll fall sick again soon, and the Malays will bring him down to the coast. I've reckoned on that."

"It isn't their job. We can't reckon on it. Would you reckon on that in my case?"

"All right. All right. But this is what will happen. You'll carry him to a place where you can't get him forward and can't get him back. Your good intention will do him harm."

"I'll watch it. I'll put it down in the diary when the child is to be kidnapped."

Norrie began to pace to and fro. He did not look at his friend. He kept up his patrol for so long that Colet began to weaken. One thing was certain. It was impossible to be fair to everybody. Doing the right thing meant that some man would get hurt. But at last, when about to pass him again, Norrie paused behind him, and rested a hand on his shoulder for a moment. Colet, touched, turned about quickly. But Norrie was not looking at him. He was watching Parsell and the Malays.

"I'll call this destiny; and there you are. That's what it means for you. Just look at the fellow. There's his view of the job in front of him. He's reciting the mantras to the men, the runes for a safe journey. They think he's a pawang, a sorcerer . . . and confound him, so he is. He's conjured something out of me."

They both watched the play for some minutes. It afforded a composing interval. Norrie then began to move towards the hut again.

"Come along, Colet. No good mooning here, listening to a shaman averting malaria and crocodiles. I've got some things to say to you. In any case, we must be off."

When they had entered the shelter Norrie selected a gun. "Just once more," he said, "I suppose it is no good talking to you?"

"I don't want to be persuaded. I might be easily persuaded."

"Then, you take this gun along, for one thing. I'm pretty sure the ethnologist has got nothing but callipers. That would stop an elephant . . . if you stop the old shaman with it, when his antics look dangerous, you won't hear a word from this admirer of his. I've still got one or two of his books to read—I've got some of him untouched, in store—so don't hesitate on my account."

He was examining the gun. "I don't like to lose it, but I suppose it must go. Another little matter, Colet. Parsell isn't aware of it, but his packs already hold some of our supplies. His medicine chest wasn't fit to apply to a village dog, and his grub was sketchy. His Malay guide knows where the stuff is. And now that there are two imbeciles instead of one, I've got to waste more time over it . . . but perhaps I ought to show some gratitude to you for offering to nurse one of my pets."

They had the maps spread out on the floor, and kneeled to them. Colet began to come down to some considerations which he had not supposed were in the journey. It looked a formidable distance, on the chart, and the greater length of it was supported by very few names. It would have been a different affair, Colet saw then, to do that with Norrie; who indeed, began to grow interested as he worked it out, as though he were projecting a new and spacious experience for himself. He lost himself in it. They were rolling up the charts, and putting them into rubber bags, when Mr. Parsell began to come their way. Norrie studied him deliberately.

"Listen. Don't let that man linger. Make him get along, short of breaking him. He'll want to sit down and become a native. Bully him. Don't forget. Bully him. Win his respect. It's the only way to treat a great scientist who doesn't know where he is. He'll never listen to reason. Order him about till he cries. If you get down to the coast you know the people who know me. . . . Here, the men are waiting."

The change in their plans was explained to Mr. Parsell. He gave it, as he listened, an apprehending and friendly nod or two. He raised no objection to Colet leaving the country by the route he himself had chosen.

"You might be of some assistance to me. Do you know anything of ethnology, Mr. Colet?"

Their farewells were perfunctory. Their men had already separated, and were on their divergent trails. When Colet turned, as he was about to enter the woods, Norrie was standing, looking back at him. They lifted their rifles, and Norrie vanished.

# CHAPTER XXXV

To face about and march away from Norrie made the land different. The very sunlight depends for its brightness on the way we are able to see it. Norrie was an old sentimentalist, easy and warm, armoured bright in guile, like most of the cynics and epicures, and was as sure to have the hump to-night as himself. What is the good of a camp-fire anywhere without a pal the other side of it? Life without comradeship would be ashes. The fire would be out. Here; better push on and take the head of the line. Set the pace. Let these fellows see who is running the show.

Old Parsell's puttees were comic. Might be an urchin's stockings; no better than dirty bandages slipping down, and the beastly leeches were active.

"Hold on, Mr. Parsell; let us fix these. They'll never last as they are. You should start them, winding the strip this way . . . see? Look at that. A bunch of worms already browsing on you. There it is—that comes of loose and unsoaped puttees. Always give 'em a strong dose of carbolic soap once they are fixed. The lather upsets the little devils."

A promising start, teaching the dear old buffer how to dress for a walk. Parsell seemed to imagine he was strolling through a Devon lane, and that the local oddities meant nothing to an important man. No concern of his. He was humming to himself now—a confident old card—considering a problem of philology, no doubt, while cheerfully humming a tune, and perhaps a rhinoceros was waiting round that bend. Where did Norrie say was the place to hit an elephant? Three inches in front of the earhole, if you could see it. But if not?

Colet, leading them, found the trail descended to an open space, a smooth and sunny lake of grass round which the forest towered rugged as basaltic cliffs. But the grass was taller than himself. You had to plunge into this lake, and walk along the bottom of it. A likely corner for sladang, the instantaneous bull which does not wait for trouble but makes it when you are not looking; and it was impossible to see a yard ahead. Queer. Now he knew how much before he had left to Norrie; he had never bothered about such characteristics of the Malay jungle while Norrie was ahead, though he knew they were there. No worse now than they used to be, but he happened to be leading. There is something in leadership, then, which the people behind never guess till the man who should be in front is not.

Through that bit. Nothing there. Just as well not to worry when you can't see anything. Wait till you do. It might be good fun to manœuvre this party through to the sea; an attractive substitute for the loss of the tin. The Malays were fine fellows. A likely lot. Stout little men. That one close behind, the guide, had a serviceable face for the figure-head of a pirate ship; coming along with its eyes at your heels it kept you brisk. Mat was decidedly a good man. His eyes saw things. He would last. And another pleasing sign. Mat had consulted him, with marked respect—which was a trifle disturbing, seeing where they were—about the point to be made that day; Mat had not gone to the pawang. Perhaps he guessed that even a pawang may be a bit weak about such a detail as the best direction to take in a forest.

Parsell, when half the day was done, showed no sign of distress. The ethnologist had no body worth mentioning, but his cheerfulness hinted that spirit could well support a purpose as well as sinew. With that big helmet, his meagreness was absurdly overcapped; it was a mushroom on a short thin stalk. He was in a mood of light confidence, when they paused for food in the early afternoon.

"I have decided, Mr. Colet, that we shall camp here for the day. This is an excellent place. I want some time to arrange my notes. The men had better make a shelter."

"Not here, Mr. Parsell. It can't be done. It's a rotten hole for a camp. We shall go on till five o'clock."

"But, my dear sir, I must have leisure for my work. It is in arrears."

"Not the place for a camp, sir. You wouldn't do any work here. The sand-flies wouldn't let you. On we must go."

Colet lumbered up, fixed his gear, slung his gun. Mat already was getting under way.

"We mustn't waste time, Mr. Parsell. Some way to go yet."

The ethnologist showed astonishment. His mind, evidently, had been settled. But he saw the men assembling their burdens and that the guide had gone.

"I don't understand this, Mr. Colet. I thought the men. . . ."

"But I do. It's not a bit of good. We can't risk the lives of these men for our fun, you know. Got to push on. I think we should get this bit behind us. It's a bad patch. Feeling tired?"

"Not in the least. I rarely feel tired. Something has occurred to me, and I wish to get to work. You don't think we could pitch here?"

"Sure of it. The men know it, too."

Mr. Parsell gave the still and monstrous foliage about them a cursory glance. It began to exist for him. No wonder he had not noticed it; it was so quiet. The last of the men was waiting for the ethnologist to take his place in the line. Colet hurried to the front. After all, the silence of the forest was a forcible persuader, once you noticed it. You could leave it to the look of the jungle at a pinch. Not even Mr. Parsell would elect for loneliness there. That was another hopeful sign.

# CHAPTER XXXVI

THE camp was not awake when Colet left it to go down to the river. Its surroundings were apparitional in the hour before dawn. The forest was uncreated. It was only beginning to come out of the darkness. Nothing had taken shape, except a few outlines on the surface. Creation had been roughly indicated. The rest was night. Substance was not alive, but was suspended in a void, germinal and suggestive. There had been no word yet.

It was almost cold, and Colet shivered. There was something in the scene suggestive of an autumnal dawn at home; the same hush and the unreality. The track led down past a tree with buttresses massive enough for a cathedral. Its exposed roots, in that light, were dank coils ambushed in a nightmare. They appeared to be a tangle of sleeping reptiles waiting for a touch to set them thrashing about hideously. The trail was easier below, almost free of obstructions. No. Something was there in the path. Only a shadow? It was not. That really was a snake; it twisted a little.

Better be careful. Colet advanced a few steps, watchful. He did not think he was mistaken. There had been a movement. The shadow then heaved, and humped on the ground. The snake uncoiled again and turned over. It was a tail. Colet stopped, with an urgent impulse to fly back to the camp. He overcame that impulse. He had a clear idea of the expression on the tiger's face. It was boredom. It had pale side-whiskers; the upward glance of its bright eyes was reproachful. It stretched itself; it yawned with a gape which Colet especially remarked, and stood for a moment sideways.

It sneered; and then it went. The forest took it in. There was no sound. It was there, and then it was not.

For a second Colet wondered whether human dignity would insist that he must go on. But dignity lost. He could not go on. The vague path left empty by that surprise was insuperable. He retired, in deliberate but agitated leisure, occasionally looking back. That was a gentlemanly beast. And if he'd had the gun with him he couldn't have hit it. It went before a thought could move.

Mat was roving about, with his morning cigarette, when he reached the hut, and after a suitable interval Colet advised the Malay that he had met a tiger when going to bathe. Mat listened to the news with a show of polite interest. These tigers! They have no manners.

Mat's own manners now, were perfect. His courtesy and patience, which were safe from the presumption of the ignorant because he did not look safe, and because of the austerity of his bearing, made him notable even on the march, when his lithe bronze figure was almost naked. The eyes of the two men met, for no particular reason, and the Malay smiled. That was well. Colet knew he was not alone in that enterprise.

The Malay wished to speak to him. Tuan! He would not hide the truth. All his knowledge of that country had been gained when, long ago, as a young man, he had passed through with a party hunting Sakais, the jungle folk, for slaves. Yet, if he might speak, he thought that time would be saved if now they took to the river. It would not be easy to pole *rakits* up against the stream, but it would be easier than carrying burdens in the forest. The river was low. The *jerams*, the rapids, would not be bad, for the season of floods had not come.

The map, Colet saw, held with Mat's opinion; the men very quickly made rafts of bamboo. That sort of craft had a dubious freeboard, Colet noticed, but the men behaved as though they had nothing to learn when they were turning bamboos into a means of transport. If the river allowed it, if there were no floods, they would be in the neighbourhood of Berching in a few days; and the idea of that mountain had been very distant, when considered in the woods. Their small flotilla of rafts began its upward journey towards the watershed.

Colet's platform of green bamboo pipes, enamelled and wet, made slippery holding. It was fairly agile, too, and demanded subtle coaxing from a rider who was unused to such a seat. It would pardon no nonsense. Its surface responded to every inequality of the current. You could feel the river alive under your feet.

Mr. Parsell sat beside Colet, but was forgotten. The ethnologist showed no interest in the world about; apparently he desired nothing better than an opportunity to meditate on what could not be imparted to a man who, in an important sense, was not with him. Colet forgot him.

Their way was now at the bottom of a chasm. The dark forest was its walls. The river was a blinding mirror, but narrow; the sky overhead was hardly any wider. That region told them that man had only then entered it; but Colet, after rounding several bends, received no impulse from the thought. He lapsed gradually into limp but enduring desire, a desire for shade, for a break in the journey. The sun concentrated its heat into that stagnant cleft in the forest, down the bottom of which waters drained from the heights. The poles of the Malays clinked, splashed, and echoed. The men cried out to each other, and their voices sped like the first flaws in the original peace. They broke the solitude at last. The stillness of the forest, in which not a leaf stirred, and the insistence of the heat, were mesmeric; they reduced Colet to a pair of eyes which travelled, that first afternoon of it, without a body. Occasionally he was brought round, and found that he was able to move, when the *rakit* was swept under a projecting bough, and globular fruits hanging in its shade, like emerald and yellow lamps, threatened to clear the deck. There was a brushing and cracking, the raft heeled, and they came clear into the sun again, half foundered, the Malays laughing.

Long sandy islands were humped in the stream, and on them had stranded trees out of old floods, trees gaunt and bleached, like the skeletons of mastodons. A dragon-fly would hover over the raft with a lustre of wing-beat as its nimbus, the only inhabitant, and then it would shoot off as a streak of prismatic light. The reach they were in was always enclosed, as though it were a brief lake, with high walls on either hand, unscaleable, and abrupt hills corrugated with the everlasting forest overlooking both ends of it. No way out. But round the corner, as they turned it, shot the uproar of rapids, and the river above was taut in glassy sheets over inclines. All had to jump overboard, and persuade the mutinous rafts to go up and over against their weighty and tricky insistence that down was the right way to go. That was a lively and cooling interlude. It was play for the men. They chanted; they raised their shrill war-cry when they got a *rakit* free from the snags and fairly on the run.

The late afternoon gloomed with the threat of the daily storm. Colet watched those pitchy masses in the sky with a concern for the coming of rain which was instinctive, but puzzled him. Here he hated rain, and that seemed unreasonable. Yet these were more than storms; they were threats to existence. The earth cowered under that savage frown, and waited, in surrender. The sky lowered to the forest in ponderous keels of bitumen solid and ominous, illuminated, so it seemed, by livid glowings from hell. The trees that had been cataleptic began to tremble, leaves and birds whirled in upper gusts, the outer branches shook in helpless desperation; and then the sky collapsed, roaring. Nothing could be seen but a screen of falling water which glittered with incessant convulsions of lightning. The raft was battered.

The storm ceased with a shocking detonation, as though on the signal of a gun-burst. In the silence which followed, when there was only drainage drumming through the leaves, they heard the crash of a forest giant. The Malays were glum now, chilled and depressed. It was nightfall when they sighted some lights ahead, and moored by a cluster of huts.

Mat overlooked the disembarkation. He knew what to do. Colet changed into a dry sarong and shirt, made coffee, and sat by himself, not wondering, after all, how much more ahead of them there was of this sort of life, but sunk in fatigue and content, a tranquillity in the cool of a tropical night, within its foreign smells, which was a hint of experience in another dimension. He was satisfied with the stars over the hills he must traverse. So when Mr. Parsell, who had been with the people of the village, appeared beside him, rubbing his hands, Colet half resented an invasion of the privacy of nature. The old fellow was satisfied with his affairs so far, it appeared. What did he want?

Mr. Parsell certainly was satisfied. It was late, but there were no mosquitoes about, and he evidently wished to be companionable. What was the matter with him, Colet wondered. For he talked. And presently, through Colet's apathy when ethnology was the subject after a tiring day, there began to penetrate an understanding of Norrie's respect for Mr. Parsell. The man was animated. He knew the secrets of the strange place already, or thought he did, by all accounts.

He made a confidant of Colet. He treated him as an equal in ethnology. Mr. Parsell forgot the difference between them. And Colet began to be stirred by surmises of a human tradition of an antiquity he had never suspected. He turned to his companion as though he had not met him before. He forgot where he was. This was the man who had taken no notice of the jungle; who only admitted its existence when he had to. Colet listened to a new voice. Mr. Parsell was murmuring, persuasive and lenient; and, leisurely, he divined the probabilities of extended human understanding with the allusiveness of a poet. He was generous, perhaps, because he had just learned of what to him was an accession to knowledge. He had a pupil; he wished to share this wealth. It was for everybody.

Colet was shown a vision of a long past humanity, few in numbers and in dire peril, the chances all against its survival, fumbling out of a darkness where the beginnings were hidden, and drifting, or impelled by forces unknown or half-guessed, to this discovery and to that, from land to land, to a partial control of circumstance.

Now and then, as Colet listened, he watched a spark wavering about the huts. Humanity was still securing itself against the powers of the night? Lightning flickered over the untraversed hills to the west. Sometimes a creature unknown called in the forest. Colet heard that interruption as though a listener had mocked Mr. Parsell's happy auguries, had derided his faith in human destiny.

Those satiric cries, and the remoteness of the stars above the mysterious penumbra of earth, did not take the scientist's attention. He went on, sometimes stroking his beard. There were tribes that, at long last, built cities; they grew haughty with a new strength. Some of them, he thought at times, had been carried a little too far the wrong way in their confidence in engines and mechanical power. If that clever fellow had found the fulcrum to shift the earth, he might only have wrecked the solar system. Mechanical power, to him, was a terrible power, easy to control, but it could be disastrous in its undesigned outcomes, as though its exactitude were a delusion and held a diabolical cheat. It interested him far more, Mr. Parsell explained, that other tribes had never come out of their original fastnesses. They were still in the woods, not far from the beginning of human impulses. Not far, in truth, from that spot. It might be true, he thought, that man had come to the steam-engine too soon for our good. The engine, very likely, had not taken us as far from the jungle as we imagined. What was worse, it was possible that we were moving at full speed on the wrong track. Eh? Perhaps we were going in the wrong direction; but that was for us to learn. We knew what we wanted. It was not his concern. No doubt we should find out presently, if things did not appear to be right, that our power had taken us too far the wrong way.

It was those other men who had taken no turning at all, but were still where they were at the beginning, who meant most to him. Mr. Parsell thrust a hand towards the unknown.

"There, Mr. Colet, they are just out there still." And he continued, coming a little closer to his companion in an odd eagerness:

"Suppose those people know what we have forgotten? Has that doubt ever occurred to you? It has to me. It has to me. They surely know what I do not. We may have thrown away clues—think of it—which these people still keep, without knowing what they are, omens that would have taken us along a better road. I am going back."

"What's that?" Colet ejaculated; for he wondered suddenly whether a clue was there.

Mr. Parsell soothed him. He explained that these original men were almost virgin documents; they were not scrawled over, they were not obscured by the palimpsest of many civilisations. They must have preserved secrets, long overlaid by civilisation, which were worth many inventions. A body of them was hovering, so the villagers had been telling him, near there. Those folk of the woods had not been seen, but they were about. The villagers called them shadows. Shy folk. Very rare and elusive people, who avoided even the Malays. But he would find them. He must find them.

The feeble glim of their lamp hardly more than suggested Mr. Parsell's face, which hovered in the dark. That faint and uncertain star at the end of a brass stalk was the sum of their effort at the illumination of the vast Malayan night. The elderly scientist's smile, as he bent forward towards the light, was all of wisdom in the wilds that Colet could see; and, when the lamp flickered, the expression of cheerful and speculative discernment was evasive, it was tremulous, as though on the verge of being engulfed.

# CHAPTER XXXVII

In that sharp confusion of forested mountains, with ridges in the clouds, and all based in an inferno of precipice, chasm, and torrent, to the depths of which the sun never reached, it was hard to say where you were, within a few miles. It was no wonder the Malays disliked the heights, and said they were the abode of spirits, and quietly declined to accompany Mr. Parsell on extravagant asides in that menacing solitude.

They were anxious to work through. Mr. Parsell was not. It was hard enough to keep to what trails there were, without adventuring on excursions from which there might be no return; so Colet stood by Mat, whose woodcraft was as astonishing in its intuitions as though the man were aided by another sense. Mat told Colet frankly that his home was by a river in the plains beyond, or else, would a man be so foolish as to do this thing?

"A man, Tuan, will find his home, even across such as this forbidden ground."

All the time they were working through the range, that expression of elation on the face of Mr. Parsell, all of him that could be seen one night by the glow of a lamp, would intrude on Colet's preoccupation with the difficulties of the day. It would return to him suddenly, a fading but troubling wraith, when toiling through the savage undergrowth of a gully; and he would see it, when, hurriedly, Mat and he were scanning the ground above, anticipating, after a storm, the irruption of a flood into a natural trap. Colet had a doubt whether any man should have a light so bright and happy on a face so worn.

P

Yet Parsell had come through it well. He could have been counted the best man of the party. He was as ardent as a little flame burning from an inexhaustible source. He was showing the marks of the experience, for the going was arduous and the food was no better than a pretence at eating, but maybe he drew nourishment from the circumambient; nothing else would account for his quiet cheerfulness. Mat, too, had observed Mr. Parsell's unconcern with what, from them, required cunning and fortitude. Mat, who had led them to a spur of the range from which they overlooked an ocean of jungle to which even the sun could set no limit, paused beside Colet, and shook the sweat from his face. He saw Mr. Parsell standing contemplating, as though it were a land of promise, that immense estrangement from man below. Mat murmured his wonder to Colet. He asked from what it was that Tuan Parsell found his strength. Colet turned to see, and felt jocular. They had done some good work that day. They were getting on.

"For he on honey-dew hath fed," he quoted.

Mat was mystified. "Tuan?" he questioned, in reproach.

Colet became as explicit as he could in the vernacular. "Allah supports him."

That, of course, was quite satisfactory, and Mat glanced again respectfully at the other tuan.

They rested for a time at that cool elevation. It was not often that they could find an outlook through the dense labyrinth of giant trees and vines, not even for a sight of the sky. They were, in a sense, travelling underground, and in the dark. When they surveyed it from above the jungle was not recognised. That aspect of it, its roof, was foreign. From where they stood then it was a sea of dusky billows arrested in its flow. It was like the sea; it was without bounds. It faded into the horizon.

Colet was awed by the magnitude of that silent and un-explored prospect. They had that before them. They had that to work through; yet always beneath its surface. That was the roof they rarely saw of the purgatory through which they usually toiled in mire, in a twilight, with thorns and leeches and the dim and questionable. There was that much more of it, to the skyline. The crests of mountains floated in the heavens on invisible vapours, regions detached from the earth. A translated peak would diminish, would vanish, and then another would appear where nothing had been seen before. Colet wondered whether his little party was not only off the map, but whether a map could contain a revelation of what was not only infinite but protean. He felt it was like his cheek, and smiled to himself, viewing his rags and dirt, to chance heart-beats against that universe.

And what a space in which to search for Sakais, or for anybody! Where were those blessed people of the woods? He would have supposed they were but a legend, a theme for camp-fires, but that yesterday in the forest they had stumbled on three huts, the most remote and forlorn human habitations which he had ever seen. They stood in a narrow rift of the jungle, which frowned down on the transient and pathetic evidence of man. They were abandoned. He thought their builders must have fled in a horror they were no longer able to withstand. And who could wonder at it? The floor was cumbered with wet leaves and forest rubbish. The day descended that shaft in the forest as far as it could, but it rested on a wall, obliquely, little more than half-way down. Mr. Parsell was absorbed by the unexpected discovery, and was in no hurry to move on. Yet nothing was there but the memorials, the sodden leaves, and the coarse webs of spiders across the uprights.

Mat dolefully shook his head about those Sakais. He himself, he said to Colet, did not know why it should be good to find them, but perhaps Tuan understood. Were they not savages? They were dirty, and they knew nothing. They were infidels, and they knew no shame. They were as the beasts. Why should they be sought, as though they were men? It was certain, Tuan, that they would not be found. They were but shadows in the forest, and moved like beasts. They saw, but they were not seen. They were as timid as deer, and feared men. He himself had hunted them, and he knew.

"There, Tuan," he whispered, pointing over the dark sea of the tree-tops below, "is smoke. It is a Sakais camp."

Colet could just discern a faint blue smear some miles away.

Mat, though, was discreet, even without hope.

"Tuan, we should never find them. Can smoke be caught in the hand?"

Colet felt that another outlooker was peering by his elbow. He turned, and saw Mr. Parsell beside him, intent on the same sign.

Mat at once led on down a precipitous shoulder of the hill; and Colet, but for a sense he had that any mishap now would mean the loss of the party, would have admitted that the land was beautiful. Streams hung in veils from upper shelves of rock, were lost, and reappeared under wet ferns and gigantic leaves to brim and shimmer in basins of granite. He paused by one clear spout of crystal, folded the waxen green of an arum leaf into a cup, on which the drops of water were globules of cold silver, and thought it was the best drink he had ever had.

Near there they camped; and again that night Mr. Parsell sat beside him, and spoke of a light that had been, and might be again for men. Theirs, indeed, was a journey of discovery. This was the true sort of exploration. Colet had little more than coffee and a pipe, and that tenuous confidence of his companion, to support him. The cicadas had shrilled to the last of the sun when Mr. Parsell began his lesson; but all was silent, and the Malays were asleep, and the fire down, when Mr. Parsell rose, and spread his sleeping-mat. His rumouring

voice, hinting at the hidden springs of life, ceased; there
was then but a sprinkle of stars overhead, and the night
around, which was the forest. Colet could pick out of that
silence even the roll of a dewdrop from a leaf. On a distant
hill he heard the imperious voice, the snarling moan, of the
lord of that region.

# CHAPTER XXXVIII

Why was Mat standing there looking at him? Colet sat up. The sun was bright on a high buttress across the valley. This was late. Time they were on the move. Mat ought to have called him; but Mat never would. That funny Malay would never waken him, of course; a very dangerous thing to do; the wandering soul might not have time to get back and re-enter the body; his soul then would be lost. He smiled, and cheered the morning to the guide. Mat looked grave. Something wrong with him?

"What news to-day?"

"An evil thing has happened, Tuan. We cannot see Tuan Parsell. Where is he?"

Where is he? Oh, spirited away, of course. Colet glanced over at the professor's corner. Why, Parsell never left the camp, unless accompanied. He never had. But his place was empty.

Nobody, Colet was told, had heard him go. They supposed that he had gone down to bathe, but no, he had not been to the pool. He had gone downhill, though; that they knew for they had found the signs. If they might say so, the Tuan had walked lightly, but as though he knew where he was going, and yet would not disturb those who slept. It was hard to follow his track below, for truly, Mat explained, he thought the Tuan had been gone many hours. There had been rain. What thing was this?

Colet was up and at his gear in the first jolt of the misgiving. That old child out alone in such a country . . . he paused. Here, cool off. Getting scared would not help. Parsell could not have gone far.

Had he taken anything with him? What had he taken? What, his pack had gone? So it had. Food, and his compass, too, and his staff. Parsell was moonstruck. Colet began to rave at the impersonal, but caught Mat's quiet and steady eye, which yet expressed anxiety; and so gazed out at the woods instead, deliberately still, seeking inspiration. He was up against it.

They would find him. After all, the old fellow could not travel far. Not alone. Not in that place. But how far need he travel to get lost? You just turned your head in the woods, lost it entirely, and there you were till domesday; and the camp about five minutes away.

He was buckled and taut. "Come," he called to Mat.

"If Tuan will allow me," said Mat, "it is not good to begin a journey without food. It is also better to sit awhile, when the liver is sick. It is hard for a man to consider what he should do while he runs."

You bet it is. Very well, then. But that old buffer would have to be found if they stayed there till the coconuts were ripe. But Mat was right. It was no good rushing at the forest. The mountains did not care. They had all the time they wanted. All the same, if old Parsell was not in camp before sundown . . . better not think about it.

"I believe he thinks he can find those Sakais."

"Truly, Tuan, that is what I fear also."

    *       *       *       *       *

No other sign of him. Time was getting on. Two o'clock now. Where was Mat?

Colet retraced his steps through the forest a little distance. Hallooed. No answer. Only something like a jackass in the woods. Naturally, it would be a jackass. Colet hurried down and back a little more—damn the rotans. He—damn the rotans, they were everywhere. Put there to stop him, probably.

Quite right, too. The thorns knew better than he did.

Fancy trying to run to some one in that tangle. He stood, collected himself, and hallooed again. This time not even a jackass. He waited, and watched the sweat trickle down the back of one hand. Not a sound.

Well, they had found Parsell's helmet at the bottom of that gully, and he was going to get to the head of it. But was this the same valley? Of course it was. He had not been paying much attention, knowing that Mat knew the business better. But it must be the same cleft in the hills. He would have to push on, guide or no guide. Mat could look after himself. He must find Parsell. No point in being there unless he did.

He shouted. "Parsell! Mat!"

Oh, don't be a damned fool. They're not on the telephone.

Better get on with it. Some hours yet to sunset. He turned, and ascended the slope. This was his own particular job, anyhow. He had asked for it. He would have to do it alone. This was the same gully, of course. Why doubt it? Parsell could hardly have gone another way without wings. The leeches had made a mess of that leg, by the look of it. Might have been stuck by a bayonet. No time now to see to it, though. When Parsell was found they'd put everything in order, and get out of that country at the double, even if they had to truss up the old boy. He ought to have been trussed up at first. He must have wandered up that valley; to what did it lead?

Those rocks and tree-trunks were inhuman, as if, in that glassy stillness, they were shapes at the bottom of the sea. No day was there; it was too far below the surface for much to show. Was it getting dark already? More likely the sides of the narrow valley were closing in; they would, of course, towards the head of it. But if you looked up, nothing could be seen. Nothing was there but ropes and wreckage dangling from a ceiling out of sight.

He stopped again and listened. Great lichened hummocks of rock, like grey couched animals, watched him. Sable pillars receded, the endless aisles of an unholy tabernacle. Shouldn't like to meet its priests. Nobody there, though. Roots were coiled and contorted in an everlasting agony. And not a sound. If Parsell was left there he would die that night—he would go properly mad. No wonder the Malays called it forbidden. He must get the old man out of it.

That fallen tree—he supposed he would have to climb over it. No way round it. But only night was beyond it. What was the good?

Anyway, Parsell's helmet was at the bottom of that valley. Where else could he have gone? But could he have ascended so far, through that stuff? It wanted some doing. Now, over that tree, and get on with it. He might as well stay there himself as go back without the old 'un.

Colet climbed the prone column, thrusting creepers and a tough raffle from his face, grunted, and was on the top of it. What was beyond? Only more of the eternal rocks and wreckage on the dim slope, in a light which told him of the end of time. The day after the last day would be the same as this. The light dying and the world a wet litter.

The tree collapsed suddenly as he was gazing ahead, and he was dropped kicking into the hollow heart of the trunk, in choking dust. Something struggled with him, and slithered out past him. He shouted when he caught hold of its hard and slippery body. And he was trapped—he couldn't escape. The desperate stuff broke away in his hands.

Hold hard. It's only a rotten tree. And oh, by God! The ants in it were like fire all over him.

They helped him out of it. He was soon out then. Now, if he continued in that trembling and mucky sweat, he'd be added to Parsell. By Jove, those little devils could bite. Like the points of red-hot wires. His job was not to get lost, but to find the old man. You are only lost if you think you are.

Parsell must have had insane strength to have struggled up through that lumber of a dead and forgotten time. What possessed him to go alone? Not to have been turned back by the very silence of it? And in the dark, too. If the old man had a faith which could turn the apparition of hell into a forecourt to be walked through with a visiting card, it would be worth knowing. He could do with a pennyworth of it now, to be going on with. Hard luck to have to do it without any.

It must be getting near night. It was dark enough for it. Perhaps the evening storm was near. That was what it was; for heaven never peeped into that valley. He was in for it, if a storm burst over such a pit. The trees were unusually still. Waiting for something? Surely he was not purblind; his eyes were all right? The trees were filmy in the dusk. They were shades standing about.

This was the head of the valley, perhaps. That was a sheer wall of rock, so he could go no further. That could not be climbed. Useless to look for a little old man when you could hardly see a precipice, and the day was only a trifle paler than the black trees. What were all those shapes waiting for? Standing about? For him to go? No good. He wasn't going. There was nowhere to go but back, and he could not go back. Not without Parsell. No point in it. To hell with the darkness and the shapes.

Perhaps the old man had been translated, gone up in a fiery chariot while they were not watching. Anything might happen there. And what had happened to Mat? That was queer. Mat had been behind him—had shown him which was the way to take a second or two before. Turned round, and nothing was there but the leaves watching him. There was more in what the Malays said about this mountain than he knew. Mat hadn't liked the job. He had been reluctant about it. He said the mountain was guarded. Well, enchantment or not, there he was and there was no way out of it now.

It sounded as if the place was talking to itself, now it had got him; got him all round. Was it safe to wait under the precipice? There was a noise, up above, like the sea breaking. The storm was coming. What about repeating the Pater-noster? Colet considered it. Couldn't remember it. The aisles filled with quivering blue fire; the trees danced. He had laughed at the men chanting the mantras for a safe journey. But he didn't know any mantras. Too late now to learn prayers and exemptions. Here it came. Poor old Parsell.

A rolling of drums, the steady booming of the coming of calamity; the hooting of bony things following the drums. Men? No, no men there. The hantus; they had a night out. The mountain was hollow and booming. They were march-ing out of it up their valley, an army of them. It was their place. He was caught, back against a wall. He strained his eyes on the cellar blackness towards the shouts. They were muttering near him now. If he could only see . . .

His prison opened suddenly, and skeletons of fire were capering round him, arms about the trees, taking the trees with them. The trees had no weight. They leaped. They had no roots. They were on quick feet. The roots were flinging out of the earth, they were lashing near him, serpents of fire.

No. That was the rain. The floods were pouring down. Torrents of romping fire. The valley was going. The moun-tain was collapsing and running down. He was going with it.

\*    \*    \*    \*    \*

If you asked him, then he'd been out all night. Was this to-day or yesterday? There was no saying whether this was early morning or afternoon. The place had been deep under water. The earth and the trees were still talking about it. His watch had stopped. He would like to know what had happened. His clothes looked as though he'd slept in the bed of a river. He must have been wakened only just in time. He had better go slow. His knees were loose.

This was very like a corner he had seen before. That rock, a kneeling elephant, might be the one where Mat had

235

vanished. When was that? Somehow there seemed to have
been an awful loss of time, or else everything was washed
out of his mind. Colet emerged through a thicket to a track,
and looked up to the gloom of the woods.

Parsell. Yes. The old man had melted into that. Parsell
had become part of the dark.

There was Mat. Hoisting his pack. Abandoning camp?
Mat stared at him, dropped the pack, and was—Colet called
out. The man was going to run away. What was the matter
with him?

"Hullo, Mat! What news?"

Mat turned, and his bronze took a queer tinge. Colet
shook the Malay's hand, and jollied him. The man was
frightened.

"I'm not a hantu, Mat. They turned me out of the forbidden gunong. They found they couldn't make a good hantu
out of me. Here we are."

# CHAPTER XXXIX

No end yet to the eternal trees and the heat. They were in the plains now, though. Areca palms and houses might be seen in the distance any time. Land ho! A little rest wouldn't do them any harm. Mat was a good man. That Malay was as good as the best. He was getting them on. Colet thought that, if the going were not too hard, he could last it out. Mat looked pretty bad himself. But it didn't matter if there was little to eat. Not much fun in food if it made you sick. He must be tougher than he thought, to walk by day and have his ague fits at night.

They could do the rest by canoe to Mat's own village, so Mat said, after this day's march. Better than walking. But there was one thing about the fever, you did not care any more. Nothing mattered. Effort was futile; it was the men who kept him going. The fever cleared the mind in a strange way. Things lost their importance. Life lost its importance. He saw even the trees farther off. They were still high and brooding, keeping their secrets. They could keep them. Not so secret as they pretended. The men, too, were farther off. They were very quiet, and looked at him shyly. He knew what it was. They thought he was going to die.

But no fear. He knew better. There were things to be done. That old blighter Perriam—but he could wait. Perriam could wait a bit longer. It was strange to see the men sweating, and yourself to feel you couldn't get warm, or keep the teeth from chattering. No good wishing he'd found Parsell. That man wasn't to be found. Parsell was taken in by what he wanted, and there was no more to be said about that; he was a successful old person.

237

Funny thing. He did not feel as though he'd failed; another symptom of the fever, maybe. His mind was cleaned to a thin clear plate of light; that was what the feeling was; no markings on it, either, except what was in the grain of it; all the scrawlings were rubbed off. Odd consequence for a fever to have. He could see things better than ever. All the fat was sweated off his brain. He wasn't sorry for Parsell, nor sorry he'd gone with the old man. It was worth it. Worth paying for. Couldn't count the gain, though. He was satisfied, if Parsell was. What was Norrie doing now, and Hale—no, Sinclair? But they were on the other side of time. He had come across the pass, and it was all right, if you didn't expect to get anything out of it; anything but dreams; bound to get dreams, when you fell asleep; but you could do without them, though.

They were just gliding out of it now. It was better in the canoe. The world had become extraordinarily quiet. Sinking down to the sea. The trees were still moving by, all on a level, a long dark line; but the country was very distant, and nothing to do with him. They'd get to the end of it all presently, when they had sunk down far enough. Everything went past, as you sank down, and there was nothing to do any more. You need not even watch it go by.

# CHAPTER XL

WHEN Colet, some weeks later, walked into the lounge of the Penang hotel, the palms in the garden were awake in a cooling draught. The wind could just be felt. It was as though you knew of the stir of the invisible principle of life. The world was alive. He was in touch with it again. This was a return from another world. Over in that corner was where Norrie had talked to him, the night before they left to go round the coast. Colet would have gone to that corner, but three young ladies had the table. They were certainly a noteworthy phenomenon, after Gunong Berching and the leeches. As good to look upon as the order and colour of the garden, and a complete assurance that he had come back. Nothing like that for a long time. What a number of women, too, and all as cool and vivacious as the wind in the palms; perhaps not a shadow of the other world in the mind of one of them. He heard a girl laugh, and it was certain then the old world was on its proper axis. He could sit down and watch this all the morning.

A hand, a hearty hand, squeezed his shoulder. Not the hand of a lady. He looked behind him. Eh?

Sinclair, by all the miracles of Fate. He stood up, but couldn't speak. Sinclair laughed, as though this was a great joke, meeting again.

"You old rascal, Colet. What have you been doing with yourself? Steering an open boat ever since on a half ration of hope? You look as if you had."

"What are you doing here?"

"Waiting for my ship to turn round. Off to London to-morrow."

"London . . . well . . ."

They talked it all over. It was good to talk, even when you had nothing more to say. Then the sailor declared that they must have another before he went back to the quay.

"Coming to Gallions Reach, Colet?" Sinclair laughed again at that, as he took the glasses from the Chinaman's tray.

"Yes."

Sinclair forgot to put the glasses on the table. He held one in each hand.

"What? You don't mean it."

"I do."

"But it's haunted, isn't it? You don't tell me you've seen so much out here that you've forgotten old Perriam."

"Not me. That's it, Sinclair. I'm going back to lay his miserable ghost."

"Here, steady the helm. I'd see his ghost to hell first."

"Well, it's not his ghost, really. It's mine, my son."

Sinclair did not answer. He was watching Colet, trying to find something to say.

"It's all right, Sinclair. You needn't look. You won't find any tile loose. You brought me out. Now, if you please, you'll take me back. We'll come full circle. We can't have ghosts hanging about, can we? They must be attended to. They run our show for us, Sinclair."

The sailor's eye roved over the colours and animation of that inspiriting morning garden of ladies.

"Well, I'm damned," he said.

"Yes, the unseen world we know governs us. Not always what you're looking at now, Sinclair, so you needn't draw my attention to it. I see it. It would move a heart of stone. But there's no fun for us in life unless we obey the order we know."

THE END